I0679172

The Christmas Cafe

Lyle Garford

All situations in this publication are fictitious and any resemblance to living persons is purely coincidental.

Copyright © 2019 by Lyle Garford

All rights reserved. No part of this book may be reproduced or transmitted in any form or by any means, electronic or mechanical, including photocopying, recording, or by an information storage and retrieval system, without permission in writing from the publisher.

Published by:
Lyle Garford
Vancouver, Canada
Contact: lyle@lylegarford.com

ISBN 978-0-9952078-8-2

Cover photo by Stacy Funderburke/Shutterstock.com

Book Design by Lyle Garford
lyle@lylegarford.com
www.lylegarford.com

First Edition 2019
Printed by Createspace, an Amazon.com Company.
Available on Kindle and other devices.

Dedication

This one is dedicated to the memory
of
Charles Dickens.

Prologue

The cafe's resident cat was named Shadow. The name was no coincidence as his fur was all black, except for a small white patch on his chest below his chin.

Savory smells emanating from the kitchen on the main floor of the old house drew the cat in, as they always did when the cafe's owner forgot to close the door leading to her second floor rooms where the cat lived. Winding his way around the main kitchen worktable Shadow reached up and placed a paw on the cook's leg to beg for a morsel. The cook, a grizzled, grey haired black man in his fifties named Willie Low, glanced down without surprise and grunted.

"You again, puss? You're going to get fat if I keep feeding you people food like this."

But the cook knew Shadow was a smart cat and, even if he could have somehow understood the man's words, nothing would change. The cat was always patient, hopeful and confident the man would relent soon enough.

Willie looked up as outside the wind howled and the rain lashed even harder yet again at the old house now serving as a cafe, drowning out for a moment the tinny sound of the Christmas music playing on the cook's small portable radio. The heavy rain pounding the house had started several hours earlier in the middle of the night and was showing no signs of letting up.

Feeling the gentle touch of a paw on his leg once again the cook sighed and reached down to scratch behind the cat's ear.

"I guess you've figured out I'm a pushover, haven't you, Shadow? Well, it's not up to me to watch your weight."

Willie cut off a generous sized piece of the roast chicken he had pulled from the oven a few minutes before. After putting it on the floor for the cat to eat, Willie went back to doing the preparation work for the daily soup they would serve in the cafe later that day and he was soon lost in the task at hand. He was so deep into what he was doing he initially shrugged off the tiny voice that came as a strange jolt to his consciousness.

He tried carrying on with thought about the work at hand, but the question of what just happened clawed its way to the surface from the deeper recesses of his mind and he stopped what he was doing. Lifting his head, he looked around in curiosity. Willie knew no one else was in the house, as the owner had closed the cafe after the early morning rush and went shopping, or at least, that was what was supposed to be happening. But he saw no one as he peered about with a puzzled frown and he rubbed his chin in thought. He tried calling out in case someone had slipped in without his knowledge.

"Hello? Is anyone there?" he said, but no answer came back.

"Huh," said Willie to himself. "Could have sworn I heard someone say something. Must be hearing things."

Willie tried focusing back on what he thought he had heard, but the voice was so ephemeral he couldn't pin down what the exact word or words had been. He shook his head and looked around one last time, intending to go back to his work.

But before he could do that he felt a light, but distinct chill touch him from behind. The sensation was faint and like nothing he had ever experienced before. His conscious mind rebelled at its touch, knowing the kitchen was in fact toasty warm from the oven being on. As he struggled to process what was happening he sensed with a flash of certainty another presence was in the room with him. Ignoring the small stab of fear that coursed through his body he turned fast to look behind him for the source, but no one was there. Willie's eyes narrowed as he whipped his head back and forth.

"Who's there?" he called, this time louder and with an edge to his voice. Once again, no one answered.

Looking down, he realized Shadow was no longer beside him and the piece of chicken he had given the cat remained untouched where Willie had left it. The strange sensation of a presence he still felt seemed to emanate from a spot near the doorway to the kitchen. With his peripheral vision Willie realized Shadow was now bottled up in the far corner of the room, the furthest distance possible away from the door. The cat was hunched into a crouch, staring hard at the entrance, and whisking his tail back and forth. As Willie continued watching him the cat uttered an unintelligible, low sound that seemed like a growl or a deep hiss of fright or maybe both.

As the stab of fear returned because of the cat's

reaction Willie turned back to face the doorway, but there was still nothing to be seen. He edged closer to the door to ensure he had a clear look down the hallway and made sure he wasn't missing anyone or anything. The slight touch of chill grew the closer he got.

"Who's there?" he said, in a more insistent tone this time. "What do you want?"

He waited, but nothing happened. Unsure of what to do, he kept waiting for several more long moments until with another flash of sudden insight he realized the chill sensation was gone. Mustering his courage, Willie left the kitchen through the doorway and went to explore the entire main floor of the cafe. Finding no one, he returned to the kitchen. The cold spot had not come back and, looking down, Willie saw Shadow had returned to eating the piece of chicken with content, as if nothing had happened. Willie looked around the kitchen one more time before shaking his head hard, as if doing so would somehow make the pieces of the puzzle of what had happened finally fall into place. Willie sighed, as nothing came to mind to explain any of it.

"Well, puss, I don't know what that was all about. I'm not even sure it happened. Maybe I'm just starting to lose my marbles or worse, maybe I'm just a stupid old man. And here you are, begging for even more chicken like its just another day in the life of a cat. Well, one more piece and that's it for you."

Willie gave him another generous morsel and scratched behind the cat's ear before turning back to his worktable with a shrug, listening once more to the heavy rain continuing to slam into the house in irregular gusts. As the radio began playing one of his favorite Christmas tunes Willie turned up the volume to drown out the rain. With effort he focused once again on the work before him, but this time he positioned himself in a spot where he could watch the door.

Chapter One

He gave in when his stomach growled for the second time, knowing it was time to find a place to stop for the night. His eyes were also tired from driving, enough to make the decision easy. He shook his head at his own foolishness, cursing himself for spending too much time wandering around in a small town further up the coast earlier in the day.

The driving, heavy rain wasn't letting up and now that night was falling trying to see where he was going would become even more difficult than it already was. He kicked himself mentally again for waiting too long to stop, but he knew the real problem was motivation to pay attention to details like that. Without a schedule to adhere to or even a real destination, he had little to force himself into making a decision. One hotel room bed wouldn't be much different than the next.

The traffic was heavy with Friday rush hour commuters going both directions, heading home to nearby bedroom communities. The next exit after he made the decision to stop had a sign announcing a nearby town with accommodations and after a moments hesitation he took it. He couldn't remember why the name of the town struck a chord in his mind, but he was sure it would come to him and soon enough it did. The seaside town he was driving to was one of many small summer vacation destinations along the coast of the Pacific northwest of America, popular with families looking for a big, pleasant beach to let the children run free.

Somewhere in his mind was a vague memory from the long dim past of his childhood of playing on that beach and staying in this town.

The road soon took him along a winding waterfront route cutting a path between cedar forests on one side and the water on the other, while following the shape of the small coves dotting the shoreline. In one such cove he found several ramshackle buildings and obviously derelict old fishing boats abandoned on the beach and he knew for certain he was right about where he was, as the town in his memory had a long abandoned, small cannery to process the catch of local fishermen nearby. He also had a memory of staying in a quaint, stately old hotel right in the heart of town and he resolved to find it.

Further along the road came dim streetlights, lighting a section running parallel to a long stretch of beach. This proved to be the edge of town and was an area dedicated to hosting several campgrounds and recreational vehicle parks. He was unsurprised to see they were devoid of customers.

The campgrounds finally gave way to the town itself, which wasn't large, consisting of a stretch of four long blocks along the waterfront where a variety of businesses clustered together. Several oak and northern pine trees large enough to testify they and the town around them were many decades old were sprinkled throughout the area, fighting for space with the numerous cedars. The small town cemetery was the only patch of ground in the business district not dedicated to making money.

Back from the shoreline and the business center were several old wood frame houses with a couple of small, but newer condominium developments mixed in. As he drove slowly through the area he got a quick impression most of the little businesses were oriented to parting tourists from their hard earned money.

His memory had not let him down about the hotel. Finding it on the main street of the town wasn't a problem as it was the largest structure in sight. The building had a sprawling footprint, taking over half of one of the long blocks right in the middle of town. The hotel was set well back from the water, with nothing but a long stretch of beach and what looked from a distance to be a path along the shoreline between it and the ocean. The view from all three upper floors of rooms would be commanding.

He parked as close as possible and dashed through the downpour to the shelter of the hotel. Even with the hood up on his heavy raincoat it felt as if the wind had driven enough rain through his defenses to soak him completely. Despite his hurried sprint from the car he had time to gain a quick impression of the stately grace and age he remembered about the exterior of the building and he realized little had changed since his youth. Someone in the long distant past had obviously banked on the small seaside town becoming popular enough with tourists to warrant making a significant investment in the property.

The interior of the hotel confirmed his quick, initial impression. The lobby was wide, with ornate crown mouldings and high ceilings. The hotel was clearly at least a hundred years old, but had along the way been given plenty of tender care over the years. Some obvious renovations had been done since his childhood visit, but someone clearly made a point of ensuring the changes had no effect on the atmosphere of understated elegance still maintained throughout.

Further past the hotel check in desk that was off to one side a huge stone fireplace was centered on the far opposite wall, framed on either side by several large glass windows looking directly out onto the beach. A number of people were sitting with drinks, alternatively watching the storm outside or the large fire roaring in a wood-burning fireplace that was converted from its original state to burn natural gas now.

On the drive in he assumed finding a room would be easy given it was now the middle of December, but the hotel seemed far busier than he expected. As he waited in line to check in behind a family with children he watched two employees struggling to find places to add even more Christmas decorations than what was already in place around the front desk. A big, festively adorned Christmas tree already stood in the lobby off to one side. The clerk finished with the family and waved him forward.

"Good evening. You appear to be a little busier than I thought you would be. I don't have a reservation, so I'm hoping you have a room to spare for the night?"

"We do, sir," said the clerk. "You would have been out of luck a few weeks back, but it's no problem now."

He watched the clerk smile in reply to the puzzled look he knew was on his face. The clerk took the identification and credit card offered and began the check in process as he offered explanation.

"Winter storm watchers always keep the hotel busy especially in November, sir. Of course, we also get storms in December, as you have obviously noticed. It slows around this time because people are busy getting ready for Christmas. We get a few more people staying with us over the holidays, but we usually aren't full again until the good beach weather is back."

Taking one last look at the driver's license and credit card the clerk slid them back across the counter along with a form to sign.

"Right, Mister—Jonathan Thomas. Welcome to our hotel, sir. If you could sign in the spots with an X beside them you will be done. Actually, I don't know if you are aware, but word is we are due for an even worse storm tomorrow night, if you can believe it. Might even be bad enough we could get a little snow. You may want to stay hunkered down with us an extra night or so if that's the case. Roads will be awful."

"I've been living back east and have snow tires, so I know how to navigate snowy conditions," said Jonathan, giving the signed form back and taking the key to his room.

He made to turn away, but stopped as he thought about it. "You know what, maybe I'll take you up on that. You don't get snow as much out here on the

Pacific coast and everyone else around me might not be as prepared as I am."

The clerk made a tentative reservation for a few more nights, assuring Jonathan it wasn't a problem to cancel and leave early. Jonathan paused again and asked for recommendations of good places to eat.

"Well, the hotel here has a nice restaurant through those doors over there. You can get meals there at all times of the day, but you might find the prices a little steep for dinner. It's primarily a high-end steak house at night. We have a few places around town, but the closest and, probably the best, if its decent food for a reasonable price you want, would be Gwen's Cafe. It's just to your right as you leave here, down the street to the end of the business district."

After thanking the clerk Jonathan made the dash to his car for his bags. His feet and the bottom of his jeans were already wet and he was too tired to get dressed up for a more formal dinner, so he decided to make the short trip to the cafe. After dropping his bag unopened in his room he made his way back to the lobby. With a sigh as he eyed the foul weather outside he stepped into the driving rain again and hurried down the main street to the cafe. He was forced to lean into the strong gusts of cold wind that buffeted every so often. He passed the old cemetery dotted with thick, ancient trees he had seen on his way in and in the dim light of the streetlights he saw numerous headstones that looked quite old. The sight did little to lighten his mood.

As he struggled against the full force of the wind

every time there was a gap in the buildings he realized it was easy to understand why people came to watch the storms. Huge waves were crashing to the shore as far as he could see in both directions on the long, downward slope of the beach to the waterline. The impossibly long waves rolling steadily onto the log and debris strewn sand seemed to stretch endlessly into the distance. If an even worse storm blew in the waves would be towering.

The cafe was a sprawling and weathered looking, two-story house with a commanding view of the beach from a verandah running along one side. Like the hotel, Jonathan immediately formed an impression of age from the outside. Relieved to finally be in shelter from the elements as he stepped inside, he sensed right away his feeling was correct.

Inside he found half of one side of the building was crammed with a dozen tables of various sizes for customers. A door leading to the verandah outside was set into the wall between windows on either side to afford customers inside a view, too. Jonathan realized parts of the house had obviously been gutted and converted to its current purpose at some point in the distant past.

On the opposite wall that divided the room someone had cut a long rectangular pass through and added a shelf with heat lamps above for plates of food orders. Through this the kitchen could be seen, where an older looking, big black man wearing a white chef uniform was bustling back and forth inside. Most, but not all, of the patrons in the cafe were white. Unlike the hotel, the cafe was decorated with only a small artificial Christmas tree in a corner of the room along with a few other Christmas decorations sprinkled about.

Jonathan slid onto one of the eight stools at the old-fashioned diner counter running parallel to the kitchen wall, amused to find it had a row of four small, old juke boxes set on the counter at regular intervals between pairs of stools. He was curious to know if they actually worked, but an attractive waitress scurrying about in the service area between the kitchen and the counter caught his attention.

"Miserable night, huh?" she said, as she bustled over with a menu. Jonathan was forced to hide a double take at how pretty she was. She had long and straight, light blonde hair tied back in a ponytail and he thought she was a true, natural blonde. He was surprised as her hair was in a style almost no one wore anymore, with her hair close to her waist in length.

Forcing himself to focus he saw beer on the cafe menu and he ordered a bottle, despite her obvious surprise. A calendar tacked to the wall told him today was December 13th and he knew there likely weren't many people ordering beer this time of year. He didn't care, as beer was his alcohol of choice most of the time, although he was happy to drink whatever was put in front of him. After studying the simple menu he ordered a small bowl of homemade chicken soup to go along with a clubhouse sandwich for his dinner. He knew he was hungry enough to eat all of it.

As the waitress went off to place his order he began looking around closer at his surroundings. He quickly judged the cafe was probably about the same age as the hotel, but could see it had not enjoyed quite the same degree of tender care. The equipment the waitress was using was a curious mix of old and new. A large espresso and cappuccino machine was obviously a recent addition, while a milkshake mixer sitting beside it that would have been new in 1955 gave contrast. Although what looked like a fresh coat of paint had been added not too long ago it couldn't hide the subtler wear around him, like the slight tears in the weathered vinyl padding of the stool next to him. The hardwood floors were scuffed and in dire need of resurfacing, while the wood tables and chairs showed a similar degree of need.

The cafe was about half full. Several people were devoting their full attention to the screen of their cell phones, ignoring both the people they were with and the food before them. Jonathan focused on the snatches of conversation around him and wasn't surprised to overhear a few people complaining about the endless rain and grey skies. A young woman staring intently at her phone excitedly announced to her boyfriend she had found a deal to a sun destination for a decent price.

With a start Jonathan realized a large black cat with a white patch on his chest had appeared and was sitting at his feet, looking hopeful he would be fed. Jonathan smiled and scratched behind the cat's ear, but as no food was on offer the cat left. The server saw the cat and came over to scoop him into her arms, scolding him as she disappeared into the back of the cafe.

As he turned his attention away he caught part of

a conversation between a group of two women and one man sitting nearby and was surprised to realize from the snippet he heard that they seemed to be talking about a ghostly presence in the cafe. The topic was so unusual he reacted by turning his head back to focus on them. The woman speaking caught his reaction and lowered her voice. Although curious, Jonathan couldn't think of a polite way to intrude and ask them about it. The waitress reappeared, coming over to set his beer in front of him, so he turned his full attention to her.

"Your dinner won't be long, sir," said the waitress with a harried look. "We're past the dinner rush now and our cook is catching up."

Jonathan smiled back. "Thanks. That was your cat?"

"Yes. Shadow and I live upstairs and he's supposed to stay up there, but the little devil likes to sneak out every chance he gets to explore and beg for food."

She hurried off again as Jonathan smiled, doing his best not to be too obvious in his appreciation of her. He judged her to be close to his own age of thirty-one. Before she scurried off he noted she wore no wedding ring on her hand.

As she left again he turned to idly browse through the song library listed on the old miniature jukebox set into the counter. The songs it listed were all over forty or more years old. He was amused when he fished a coin out of his pocket, dropped it into the machine, and found it still worked as he punched in the number for a song. A rhythm and blues tune from the late sixties blared out of the tinny sounding speakers, just loud enough to catch the attention of a few of the other patrons sprinkled throughout the cafe. Despite being obviously deep in their conversation, the nearest group looked over from their table at him for a moment before turning away again.

His thoughts drifted as he turned his attention back to the music and the sound of his stomach still growling, not satisfied with just having beer to fill it. The time showing on his cell phone told him it was far later than his stomach was used to being fed. He debated checking his emails, but knew there was little point. Nothing he really wanted to see would be there.

As the song finally ended he thought of dropping another coin into the jukebox, but he couldn't make up his mind. In the silence following the song's end the conversation of the other patrons filled the void, so he kept his money in his pocket. Idly sipping at the beer that was disappearing too fast and making him lightheaded, he couldn't help focusing on trying to listen to the people talking nearby again.

The conversation had grown more intense and, to his surprise, he realized they really were talking about the cafe he was sitting in being haunted. He turned his head slightly to hear even better with one ear while keeping eyes forward to the cafe counter in front of him. He focused on the female voice speaking that had originally caught his attention. She sounded mildly exasperated.

"I tell you, I thought I saw something. I definitely felt it, because that's what drew my attention to look in its direction. It was like a cloud—a wisp of energy. I don't know how else to describe it. I know I never said anything at the time, because it just seemed so odd and I've never had anything like that happen to me before. I have no idea what it was or why it was there. Look, I realize this may be hard to buy, but I'm telling you the truth. There are great mysteries in life and nothing is impossible, you know."

"So do you not see a certain irony here, Miriam?" said a male voice. "You're telling me you run a new age shop selling all this esoteric, metaphysical stuff and this is the first time you've actually seen a ghost?"

"James, for God's sake. Don't be stupid. She's being serious," said the other woman at the table. "Miriam, he's just trying to tease you."

"I know. Some things about people change and some things don't. You always teased me in high school, so I'm not surprised. And for the record, James, I prefer to think of it as a spirit, because that's what a ghost is."

"Well, I am at least partly serious," said James with a laugh. "Is this really the first time you've seen a spirit?"

"Yes. Look, the metaphysical world is much more than silly television shows with people chasing ghosts around trying to get video clips of them. That sort of nonsense really isn't my focus. I suppose I am more attuned to the spiritual world and that is why I sensed it. I've certainly tried to grow my understanding of it. But I don't know why it's a surprise I've never encountered this before. If there really is a spirit in the cafe it has to be one that is unwilling to let go and transition from its former life for whatever reason. I don't believe for a second this is an everyday occurrence. I think the vast majority of people really do move onward when they pass away."

"So you say you saw it in the hall over there on the way to the washrooms? I find it interesting that's where it was. I wonder why it would be there?" said the other woman at the table.

"Yes, like I said, it seemed like a faint cloud or swirl that was there for the barest moment. It disappeared into that passage off the hall that leads to the kitchen and the storerooms in the back. But why do you find it interesting, Melanie?"

The woman sighed. "Well, I'm going to confess here. Keep in mind I've never really believed in this kind of stuff or given it much thought, which is why I discounted what I felt last week when I was in here. I went to use the washroom and as I came out I felt a very faint chill as I passed by that entrance to the kitchen. It was just enough to make me stop in my tracks and look around, because this place is always a bit stuffy and warm. But there was nothing there and in seconds it was gone. So it just seems weird and more than coincidental you are telling us about seeing a spirit in the same general location this happened to me."

"Huh. I guess I'll be paying more attention when I go to the washroom," said James. "But why would this place have a gho—I mean, a spirit?"

"No idea. Could be a host of reasons why a spirit might be about," said Miriam. "Like I said, this isn't an area of the metaphysical realm I've ever spent much time on."

"Were you scared, Miriam?" said the other woman. "I'm going to confess again here, it kind of scared me. I didn't like what I was feeling at all."

Curious to know how she would respond, Jonathan turned his head in time to see the woman named Miriam frown before answering.

"Well, come to think of it, no, I wasn't scared, although I don't know why not. I probably should have been, but it was such a fleeting experience I didn't have time to be scared, I guess. Mind you, I was much further away from it than you obviously were."

The sound of a bowl being set on the counter in front of him announced the arrival of his dinner. Jonathan gave the waitress a grateful smile and ordered another beer before reaching for a spoon to dig in. The soup was delicious, thick with bits of chicken, noodles, and vegetables, and he was soon scraping the dregs from the bottom of the bowl, wishing he had ordered more. Even as the thought came he saw his dinner appear on the pass through counter from the kitchen and the waitress bustled over to bring it to him.

As he began eating the sandwich and fries that came with it he thought about what he had just heard. He had no experience with the supernatural and had never known anyone that had any, at least to his knowledge. He felt a mild curiosity nag at him to learn more, but he knew it was unlikely he would. He was half way through the meal when the waitress finished tidying her counter workspace and came over to him.

"How is your meal, sir? Everything tasting good?"

"Wonderful. I was starving when I came in here. Say, it looks like you've had a busy day."

She gave him a tired smile and brushed aside a stray strand of her hair. "The dinner rush is always crazy. I'm the only server so I always need to soak my tired feet when the day is done."

She made to turn away, but he forestalled her with another question.

"So I'm assuming you are the Gwen lending her name to Gwen's Cafe?"

"I am," she replied, reaching out to briefly shake his hand. "Gwendolyn Fairchild, sole proprietress, in addition to being the only server on staff. You are new here, aren't you? Just passing through?"

"I am, but I might stay a little bit longer. It says Jonathan on my driver's license, but you can just call me Jon or whatever suits you. This seems a lot of work for just one server, isn't it?"

"It is, and thank you for noticing. Most people don't. The restaurant business is hard, harder than I thought it would be. Long hours and it's a struggle to stay afloat."

"Harder than you thought? I take it you haven't been in business long?"

"I opened the doors in late August at the end of the tourist season, so it's been less than six months. It helps the place came with a few regular customers because I already knew people in town, but my timing was lousy. Mind you, I hadn't planned it that way, but circumstances forced the bad timing on me. It's a long story."

She made to leave, but he forestalled her with one more question. "So you're from here are you?"

"Yes, but my husband and I moved away for a few years before coming back to open the cafe."

Jonathan inadvertently glanced at her hand and she saw the look on his face, so she answered the question before she could ask it.

"My husband passed away."

"I see. I'm sorry to hear that."

Someone looking for their bill waved at Gwen from the other side of the room to catch her eye and she nodded to acknowledge their need.

"I'd love to chat, but I really must go. More customers to help."

She turned to leave, but Jonathan thought he saw her gaze linger deliberately for a bare fraction of a second on his own left hand. The moment was so fleeting he couldn't be sure, but it seemed to be her own obvious attempt to see if he wore a ring, too. As she began walking away he realized his second bottle of beer was now almost empty and after a moment's deliberation he called after her once more.

"I normally don't have a third beer, but what the heck, you can bring me another when you get a second. All I have to do is stumble back to my hotel room."

She gave him a quick smile and nodded over her shoulder as she walked away. Jonathan watched her go, feeling the stirring of the kind of desire he hadn't felt in a while. She really was quite pretty, with a slim and willowy body. As she disappeared from his line of sight he turned his attention back to finishing off the remnants of his dinner. He watched the cook moving back and forth in the kitchen, presumably busy now with clean up as no new orders were coming in. The beers were doing their job and he felt a pleasant buzz from the alcohol, but he chided himself for ordering a third. He knew it would be all too easy to succumb to an alcoholic haze on a regular basis and that it would be a bad idea to do so.

He was just finishing the last of his meal when the fresh bottle appeared in front of him. He smiled up at her, but she didn't stay as yet another table was looking for their bill. He stared at the beer and asked himself why he had ordered it, before shrugging and grasping it to take a sip. He knew he should have just paid the bill and left too, but something had kept him from doing that.

The beer was affecting him, but it was also obvious there were only two possible reasons to stay. The owner Gwen held some allure and he felt the stirring of his need, although a sense of trepidation came with it and he knew acting on his need could complicate his life even more. But the other thought nagging at him was the curious talk of the cafe being haunted. He wondered if Gwen had ever encountered the spirit herself and what her thoughts would be about it.

Jonathan sighed, mentally kicking himself one last time for the third beer and for getting himself lost in what somehow seemed trivial matters when he had far larger questions to deal with and answer in his life. With a sigh over his weakness he caved in to the urge to check his email and pulled out his phone, but he soon regretted the decision. A number of concerned emails from friends asking how he was doing, a sarcastic note from his lawyer telling him matters with his ex had improved as she was now asking for only 99% of everything, instead of the 100% she had started with, and a whole bunch of emails trying to sell him something were all he had waiting for him.

In addition to the emails a few people from his workplace had sent him texts to ask how he was doing, but he decided to leave them for response later, knowing he would risk succumbing to the urge to tell everyone what he really felt. If there was one thing he had learned over the years, it was never a good plan to start sending emails or texts on sensitive topics after drinking a few beers.

Putting his phone away Jonathan focused on the conversation behind him once again and realized they were still on the topic of a spirit in the cafe. The greying, older black man Jonathan had seen working in the kitchen came out carrying a rack filled with small plates and coffee cups that looked still warm from the dishwasher and he began adding them to the counter shelving to replenish what was already there. As he finished rearranging them to suit his preference, he stopped and took a moment to catch his breath and look around the room. Catching Jonathan's eye, he smiled.

"Hope you enjoyed your meal, sir?"

"I did. You make that soup from scratch, did you?"

"Yes, sir. Made it fresh today."

"It was awesome. I could have made a meal of

that alone."

The cook smiled and nodded, turning to look around at the rest of the cafe. No one new had come in and the place was now barely a quarter full. The cook wiped his hands on his apron, as he appeared to focus on the three people still in deep discussion about a presence in the cafe. As Jonathan watched a strange look came over the cook's face, as he stood rooted to the spot obviously listening to them. After a few moments he gave a small start and Jonathan knew the man had realized he was being watched. The cook turned away and went back into the kitchen, returning a short time later with more racks of dishes to put away. But as he finished this time he remained, wiping his hands on his apron before taking it off and putting it aside to step around the counter.

Jonathan was still focusing on the nearby conversation, which had finally shifted to another topic. As he continued watching the cook from the corner of his eye he saw him perch on one of the nearby stools, close to the people at the table that had been talking about a ghost. The male at the table was in the midst of talking to the women, but he saw Willie approaching and finished what he was saying before acknowledging his presence.

"Yeah, well, believe it or not, it's true. Paula ran into him and confirmed that Dunstan has in fact returned to town. God knows why since he told us we were all losers and left years ago, swearing he would never come back, but she said to expect he is going to pop in here," he said, turning finally to face the cook.

"Evening, Willie. That was a damn fine meal, as always. You must have been a chef for a long time to get this good."

The chef shrugged and offered him a sour grin. "Maybe not as long as you think, James. Let's just say I had the time and motivation to pay attention and focus on a skill for the first time in my life once I got older. But say, I heard you talking about a ghost in here?"

James grunted, stifling a bigger laugh as he replied. "It's a spirit, Willie. Miriam is insisting we call it a spirit. Oww—"

"Yes, Willie, we were talking about a spirit," said Miriam, although she was still giving James a mock glare of frustration after punching him on the arm. She turned to the cook once she was satisfied he got the point.

"Why do you ask?"

"Well, I don't know why you are all talking about this, but I confess I had a strange experience in here earlier today when I was on my own."

Jonathan shifted slightly to get a better view of their reactions and he saw surprised looks flit across their faces. Their response seemed enough for Willie to launch into the story of what had happened to him in the kitchen without further encouragement. As he finished he gave them a wary look, almost as if he was expecting them to discount what he was saying.

"Well, isn't that interesting?" said Miriam. "Yes, we were indeed talking about the possibility there is a spirit or two here. I thought I saw something over there by the kitchen entrance and Melanie here said she felt a chill in the same area a while back. This is more than a coincidence we are all sensing a presence in the same general area at different times."

"Willie?" said Melanie. "Is this the first time you've encountered this? Have you ever seen a spirit before?"

"Uh, never encountered a spirit before and don't really want to again. This was the only time I've felt anything like that, at least while I was awake."

"What do you mean by that?"

Willie looked uncomfortable, but continued. "Well, as you know, Gwen gave me a room in the cafe here to stay in. I dunno, the mind plays tricks sometimes, especially when you are sleeping and on your own."

"Go on."

The cook sighed. "Look, all I know is I was in a real deep sleep before waking up from the strangest dream I've ever had. This was a couple of weeks ago. Something was in the room with me. I—sorry, all I can tell you is it was very strange.

"My God," said James. "What happened?"

"Well, look, I think my mind rebelled at what was happening and I forced myself awake. It just didn't—feel right. Of course, once I was actually awake there was nothing in the room with me."

"Did you feel a chill or anything like that?" said Melanie.

"No, but then I had a blanket on me. To be honest I can't be certain, as I was focused on getting my bearings and figuring out what just happened to me. I was really disoriented when I woke up. Look, I wasn't going to tell you about this, but you asked. I don't know if it was a dream or what, but if it really was just a dream it was the most vivid and real dream I think I've ever had."

"I understand it's hard to explain. Did you find any of this frightening, Willie?" said Miriam, a thoughtful look on her face.

Willie grimaced. "Yes, today I was scared, but you know what? I'm not sure I could tell you why. I came away with a sense it wasn't trying to hurt me, but I don't know why I know that. As for the dream, yeah, I guess I was a bit frightened by it all. That may have been why I woke up so fast."

They were all silent, obviously contemplating what they had heard. By now Jonathan wasn't surprised it was Miriam who broke the silence, given her interest in the supernatural.

"Willie, has Gwen said anything about this?"

The cook shook his head. "If she's felt something like this it's news to me. She hasn't said anything."

As one they turned to look for the owner. Jonathan did the same, unable to stop himself. Gwen was on the far side of the room with the only two other people in the cafe. They had just finished paying for their meal and the couple was now rising from their chairs to put their coats on. Jonathan looked down at the beer bottle in front of him and realized it had been empty for some time now.

With a shake of his head he sighed, wondering why he was still sitting here. Listening to ghost stories was the immediate answer, but the lassitude he felt had a deeper source. He pulled out his credit card and waved it at Gwen, who detoured over with the machine to process his payment. Jonathan knew the conversation beside him had stopped, as they were watching and waiting for Gwen.

Jonathan gathered himself and gave her a winning smile as he finished paying and stood up. He said goodbye and complimented the cook while she picked up the empty bottle and wiped the counter. She gave him a tired smile in return and walked away. He turned around to look at the still waiting group of people as he put on his raincoat again. One of the two women locked eyes with him, lingering long enough to make her frank appraisal of him obvious.

She appeared to be similar in age to the owner Gwen, but the similarity ended there as this woman had vaguely East Indian features. Sultry was the word that instantly appeared in his mind and for a moment he couldn't place why it did, but then he realized it was her midnight black, dark hair framing her alluring, pretty face and the air of sensuality she emanated.

With the rest of her body hidden by the table and a large shapeless sweater he knew he wasn't going to learn more that night, but even as that thought came he felt a strange certainty a simmering, powerful desire lay behind her dark eyes and it was focused entirely on him. Jonathan knew most women considered him handsome enough and at six feet tall with a lean, fit looking frame he would garner attention. Other women had in past set their sights on him, but he had never felt anything quite like this from anyone else.

He finished zipping up his coat and stepped out

into the night, standing for a moment in the light of the doorway to get his bearings. The rain had finally turned to a steady, light drizzle and the wind had eased significantly, although occasional gusts still buffeted the trees along the street. The thought of going straight back to the hotel appeared in his mind, but he dismissed the idea, knowing he would just be tempted to sit in the bar and get loaded.

Since the pounding rain had lessened, at least for the moment, he decided to try a walk along the beach. A vague memory from long ago told him the town had some sort of a big promenade between the edge of the beach and the buildings of the town. Thinking back to when he checked in he remembered seeing the path outside the bar windows and knew it must be the promenade he was thinking of.

He went further past the end of the cafe's empty verandah and saw a small, tree lined, but unlit pathway in the gap between the cafe and the building next door leading to the beach. He let his eyes adjust to the darkness before following it along the edge of the verandah and was soon standing on the edge of the beach. The gusts of wind here were stronger and every so often a stronger bout of rain lashed him like the touch of a whip, but he stayed where he was for a long time before finally turning to walk along the promenade, heading even further away from the center of town and the hotel. He couldn't remember how far the walkway went, but he would find out.

No one was outside on the walkway with him, but as he got further away from the business center he found there were homes sprinkled along the shoreline. Several had lights on inside, as it was only just past nine o'clock. Many had Christmas light displays outside, varying from a few simple strings of outdoor lights to ostentatious, massive installations of lights and huge lawn ornaments.

Being alone felt appropriate, as it fit his mood. With a sigh he turned his thoughts back to the problem at hand, knowing he would have to make yet another decision about what to do the next day. The absence of a goal of any sort made this a daily issue and it was becoming more of a burden each day. With nowhere to go and no one to see, both everything and nothing seemed possible.

The visit to his sister up north in the small coastal town they were born in had seemed a good enough plan for lack of anything better to do. He had not seen her or been back home for over five years. With both of their parents gone and no other siblings, she was the only close relation he had. But her husband was the same curmudgeon he remembered, a small town traditionalist dismissive and distrustful of anyone who lived in one of the big cities back east. Jonathan soon grew tired of the attitude and sarcastic remarks and left early, despite his sister's invitation to stay for Christmas. He knew she was in reality secretly relieved he had left, as a Christmas filled with tension was not what she wanted to have.

The paved walkway ended soon enough, turning into a gravel path that wound its way along the shoreline into the distance. The homes lining the shore grew further and further apart while the small street lamps that lit the paved walkway ended when the gravel path began. In the distance Jonathan could see the vague outlines of what looked like mobile home trailers.

Jonathan finally stopped and began retracing his steps, deciding he should have made a point to use the washroom before he left the cafe. With no one about he relieved himself in a patch of brush near the shoreline. Although the weather was moderating and the gusts had finally stopped, he knew he was growing chilled from the still steady wind and damp weather. The thought of sitting in front of the gas fireplace at the hotel with a glass of liqueur to warm him seemed appealing. At least it gave him something to do and if nothing else he could surround himself with the presence of other people, as he had been spending far too much time alone with his thoughts.

Back at the hotel he shed his wet clothes in his room and changed into something dry before making his way to the lounge and ordering the drink he had promised himself. Within moments a glass of the cognac he ordered appeared. Cognac wasn't a drink he normally enjoyed, but he felt the need to sip something slowly as he contemplated his future yet again.

The high ceilinged room he was in was built in a large semi circle jutting out toward the beach to afford as many view seats of the ocean as possible. On closer inspection he realized the large glass windows that stretched from the floor to the ceiling were a recent modification, similar to the gas fireplace, for his childhood memory was of much smaller windows. But at this time of night there was little to see and there were few people in the lounge. No obvious opportunity to talk to anyone arose and Jonathan didn't feel like making one, so he nursed his drink in silence as he stared into the gas fire.

When it was almost empty the server came by to ask if he wanted another, but Jonathan shook his head. No flashes of insight had come to him and Jonathan wasn't surprised, as he knew all too well there weren't answers to be found in an empty cognac glass. He paid his bill and went to his room, mechanically readying himself for bed.

When sleep came it was fitful, and he found himself tossing and turning. He was semi awake when he realized it sounded like the rain and wind had started again, loud enough he could sense it flaying the hotel. Turning, he looked at the bedside clock and saw it was now three o'clock in the morning. Sighing, he sat up and got out of bed, going to the window to pull aside the curtains. From the darkness of his room he could see the main street outside and in the cones of light from the streetlights it was clear fresh waves of rain were lashing a large puddle of water around a street drain clogged with leaves.

He stood at the window for a long time before he finally shook his head. The dream he had been having before he awoke grew more vague with every second, but he knew it had revolved around an ephemeral feminine presence drawing him ever closer. The problem was he had not been close enough to grasp her.

"My God. I guess I need someone tonight," he

whispered to himself as he stood watching the rainwater pour down the street in steady rivers.

He knew he had questions that needed answers, but he had no idea what they would be or how he would find them. As he was about to turn away yet another dim memory of his long ago stay in the town as a child surfaced, a memory of playing on the beach in the early morning sunshine with a host of other children turned loose by their mothers. The simple joy of finding a kind of small, strange looking flat fish none of them had ever seen before marooned in a tidal pool was followed by the thrill of discovering a Dungeness crab that had buried almost its entire body in the tidal mud to await the return of the water with the tide.

The memory lightened his mood a fraction and he came to a decision, taking the memory as a sign. He wondered if more such happy memories could be found or new ones made if he stayed a bit longer in the town. With images of the pretty owner of the cafe and the sultry, dark haired woman that seemed interested in him in his mind the notion seemed worth the chance, but he still wasn't certain it was what he really wanted. Jonathan shook his head, closing the curtains before going back to bed.

Chapter Two

On the third night in a row Jonathan showed up for dinner in the cafe Gwen raised an eyebrow as she passed him the menu. Before he could speak she bustled away, having obviously assumed he would want the beer she soon returned with. She poured the beer into a glass and pursed her lips as she set it on the table before him.

"You're becoming another one of my regulars, Jonathan."

"I like the food and the atmosphere," said Jonathan, giving her a winning smile.

Gwen lifted a corner of her mouth in a tiny smile of her own. "Chef Willie has a special tonight, a shepherd's pie. I know that may not sound special, but I highly recommend it. I don't know how he does it, but its better than any I've tasted elsewhere. You won't leave here hungry."

"I'm sold," said Jonathan, handing her back the unopened menu.

As she smiled and left to put in the order Jonathan turned to look around the cafe. Not as many people were present as on the first day he had dinner there, but of interest the three people who had engaged in a conversation about the spirit were back after being absent the night before. He immediately locked eyes for a moment with the sultry, dark haired woman who had shown interest in him before realizing they had more people at the table with them. Yet another woman of about the same age was present, along with a girl of maybe ten or eleven years of age. Jonathan realized the woman was sight impaired when he saw a young golden retriever dog wearing a harness lying on the floor beside the woman.

Instead of sitting at the counter this time he had sat at a nearby table for two set against the far wall with what would have been a commanding view of the beach if it hadn't been full dark outside. Jonathan sighed and pulled out his phone to check his messages and emails, knowing it had to be done. As there was nothing of consequence to deal with he was soon able to put it away and stare into the distance. The disadvantage of sitting where he was meant he was too far away to hear clearly what the people were saying, so his mind drifted back over the last two days.

The churning, heavy storm that had rolled in as predicted by the desk clerk at the hotel made for interesting watching in the view lounge on his first full day in the town, in between periods focused on reading a book, but it all left him with little motivation to go outside. A quick dash out to the cafe late in the evening when the storm finally began to ease was his only sojourn out, but today had been vastly different.

Although the weather was cloudy and threatening the possibility of change at any time, it was calm enough to actually be pleasant to walk the long shoreline. He loved smelling the fresh scent of cedar trees washed by the storm, mingling with the salt-water tang of the clean ocean air and the smell of new debris on the beach brought up by the storm. He enjoyed it so much he was out long enough to get chilled to the bone.

The long walk along the curve of the seemingly endless shoreline brought back more long buried memories. He now remembered being all of perhaps seven years old when his mother had brought him and his sister to the town for a week. His mother's sister had brought her children too, and they had stayed at a small cottage a block off the beach. Jonathan recalled doing a sleepover in it, so on the way back to the hotel he detoured from the beach path to search for it without success. But he felt refreshed from the walk and, enjoying the positive memories, he made a booking with the same hotel clerk for a few more days before heading to his room for a long nap.

Gwen interrupted his thoughts by placing dinner in front of him and he was soon devouring it with gusto, since it was even better than she had promised. She was bustling about the cafe tidying up as customers left, but when he finished she brought over the second beer he had signaled her for and this time she remained to talk to him. They were still talking two minutes later when the dark haired woman at the other table called over and interrupted them.

"Gwen? Why don't you take a break and join us? You've pretty much got everything tidied up already and you can introduce us to your new friend while you're at it."

With a start, Jonathan looked around and realized that once again he was the only other patron in the cafe. But Gwen smiled and turned to catch his attention.

"Yes, I should introduce you, since you seem to

be my newest regular customer. You may as well join my other regulars, who also happen to be very good friends of mine. Pull a chair over."

Gwen introduced him as he complied and the others shifted to make room at the table. As he settled into his chair again he eyed them with the same level of interest they all seemed to be displaying toward him.

The dark haired woman smiled. "We didn't see you last night."

Jonathan shrugged. "I was in here kind of late. Must have been the last customer."

The first to be introduced was Miriam Christopher, the woman he had already identified as the one who owned the new age shop. She had short, sandy brown hair and was wearing a flowing, flowery dress that matched her hair, reminding Jonathan of the style of clothes worn back in the sixties. Her most unusual feature was her striking, hazel colored eyes with flecks of gold in them. Beyond the dress, the only other outward sign she might be the owner of a new age shop was a large, beautifully cut crystal she wore on a chain around her neck. She grasped it in her hand as she told him about the shop she owned.

The dark haired woman who had invited him over was Melanie Patel. Today she was wearing a blouse tight enough that Jonathan had to force himself to focus on her dark eyes as they shook hands. She gave him a knowing smile and she left her hand in his grasp longer than necessary. Although her interest was obvious, the wedding ring on her left hand made him wonder what she was really thinking.

The newcomer to the group introduced herself as Paula Meeker. She was a petite woman with plain features and curly hair, but she was pretty enough in a simple way. She smiled in his direction as she introduced the child beside her.

"This is my daughter Cate," she said, placing a protective hand on the girl's shoulder. "And as I'm sure you've realized by now, I am sight impaired. My friendly dog is named Joker."

Jonathan laughed. "So how does a guide dog get a name like that?"

Paula grinned in return. "I don't know why they gave him that name, but I have my suspicions. I've only had him a little while, so we're still learning about each other. When a guide dog is in harness he knows he has a job to do, but when you take it off he's free to just be a dog. I'm finding this one wants to make up for lost time and party when he's free of the harness. He seems to have a penchant for running off with things like my slippers, so maybe that's where his name came from."

"You only just got him? He does look rather young."

"Yes, he's pretty much fresh out of training school. I've not had a dog before, but the minimal eyesight I have left has worsened to the point I need him. In point of fact I think he's better trained than I am, but we'll get used to it. With his help and my smartphone apps I'll get by."

"And your daughter doesn't have the same problem?"

Paula sighed and hesitated a brief second before

replying. A worried look appeared on her face.

"It is starting to look like she may have inherited problems similar to mine. We're actually just waiting for more test results to tell us for certain. There was a good chance she would be okay, but we didn't get a break. She's had glasses since grade two and her eyesight keeps getting worse. There is talk they might be able to do something with lasers, but it would be very expensive and experimental. It's too late for me, but it might help her. The problem is I can't afford it, but I guess we'll see."

"Well, everyone is different, so maybe it will be okay."

"You know, if I was going to have a dog, it would be one like this," said the male beside her, reaching down to scratch behind the dog's ear before turning to Jonathan and sticking out his hand. As Jonathan grasped his hand and shook it, the man introduced himself as James Straith.

Jonathan pointed at the t-shirt James was wearing as he withdrew his hand. Emblazoned on the chest area were the words Fire Rescue in bold, capital letters along with the fire department logo of a town almost an hour drive further down the coast.

"A fire guy, are you?"

"Yep. Been in the service for ten years now, ever since I left here. I'm just back to visit my folks for Christmas."

Jonathan wasn't surprised to be right, as the man before him filled out the t-shirt with well-defined muscles and a strong neck from plenty of time spent working out. A number of tattoos ran up both arms, while a small burn scar running down the side of his face past his jawline gave him a daring, rakish air that Jonathan knew the women would likely find irresistible.

"So I get the sense you all know each other rather well?" said James. "Is everyone from around here?"

"Yes," said Gwen. "We all went to the local high school and if you were wondering about why we are all look around the same age that would be your answer. There were lots of other people we hung out with, but many of them have moved away. Some of us, like me, actually came back, although the rest of my family is gone. I'm glad my friends are still here, because they've become my surrogate family."

"And you?" said James. "What brings you to town?"

Jonathan explained how he had been visiting his sister and was otherwise for the moment just travelling and taking his time about it. He continued after seeing their puzzled looks at the vagueness of his response.

"I work back east, but I'm taking some time off just now. My parents are gone and I hadn't seen my sister for a long time, so I came out for a visit."

The girl Cate spoke up for the first time, with a puzzled look on her face. "Couldn't you stay with her for Christmas?"

"Ah—well, no. Um—they were going away for a visit to her husband's side of the family for Christmas."

The puzzled look remained on the little girl's face, but her mother seemed to sense Jonathan was struggling with his answer and she forestalled any further questions with a squeeze of her daughter's shoulder. She smoothed it over further with her own question.

"So what do you do for a living back east, Jonathan?"

"I'm a—financial specialist. I work on high-level private sector analysis for the government and I manage a small team of people. It's all rather boring and dry stuff to be honest, unless you like lots of numbers and spreadsheets."

Jonathan could see from the looks on their faces they were all puzzled at the bland lack of detail in his answer, but they seemed willing to accept they weren't going to get any more information out of him.

"Well, that's all fine, but to me the interesting part is why you are still hanging around here?" said Melanie, with a teasing look on her face.

Jonathan laughed. "Good question. As I said, the truth is I don't really have a deadline to be anywhere at the moment. I was thinking about maybe finding some sunshine and doing a beach vacation down south, but as you know I stopped in town overnight here a few days back. I remembered staying here on vacation when I was a kid and I like it, so I've stuck around. I enjoyed watching the storm the other day while at the hotel, too. As for the cafe, I expect I don't need to tell any of you how good the chef's cooking is here and I have to eat somewhere, so here I am. And since I'm being honest, I guess I got curious, too."

"Curious?" said Gwen. "About what?"

Jonathan shrugged, allowing an apologetic look

to appear on his face.

"I wasn't deliberately listening in to your conversation the first night I was here, you understand, but I couldn't help overhearing you folks talking about a spirit or spirits haunting the cafe. I've never experienced anything like that before and I'm curious."

They all looked around at each other before Paula spoke up in response, a puzzled look creasing her face.

"A spirit haunting the cafe?"

"Yes," said Miriam, as she quickly outlined what had happened, before turning back to Jonathan. "I was actually just about to tell Paula all about this, so we could talk about what we can do to help it."

"Do to help it?" said James. "What can you do about a spirit?"

Miriam was about to reply when the door to the cafe opened and two men came in. One of them was an older, grey bearded man dressed in a Santa Claus suit who was carrying a small plastic kettle with a slot in the top for people to make donations. Everyone turned to look at them in surprise, as it was now well past the peak dinner hour and it was unlikely anyone new would come in now.

"Good God, he really has come back to town," said Melanie, as the newcomer not wearing the Santa suit came over with a big grin on his face.

This man was about the same age as the rest of them, but he sported more signs of age than everyone else. He face was deeply tanned and lined, with sun bleached, dark blonde hair, while the rest of his body frame appeared thin. He pulled up a chair and slumped into it, unzipping his jacket and dumping his cell phone and a pack of cigarettes on the table in front of him.

"Hey, losers! I'm back. Did you all miss me?"

"Of course not, Dunstan," said Gwen with an edge to her voice, before she turned to the man in the Santa suit who was looking directly at her for attention. "Say, George, thanks for bringing the donation kettle. Stay for a drink? I could pour you a hot coffee with a little something in it."

"Donations?" said Dunstan. "Why would anyone want to give away all of his hard earned money? Probably going to give it to a bunch of failures and street scum. Are you sure he isn't running some kind of a scam?"

The man in the Santa suit turned to Dunstan with an incredulous look on his face, but before he could respond Gwen sighed and spoke again.

"Ignore him, George, he's an idiot. Drink?"

George scowled briefly at Dunstan and shook his head, before turning to Gwen. "No, thank you, my dear, another day. I have a few more to drop off. I'll just leave this on the counter here and be off."

James spoke up as the door closed behind the Santa. "Still the same jackass you were ten years ago, huh?"

"Depends on your point of view, straight man. I prefer to think of myself as a winner, probably more so than any of you. Any of you become a millionaire and are swimming in money like me yet? I expect not. Hey, Gwen, the old guy didn't want a drink, but I sure do. Got any beer?"

Gwen sighed and got up. "Yes. I have some

choices—"

"You know what kind of beer I like. I haven't changed."

James and Jonathan both signaled to Gwen they wanted a refill too, so she went over to the nearby fridge and came back with their orders as the conversation continued.

"Yes, you sure seem like the same jackass, Dunstan," said Melanie. "Has the lesson that money isn't everything never sunk in with you?"

"Of course money is everything. Makes the world go round. Far as I'm concerned, when it comes to money, there are only winners and losers in this world. And I assure you, I haven't spent the last ten years in Las Vegas being a loser. Vegas is the holy city I worship in, baby."

Melanie sighed. "My God, you've gotten worse, not better. And I'm not your baby, asshole."

"Suit yourself, hot stuff. Well, you can believe me or not, but I actually have missed all of you. It's been a long time."

Dunstan paused and looked at Jonathan. "So who's this dude?"

Jonathan introduced himself and Dunstan immediately asked him what he did for a living. Jonathan gave him the same explanation as before and Dunstan raised an eyebrow.

"Government, huh? You some kind of spook?"

Jonathan smiled, folding his arms as he sat back in his chair before responding. "Define 'spook' and I'll tell you whether I am or not."

Dunstan gave him a dark look and turned away. "He's a government spook. Don't trust him."

"So what are you doing back here, Dunstan?" said Paula. "I think you're right, it must be all of ten years or more since we last saw you. What have you been doing?"

Dunstan shrugged. "Making money in Vegas. Yeah, I was up, I was down, damn near went into bankruptcy more than once, but if you know the right people and you're prepared to do what you have to do, you can get it done. It's all about whom you know, who your friends are, and doing favors when you have to. Well, sometimes it also includes stepping on these friends since they really aren't friends. Like I said, you do what you have to in order get somewhere."

"Well, if you're so busy trampling on other people, why the hell are you back here?" said James.

"Came to see the old man, I suppose. Needed a break from Vegas after ten years. And, of course, I miss the rain here. Or not. Or maybe it's because I heard she was single again," replied Dunstan with a grin that seemed suspiciously like a leer, nodding in Gwen's direction. "Or maybe all of the above."

Everyone turned to look at Gwen, who wore a frozen, unreadable look on her face for a long moment before she spoke.

"Yes, I remember now, it was your caring, sensitive nature I fell for during a brief moment of temporary insanity all those years ago. Lord."

Turning, she looked around at the rest of them as she continued.

"Can you believe this? No mention of being sorry for my recent loss. The big man is back in town, so

I should just invite him in, take my clothes off, and await him in bed, huh?"

"Uh, people, can we please remember we have a child present here?" said Paula.

Gwen turned, a mortified look on her face. "Sorry, he's just setting me off."

"Oh, come on, I'm not that bad, Gwen," said Dunstan. "I was at least planning on taking you out to dinner first. Besides, he's gone and isn't coming back. Dead is dead. You gotta move on sooner or later."

"Well, good luck with that, Dunstan," said James, with the hint of a sharp edge to his voice. "She doesn't sound interested to me. So you're back to see your parents?"

Dunstan shrugged again. "I suppose. Mom passed away, just the old man left."

Miriam looked skeptical. ""You suppose? Can you be any fuzzier than that? And it's just your Dad you came to see? Last I recall the two of you weren't exactly close. And what about your sister?"

"She's gone too. Overdosed on some bad shit out on the street and they didn't get to her in time."

"My God, I'm sorry to hear this, Dunstan," replied Miriam. "Did you come back for their services?"

"No. Dad never organized services or put notices out. He thinks like I do about it. They're dead. What's the point of going to a service? They're not around to know if I don't attend. You may not agree, but I think those things are a waste of time and I'd be a fraud if I went despite feeling that way."

"Well, I guess I can't argue with that approach if this is how you feel about it, but I can't say I feel the same way," said Paula.

Dunstan turned the conversation to what everyone had been doing for the past ten years and they spent the next several minutes taking turns filling him in. Jonathan was interested to learn more details about the people at the table as one by one they gave him a brief summary of their own past ten years.

Gwen had married one of her high school friends and moved away, but he passed away just after they came back to open the cafe. James had married and divorced twice after moving away for his work. Paula never married the father of Cate and their relationship ended years before. She had found work as a clerk for the town administration to support herself and her daughter. Miriam had never married and had come back to town to run her shop. Jonathan was interested to learn Melanie had married and her husband travelled a lot, but she was now divorced and working remotely from home in the insurance business.

As she finished speaking everyone turned to look at chef Willie as he appeared from the kitchen and came over, obviously looking for Gwen.

"I'm all done in the kitchen, Gwen. You need a hand with clean up out here before I head downstairs?"

"Thanks, Willie, but I can manage from here on. There isn't much left to do."

"This guy your cook, Gwen? What do you pay him? I'll bet it's more than you need to. Guys that can cook are a dime a dozen in Vegas."

Willie had been turning to leave, but he stopped and glared at Dunstan in disbelief. Gwen held up a hand to forestall Willie and rolled her eyes as she spoke.

"My God. What I pay him is none of your business, you a—I mean, you idiot. Willie is a fine chef and is worth every cent I pay him."

The others at the table all chimed in and voiced support for Willie, who gave them a small smile before turning away without speaking. He was stopped from leaving once again by Miriam.

"Willie? Don't go just yet, please. You were telling us the other day about your experiences with the spirit here. Our new friend Jonathan here is curious about what happened and was asking about it. Paula was, too. I want to talk to everyone here about what we can do to help the spirit, but I need more information. I'm wondering if you could maybe take a stab at finding the right words for what happened to you when you were sleeping that night. I know it's tough, but I'm hoping you can try? Maybe you could tell us about what happened in the kitchen again, too, since Paula wasn't here to hear you."

Willie had let his head droop and he was staring at the floor as she was speaking. When she finished he took a few long moments before giving a deep sigh and looking up.

"All right," he said, describing what happened to him in the kitchen again. When he finished that story, he took a moment to obviously compose his thoughts before continuing.

"As for my dream, if I can call it that, I guess I've had a couple of days to process what happened a bit more. I never expected to be talking to anyone about it, you see? Look, as I told you the other day, I was in a real deep sleep. For lack of a better description, I felt like I was under pressure, something was forcing me to wake up. It wasn't exactly pleasant, but I didn't feel scared, at least not at that point. The thing is, though, I didn't actually wake up. The pressure just built up until, in my dream, I got out of bed and stood up. I got scared when I looked down and realized my body was still on the bed."

Willie stopped a moment to shrug. "I know, that sounds crazy, even for a dream. I could see my eyes were closed, but my face was looking like I was under stress and I was kind of writhing on the bed a little. I turned around and looked behind me, and there in the middle of the room was this sort of— well, a blob of something. It was like a swirling mass, wisps of light, or something. I could sense the stress I was feeling was coming from whatever it was doing to me and at this point I really, and I do mean really, just wanted this to stop. I reached out my hands to kind of ward it away and told it in my mind to stop with all the strength I could find. And that is when I really did wake up."

"My God, Willie," said Miriam. "Were you all right when you finally woke?"

"Yes, but I was real disoriented. The whole thing had been so vivid and strange. But there was nothing in the room with me. I dunno, it hasn't happened to me again, but I go to sleep every night wondering."

"Well, that just seems like a load of total bullshit, Miriam," said Dunstan. "I don't know what all this crap about a spirit being here is, but far as I'm concerned if the basic five senses we all have don't work on something then whatever that something is doesn't exist. He had a weird dream, that's all. Or maybe he's been in the back smoking some of that same wacky shit you were always getting blasted on in high school and he smoked too much."

"I doubt that, you asshole," said Miriam. "You know, I haven't touched any of that stuff for years now, but your presence is making me wish I had something like it to scrub you from my mind. So congratulations on making me say a bad word for the first time in months. As I suspected, you haven't changed much in ten years, have you?"

As Dunstan laughed Melanie spoke up, summarizing what she and Miriam had experienced in the cafe before continuing.

"Think what you like, Dunstan, but I agree with Miriam that something is going on here. What you two don't know is Gwen told me she's also had a few strange experiences since she took over here, although she didn't give me much detail. Who knows, maybe we'll all catch a glimpse of the ghost if we keep hanging around. It sure seems to want to show itself."

Dunstan grunted. "Damn, I'll make sure to bring my camera next time I'm in here. Hey, if someone uses their cell phone to grab some video we can post it online and get a few million views. Maybe we could flog it and make a few bucks, too. We'll be famous. Oh, hey! We could start a business, get some costumes and a funky car with a siren, like that movie back in the eighties, and make a pile of money cleaning up ghost slime."

"Miriam is right, Dunstan," said Melanie. "You really still are an arse."

"Yes. Yes, I am. None of you expected that to change, did you?"

Ignoring him, Miriam turned to Gwen. "Is that true, Gwen? You've encountered the spirit too?"

Gwen looked uncomfortable before shrugging. "I don't know. I've felt a weird cold spot a couple of times, but didn't think much of it. One was just the other day, outside my bedroom. I didn't really pay much attention as I was in a hurry to get back down to the cafe. To be honest I can't really say it was a ghost or something."

"You people really are serious about this nonsense, aren't you?" said Dunstan. "Even if any of this is real, which I don't believe, why do you care anyway? It's not like you can do anything about it."

This time Jonathan spoke up, gaining him mild looks of surprise from the others. "Well, I'm not sure about that. Look, I'm on the fence here as to whether I believe it all or not, but I'm willing to keep an open mind. And if it is real and the spirit or spirits in here need some help, as I think Miriam suggested she wants to offer, then why not do so?"

Miriam smiled. "Thank you for that, and yes, I do want to help. Look, all of you, since we talked about this a few days ago I've spent a fair bit of time meditating about it and contemplating the situation here. I feel this is happening for a reason, although it's not at all clear why. I'm not even certain this is just one spirit. It may be more than one. The thing is, the more time I spent focusing on this the more certain I became that we have been given a task."

"A task? What does that mean?" said Jonathan, a puzzled look on his face.

"It means exactly that. Look, I'm no expert on this. All I can tell you is what I feel and believe. We are faced with a situation that is wrong, you see? This is a spirit, or maybe more than one, that for whatever reason has not let go and truly passed onward. That isn't supposed to happen, but obviously it sometimes does. I think it needs help to deal with its situation, to free itself, and I believe this is where we come in. I don't know for certain how to go about helping it, but it feels to me that doing so is our task."

The sound of Dunstan's chair scraping across the floor came as he shoved it back and stood up, making everyone turn to look at him. As he made his way over to the beer fridge he looked over at Gwen.

"I decided not to bother you and go get a refill for myself. I expect you aren't going to let me smoke in here, are you?"

"Certainly not. There's a local bylaw that says no smoking in restaurants. You'll have to go out onto the verandah."

Dunstan came back with his beer and grabbed his pack of cigarettes off the table before heading to the door.

"I'll gladly go outside. If I stick around in here someone will assign me some kind of crazy job to do, like go out and buy one of those boards where everyone puts their hand on the marker that moves around and spells out words. Hey, maybe we should get a crystal ball while we're at it. You can decide which of those you want to try while I'm gone."

A silence descended as the door closed behind him, broken finally by Jonathan.

"I hope you'll all forgive me for saying this, but how did a nice bunch of people like you find yourselves stuck with him as a friend?"

Several of the people around the table either stifled grins or looked away to hide them, but James burst into laughter and replied.

"Yeah, we've wondered that ourselves. Seriously, this town isn't that big. Only one high school and that means everyone pretty much knows everyone, right? Dunstan was always the guy that came close to the line with his friends, but never crossed it. I think he secretly enjoys goading people, or at least, he did when we were all younger. Reason he never crossed the line is he needs an audience to give him a standing ovation every day. He hasn't changed much."

Turning serious, James focused on Miriam. "So Miriam, back to this task you are talking about. Look, you know me. I'm a pretty straight guy. I don't agree with the way Dunstan is getting his message across, but I confess I understand his thinking more than all this talk of having a task to help a spirit. What makes you so certain we need to be doing something?"

Miriam was silent for a long moment and looked around the table before she spoke.

"I respect that everyone has their own perspective about the spiritual world and this is as it should be. For me, I've come to understand each of us is a spirit housed in a material shell that is on a journey to learn and grow. Heaven knows I didn't understand that when I was younger. What the ultimate purpose of it all is I don't know, just like none of you know either. However, I am certain that the universe has purpose and so do we. I think life is like school and we are here to learn. Learning means being given homework, if you will. Each of us is given situations in life and tasks to deal with, and our job is to perform them to the best of our ability and learn. And among other things, one of the big lessons I believe we are all here to learn is how to show compassion for others. For the record, I'm not alone in thinking like this. There are plenty of books out there I could share with you which talk about this."

She paused a moment, looking directly at James again.

"If you look in your heart, James, you know I am right, because you already have a lot of compassion for others. You are a firefighter. You put it on the line every time you answer a call. You run into danger when the rest of us are running away."

"Miriam, they pay me to do that, you know."

"They do, and that too is as it should be. But I know for you it is more than money. You have a genuine desire to help others in your heart. You may have your warts, like the rest of us, but at heart you are such a good man, James Straith. But where I'm going with this is I've looked into my own heart and contemplated what is happening here. One or more spirits have reached out to us here and I am certain our job is to find the compassion in our hearts to help fix this. I can feel it. And I think we need to do this sooner rather than later."

"But are you sure they need help?" said Jonathan, a puzzled look on his face. "Perhaps the spirit or spirits aren't as friendly as we might think. Maybe they don't want to be helped and they are instead trying to harm us for some reason?"

"No, the spirit needs help," said Cate.

Everyone turned to look at the girl and as Paula spoke to her daughter amazement was written on her face.

"You seem rather certain of that. How do you know?"

"I'm not sure how I know, I just know it," shrugged Cate. "I can feel she is right."

"I agree," said Melanie. "I don't know why, but I feel that too. It feels right that we offer help. Maybe the spirit or spirits won't want it, but we have to try."

"Well," said Gwen. "I suppose I can go along with that, although I have no idea what to do. I confess this place has felt odd to me ever since I moved in close to a year ago. We've certainly got enough people experiencing strange things here and what Miriam thinks she saw kind of sounds like what Willie saw in his sleep, so I don't think it's our collective imagination. But I guess I don't understand why it's only recently that things have been happening."

"When did you first notice something, Gwen?"

said Miriam.

Gwen grimaced. "I don't know. The first time I felt a cold spot must have been maybe five or six months ago, around when I first came back here."

"And you, Willie?"

"That dream I had was maybe a month or so back. And then, of course, there was the other day in the kitchen."

Everyone was silent for a long moment, before Miriam spoke.

"Well, that would be a mystery for certain. Who knows? Perhaps the spirit has in its own way been contemplating its fate and is slowly moving to seek help?"

"Miriam?" said Cate. "I thought ghosts were bad and they try to scare people."

"No one knows, but I don't personally think all ghosts are bad. Maybe some of them do try to hurt people or scare them, although I don't know why they would. Remember, spirits are just people that have passed, but not fully let go. If the person had behaved badly in life, it would be logical the spirit would bear the burden of those same characteristics."

"So why do they stay in one place? Why don't they go wherever they want?"

"Good question and I don't know. I suspect it's because they felt an attachment to a place for some reason and they simply cannot let go. Or maybe something really bad happened to them in it? For example, I could certainly see if someone was hurt they might now feel tied to the place by the trauma. Look, all I know is there are great mysteries in life and maybe in death, too."

"This is interesting," said Paula. "You know, because of my sight impairment I'm kind of used to paying attention to my other senses and that certainly includes how I feel at any given time. I haven't felt or sensed anything in the few times I've been here. However, I've been sitting here trying to sort out how this place feels to me right now and, near as I can tell, there actually is kind of an odd feel to this old house. It doesn't necessarily feel bad or wrong, but it doesn't feel right either. Does that make any sense?"

"Does anyone have any really bad feelings about this place?" said Miriam.

A silence descended as everyone considered the question. James frowned and rubbed his chin in thought, while Gwen looked like she was about to say something and thought better of it. No one seemed ready to answer the question, so Jonathan spoke up.

"You know what? This place does feel—odd. Don't know why I know that. But I don't have any real bad feeling about this. Its not like I'm in some horror movie where there's a sense of something evil waiting for me."

"I don't know," said Willie, a frown creasing his face. "I didn't come away from my encounters with whatever this is feeling happy."

"Well, I'm no expert, but this just doesn't seem like an average kind of haunting, if there is such a thing. It certainly isn't anything like you see in the movies. And I still don't get why it's happening more now than it was when Gwen first moved in here," said Jonathan.

"I think this is happening now because Christmas is coming," said Cate.

Once again everyone turned and gave the girl surprised looks. After a little pause, Miriam smiled and replied.

"Who knows? That just might be the most perceptive thing anyone has said here all night. Well, look everyone, all I know is something is going on and I have a really strong feeling we need to do something about this and do it sooner than later. So who is with me on this?"

Before anyone could respond the door to the verandah opened and a cold blast of chill air followed Dunstan in before he closed it. He came over to the table and shrugged out of his coat, draping it over the back of the chair.

"God Almighty, I've forgotten how the chill here on the coast just seeps into your bones no matter what you're wearing. This sure isn't Vegas. Gwen, you got anything warm with booze in it to offer?"

Gwen shrugged. "My license says I sell beer and wine, but I happen to have a little bottle of brandy under the counter. I still got some coffee warm, so I can pour some of that together for you if you want."

"Oh, yes, please," said Dunstan, rubbing his hands together and sitting down as Gwen went to get it for him. "So, are we done talking about all that spooky crap, I hope?"

"Actually, no," said Melanie. "Miriam just asked us if we were prepared to help her do what we can for the spirit or spirits stuck here."

Dunstan groaned, but Melanie gave him an arch

look before turning to Miriam to speak.

"Miriam, you can count me in, although I'm not entirely sure what I'm getting into here."

One by one the rest of the people around the table echoed Melanie and agreed to help out, leaving only Gwen and Dunstan to respond. Gwen came back and dropped a steaming cup in front of Dunstan along with a big bottle of brandy before sitting down again.

"Help yourself, Dunstan," she said, before turning to Miriam. "I guess I'm in, but I sure wouldn't mind knowing what the plan is."

"I'll bet it's a séance," said Dunstan, pouring a generous amount of brandy into the coffee. "Better make sure you get the right phone number for the spooks in this place first, though. You could end up bringing Genghis Khan or some serial axe murderer in for a visit."

"If you're going to be the first victim, I'll be the first at the table for the séance," said Gwen.

"Damn, I knew you still loved me," said Dunstan with a huge grin.

This time it was Gwen that groaned in response and she was joined by a few of the others at the table. Jonathan cleared his throat before speaking to catch their attention.

"So—joking about séances aside, since we've all agreed something needs to be done and I am still curious enough about this, I hope you're all okay with my sticking around to help. So what is the next step?"

Everyone turned once again to look at Miriam as James spoke up.

"I think you need to point us in the right direction on this, Miriam. You're the one selling crystals and new age stuff, which is more qualification to guide us than anyone else here. So do we just sit around and wait for the spirit or spirits to contact us again?"

"Well, I don't know about my being more qualified, but I do think we need more information. More contacts might well help us understand better. But I think I'd like to know more about the history of this place. I should think getting a better sense of who lived here before might help. Do you know anything about that Gwen?"

"Not really. We had a building inspection done before we purchased it, but that didn't give much in the way of details about the history. I do know its over a hundred years old. The place was built in 1906, so it's been around a long time. Probably had many owners."

"Hmm. Well, I—"

A low whine from Paula's dog caught everyone's attention. He had been sleeping on the floor at Paula's feet the whole time they had been talking, but as everyone looked under the table at him they saw his head had come up and he was staring with intent in the direction of the entrance to the kitchen.

"What is it, Joker?" said Cate, placing her hand on his head.

Joker remained staring, this time in silence, at the entrance. Everyone followed his gaze, but there was nothing to be seen. After a long moment James stood up.

"Perhaps our spirit friend is paying us a visit? I'll go have a look."

He made his way to the entrance and stood there for a few seconds before disappearing into the kitchen and the storerooms out of sight. A minute later he reappeared and came back to sit down. He shrugged in response to the questioning looks.

"Nothing. Didn't see anything, didn't feel anything. And I see Joker has gone back to sleep."

Everyone looked down to see the dog was once again resting with his eyes closed and head on his paws.

Dunstan grunted as he poured yet another big shot of the brandy into his now empty cup.

"Don't know what you were all getting excited about. The dog was probably dreaming about chasing that black cat I almost tripped over when I came in."

"Miriam?" said Paula, with an odd tone to her voice. "Did you see anything? You said you thought you had seen something before."

"No. Not this time. Paula, are you all right?"

"Ah—yes, I'm okay. It's just I thought I felt something strange there for a moment. I don't know how to describe it. Although the feeling is gone, I—this may seem weird, but I've got a sense we need to act on this soon too, just like Miriam. I don't know. Anyway, before Joker interrupted us I was about to suggest we talk to Tom and Athena if we want to know more about the history of this place. We could stumble around doing research on our own, but what's the point? I'll bet at least one of them will have some useful intelligence for us. If not, they will certainly point us in the right direction."

"Well, I think we are all in this to help, since

everyone seems to agree we should do something. Contacting Tom and Athena is a good start," said James. "Hadn't thought of them."

"Yes, I agree," said Miriam. "Can you talk to them for us, Paula?"

"Sure. I might even be able to get them to come here tomorrow night to talk to us."

"Sorry, folks," said Jonathan. "Who are these people and why could they help?"

"Tom is a high school teacher here in town," said Melanie. "We all know him because we were all in his classes. He's a wonderful man. And his friend Athena is a senior manager with the town who's been around as long as him. Paula is right, if anyone can help out here it would be them."

"Athena is my boss," said Paula. "She's a lovely person too. I'll ask her about this first thing in the morning. Come to think of it, I do have to work tomorrow and it's time for Cate to get to bed. I'll let Gwen know if they can make it and we can maybe meet tomorrow night after the dinner rush around the same time?"

A few of them took quick looks at their watches and cell phones for the time. Everyone agreed with the idea and as Paula and Cate rose to leave their departure turned into the catalyst for the rest of them as well. The next few minutes were occupied with people paying their bills and leaving in a steady stream.

The one exception was Dunstan, who remained sitting and swirling the brandy in his cup while staring at Gwen. Jonathan was one of the last to pay and as he shrugged into his coat he saw the only people now left were James and Dunstan. James had already paid, but he hadn't put his coat on yet and was standing there holding it in his hands as he eyed Dunstan still sitting where he was.

"You coming?" said James.

Dunstan shrugged and looked at Gwen, who had finally turned her attention to him.

"Actually, I was hoping to stick around for a bit and reminisce with Gwen about old times. Besides, I haven't finished off this bottle of brandy yet."

Gwen reached over and grabbed the bottle, marching back to the counter to put it away while she responded to Dunstan.

"Sorry, Gwen's Cafe is now officially closed for the day. I'm tired Dunstan. If you really must talk to me, try another night."

Dunstan stared at her for a few moments before turning to look at James, who still hadn't made any moves to put his coat on. The two men stared at each other long enough that Jonathan began to wonder what would happen next, but Dunstan abruptly shoved his chair back and stood up. He threw a bunch of money on the table and shrugged into his coat. Seeing Dunstan readying to leave James finally did the same.

"Tomorrow night, same general time, huh? I'll be here. I may even come down early and have dinner with you Gwen."

Gwen glared at him. "I'm the only server around here so I eat on my own either before or after the rush. If you're coming down to be a paying customer I'll happily serve you whatever you want."

"Whatever I want, huh?" said Dunstan, giving her

a leering grin. "I'll remember that. May have to think about what I want to order. See you all tomorrow."

As the door closed behind him Jonathan turned to the others and spoke.

"Wow. Hope I'm not offending anyone, because he is your friend, but he really is a bit of an asshole, isn't he?"

"More than a bit," said James. "Gwen, are you okay? You want some company for a while?"

Gwen looked up at James with a look on her face that Jonathan could only call mild disbelief.

"Not you too, James. Look, thanks for the offer, but no. Now off with both of you, please. I have to finish a few things so I can enjoy a little time to myself before bed and I have to get up and do this all over again."

The damp chill of the night air proved a stiff contrast to the pleasant, stuffy warmth of the cafe and it made Jonathan pull the folds of his coat tighter around himself after shaking hands with James. The two men went their separate ways and as he walked back to the hotel Jonathan thought about the people he had met and what he had learned about them over the course of the night. They were an interesting mix of people, but Jonathan felt comfortable with all of them, although Dunstan was the clear exception. An image of one of those strange corpse flowers sitting in the middle of an otherwise fragrant flower garden while smelling of rotting flesh when it bloomed came unbidden to his mind. He couldn't help laughing to himself at the thought.

As he walked into the warmth of the hotel lobby he eyed the distant lounge bar with its welcoming gas fire and he caved into temptation instead of going straight for the elevator to his room. A glass of cognac was now a nightly ritual and he had just finished shrugging out of his coat once again when the pretty young server set a glass of it on the table in front of him, having ordered it the second she saw him walk in the door. He smiled and nodded up at her before she turned and walked over to another customer.

Jonathan swirled the cognac in his glass before taking a sip and once again asked himself, for what seemed the hundredth time, why he was still here. But even as the thought came he dismissed it and resolved to try to stop asking the question. He liked these people and the pretty owner of the cafe in particular. He was beginning to wonder if he had competition for her attention, but there was no harm in finding out. The sultry good looks of Melanie came unbidden to his mind too, but the fact she was still wearing a ring made him dismiss that thought. He realized his curiosity to find out if they really could help this spirit was still strong.

The alternative was to simply move on, but the hard reality of having little reason to be anywhere else was unchanged. As he took another sip of the cognac he decided to stop at the front desk and extend his stay even longer.

Chapter Three

Having restricted himself to long walks along the beach to this point Jonathan spent most of the next day thoroughly exploring the town, which was actually a bit larger than he realized. The still reasonably calm weather made it more of a pleasant experience than it otherwise would have been. The nearby mountains that stretched in a line along the coast in either direction stood bold in the sunshine and crisp air, giving an illusion they were close enough to touch. Those in the far distance displayed caps of fresh white snow, while the lower hills wore wreaths of low mist that would soon burn off. Out on the water a few smaller, much weathered rocks whittled down by the endless waves from the size they once were nevertheless also stood clear enough he felt he could almost reach out to touch them.

The business district housed an even wider variety of small businesses than he realized. Everything from antique furniture stores, to small bookshops, and a few tiny art galleries selling the works of local artists lined the main street. Jonathan found a new age metaphysical shop named Mystic Crystals and he looked in the window. Miriam was there, absorbed in conversation over a display case with a customer while two more browsed the shop.

Miriam seemed a pleasant enough person, but Jonathan knew he felt no attraction to her, although he couldn't put his finger on why. Seeing she was busy he decided not to bother her and moved on, amused to find the shop right beside her selling every possible kind of paraphernalia anyone could need for the purpose of smoking cannabis. On the other side of her was a small travel agency. He laughed at the odd congruence of three shops all offering very different kinds of journeys being located right beside each other.

By early afternoon the sidewalks were a lot busier with people working on their Christmas shopping lists, struggling to carry shopping bags in one hand while staring at their smartphone in the other. As he strolled along the street he ran into Paula, who told him the two people they had hoped could help them out had confirmed they would be at the cafe that night before she went on her way.

Impressed that the town still supported the presence of small, local booksellers, Jonathan decided to spend the rest of the afternoon taking a deep dive into one of the stores, coming out with a half dozen books to read. By the time he made it back to the hotel the Christmas lights decorating the homes and businesses in the town were already coming on.

That night the cafe was busy enough Gwen was kept going at a steady pace, not leaving her with time to talk to Jonathan. This time Willie had conjured up a delicious fish and clam chowder soup filled with plenty of seafood and potatoes, and once again Jonathan cursed himself for not simply ordering a large bowl of the soup for dinner. When the fish and chips he'd ordered for the main course appeared Jonathan could only laugh at the size of the piece of fish, knowing it was unlikely he would be able to finish it.

He was halfway through the meal when Dunstan

came in and joined him at the table. He ordered the same meal after seeing what Jonathan had. As Gwen walked away from delivering beer to the table the two men eyed each other. Jonathan was sure the speculative look on Dunstan's face was mirrored on his own.

"So what are you up to here, spook? Doesn't strike me this one horse town would have much of interest to the government, but I suppose you never know. You spying on the local crazies that believe in ghosts or something?"

Jonathan almost choked on the last piece of the fish he was eating as he tried to stifle a laugh. After downing some of his beer he shoved the plate away and replied.

"Nope. Can't imagine why the government would be interested in anything like that anyway, even if I was what you call a spook."

"So what are you hanging around for then?"

Jonathan shrugged and explained about being on his way back from visiting his sister. Dunstan raised an eyebrow.

"That doesn't answer my question."

Jonathan eyed him for a moment before he responded.

"Got nowhere better to be and I'm curious about what's going on in this place. You got anywhere better I should be?"

"Huh. Well, whatever you say. Some place better for me would be Vegas. Helluva lot warmer than this town."

"Well, that just makes me wonder what you are doing here. You weren't any more specific than me the other day about why you are back here."

Dunstan simply shrugged and Jonathan went back to his meal in silence. Gwen finally interrupted them by dropping a steaming plate of fish and chips in front of Dunstan. As she did the door to the cafe opened and several people came in. Gwen looked at them and smiled, before turning to Dunstan and Jonathan.

"You guys need to shove over and make some room so I can add a table here. Almost everyone is here now."

The same people from the night before came over along with two newcomers to join them. James was the only one missing, but he appeared in the doorway just as everyone was removing their coats and sitting down. As they settled in Jonathan studied the new arrivals he had not seen before with interest.

Both appeared to be in their late fifties or early sixties at most. The male had Asian features and was relatively short, while the woman was white. Both had a few wrinkles and the greying hair to be expected of people their age, but they also had an aura of good health and fitness about them. At the same time they radiated a distinguished air of accomplishment too, as people who were comfortable with who they were and what they had done in life. Neither wore wedding bands on their hands, but Jonathan recalled someone mentioning the woman was the friend of the man. He wondered what being a friend really meant for these people.

The two of them were eyeing him with equal interest. The male introduced himself as Thuan

Tranh, although he emphasized everyone just called him Tom. Recalling someone had mentioned he was a teacher, Jonathan introduced himself before asking him what he taught. Tom laughed.

"Pretty much everything, although my favorite subject is history. In a small town like this you have to multitask as a teacher."

The woman's name was Athena Locklear. When he learned she was an engineer Jonathan's interest in her went up, knowing that there would have been few female students studying the subject along with her at the time she went to university. Curious for more, Jonathan asked if they were both from the town, too. Tom smiled, but shook his head.

"I am from Vietnam and I came to this country when I was very young. When I got out of university I found a job in town and I stayed because I like it here."

"I, on the other hand, was born here," said Athena. "I too went to university, but finding a job in the man's world of engineering at the time was easy to say, not so easy to do. Times have changed out there and it's easier for women in the field now, thank heaven. But I was fortunate that an opening in the engineering department for the town came up and I got it. I'm head of the department now and, as with Tom here, I like this town and the area. So we've both been here a long time, haven't we, Tom?"

The two of them smiled at each other in a way that conveyed more than cordial agreement. Jonathan would have bet a large sum with anyone that the two of them were more than just good friends.

"Hey, teacher! Aren't you happy to see your best student again?" said Dunstan. "Bet you haven't had any students like me since."

"Fortunately, Dunstan, that's true. I really haven't had anyone quite like you since your time in my classes and that's good, because you know you were the worst student I've ever had. You scraped by, but I can't claim it was any of my doing. It could have been otherwise."

Dunstan laughed. "I've done okay in Vegas and, believe me, that can be a tough place to succeed."

Tom was about to reply, but Gwen appeared with their drinks. Before she scurried off again she told them not to wait for her. Jonathan looked around and saw she was still hurrying about, dealing with the rest of the customers in the cafe that were either done their meals or close to it.

Athena peered at the people around the table, a quizzical look on her face.

"So, we were busy at the office today and Paula didn't have time to tell me much, but Tom and I are curious. I gather there have been some strange things happening here?"

Miriam took a few minutes to summarize what had happened to date. Tom and Athena listened with obvious interest, interrupting her a couple of times with questions. By the time she was almost finished, both were looking thoughtful.

"So you see, we thought of you two when we were considering what to do. We thought you might have some knowledge of the history of this place, as a starting point for clues as to how this came to be."

Tom frowned, still in thought, before he turned to Athena, who had pursed her lips as if she wanted to say something, but the right words weren't coming to her.

"Athena, there was something happened here in the long distant past. I can't quite place it, but it might have been a murder or murders. I think there was some kind of bad event here."

"I agree something happened, but it was long before our time. That's what I was sitting here trying to remember just now. The nineteen twenties, perhaps? The thirties?"

Mention of murders taking place in the house made everyone sit forward and take notice. A few of them couldn't help involuntarily looking around before focusing back on the two older people.

"Hmm," said Tom. "Before our time, that's for certain. I suppose I should be embarrassed I don't know the answer, since I'm the history buff around here. We will have to do some digging if that's what you want to know more about."

"What kind of digging do you have in mind, Tom?" said Miriam.

"Oh, we will need to check the usual sources. A good place for information would be the archives of the newspaper. The only problem with that is we would have to scan through a big pile of papers in order to find what we're looking for, unless we can narrow down the timeframe to look in."

"What about that town history book that was written back in the seventies, Tom?" said Athena.

"Yes, I was thinking that would likely be a better place to start. Been a long time since I worked my way through it, but maybe that's what is tickling my brain. I have a vague memory of a few references to this place."

"Well, Paula and I can always spend a little time in the town archives, too. Might be some references to unusual things happening in the town council minutes. This was all a long time ago, though, and maybe this is perhaps a dumb question, but why are we only now hearing about this place being haunted?"

"Not a dumb question. I don't know much about ghosts, but it seems weird to me, too. Who lived here before, Athena?" said Tom. "I have a vague memory this was a cafe long ago, before Gwen acquired it. It didn't stay open very long and closed its doors."

Athena looked around and saw Gwen was just finishing clean up on the last table, so she called her over and asked whom she bought the building from. Gwen frowned a moment before responding.

"It was an estate sale. I think no one had lived here for quite a while before we bought it. I didn't pay much attention to who the former owner was."

As Gwen went back to what she was doing everyone stayed silent for several moments as they digested that. Athena finally broke the silence.

"So. We've got some digging to do. I've got some time I can dedicate to this for you and I expect Tom can help out too, since school is out now for the Christmas break. But I confess to having little knowledge of this whole topic. Miriam, can you help me understand, please? Why does a spirit hang around?"

Miriam took a moment to explain everything she had told the rest of them the day before and Athena nodded as she spoke in response.

"Well, if someone was murdered here that would certainly count as a trauma that could trigger a situation like this. But I'm wondering if there couldn't be more to it than that. Suppose the trauma wasn't a criminal act and instead was an abusive situation? Or maybe a dispute over something important to the spirit could be involved? Throw in possible mental illness issues? Now I think about it, I guess the reasons could be countless."

"I think anything is possible, Athena," said Miriam. "That would be why we really do need to know more about the background of this place."

"Miriam?" said Jonathan. "I think I read somewhere once there are different kinds of ghosts and there are different ways they can appear?"

"Yes, that seems to be true. I was doing a little research on that last night and there doesn't seem to be just one simple way they reveal themselves to us. For example, you've all heard of poltergeists, right? I think of these as naughty spirits. They move stuff, they slam doors, or they knock stuff over, maybe turn lights on or off. They make noises when there is nothing to make noise with. Why I have no idea, but they are intrusive. And in case you are wondering, no, I don't think what we have here is a true poltergeist. What has happened so far doesn't seem to fit."

"So what other kinds of ghosts are there?" asked Melanie.

"People have reported seeing what they describe

as an orb, a circular ball of white light moving about. Others talk about what they call a funnel ghost, a swirling funnel that is tall and thin. Neither of these seems to fit the picture here, but there are also reports of a swirling mist like apparition occurring. That does seem to fit what Willie experienced and what I think I briefly saw. But the kind of ghost or ghosts I think we have on hand here is an interactive one. That means sometimes it might speak or say something, there are cold or cool spots. I gather there could be many ways for it to interact with living people. The interesting part about this is there are references to these spirits behaving like this sometimes because the living have need for it to contact them."

"Need?" said Dunstan, before laughing aloud. "My God, why would I have any need for a ghost to get in touch with me? Oh, hey, I know."

Dunstan put a hand over his mouth and made a fair imitation of an old-fashioned telephone ringing. Continuing his act he mimed reaching out, picking up a telephone handset, and answering it.

"Hello? Yeah, thanks for getting back to me, we gotta talk. Since you're a real ghost I could book you just about anywhere in Vegas and we would make a crap load of money. Every freak and crazy in town will want to be there. If we time it for Halloween next year we could cash in big time. Think about it and call me back."

Athena stared stone-faced at Dunstan for a moment before shaking her head and turning to Tom.

"So how did you manage to deal with that as his

teacher?"

"A whole lot of patience. I kept hoping at least something I was teaching would eventually sink in, but with some kids it's always an uphill climb," said Tom, before turning back to Miriam.

"So Miriam? Do you think that is what is happening here? The spirit is definitely manifesting to more than one person, so I would think that knowing this there would have to be some kind of reason for it to do so that was common to everyone. Does that make sense?"

"It does, Tom, but if you are hoping I know what the common denominator is I'm afraid you are out of luck. Remember, folks, I am not an expert in any of this."

"Maybe it's all about the bad stuff, whatever it may have been, that tied the spirit or spirits here?" said Paula. "And maybe somehow it's linked to us?"

"How can that be, Paula?" said James. "Sorry, this is getting a little too out there for me. You need to help me understand how that works."

"James?" said Miriam. "I'm not certain if Paula is right or not. I think the thing you need to consider is the universe has purpose, like I said the other night. The principle of cause and effect is very real and is a constant that applies all of the time, without exception. Now, I know what you are thinking, there are plenty of situations out there where things happen, sometimes really bad things, and they seem to be random events. Personally, I don't believe that. I think there are many, many variables that come into play and other principles at work, all of which result in this confusion. In other words, if we can't see a logical reason for something to happen, it simply means we have an imperfect understanding of the factors at play, some of which may be in the spiritual world. And that means she may well be right, this is all happening for a reason."

"God, the only principle I'm sure of when I'm playing roulette is the house is going to win in the long term," said Dunstan.

"Well, that would be cause and effect, wouldn't it?" said James. "The game is designed to work that way."

"So Miriam?" said Melanie. "I guess I'm still stuck on what the common denominator with us could be?"

Miriam shrugged. "Well, let's face it, everyone has bad stuff they have to deal with in their lives, sooner or later. Conflict is a part of life. Bad stuff with families or lovers or colleagues at work, who knows? Sometimes the problems we face stem from things that happened long ago and we just can't let them be. So maybe part of our task is to figure out what the bad stuff we have in common is that is attracting the spirit?"

A silence descended on the conversation once again. The range of expressions on the faces around the table fascinated Jonathan. Dunstan was uncharacteristically silent, but wore a bored, disbelieving look on his face. Melanie was looking down at the table, trying to hide a distinctly troubled look on hers. James was scratching his head, wearing a puzzled frown, while the two older people wore bland looks as they stared into empty space. Sensing the discomfort, Jonathan decided to break the silence by asking about another puzzle that had yet to be answered. He let a wry look appear on his face to ease the tension as he spoke.

"Well, I don't know about the rest of you folks, but I've had my share of bad stuff to deal with. In fact, the spirit has too many options to link with. But look, I'm curious to know how we're going to figure out how many spirits there are in this place. Miriam?"

Miriam shrugged. "We need to know more about the history and, obviously, we need more contact with the spirit or spirits. I don't know how, but I'm sure we will figure it out."

As she finished speaking both Gwen and Willie came over to join them, having finally finished clean up for the night. Miriam filled them in on the conversations to that point and as she finished she looked directly at Gwen.

"So Gwen? I don't want to pry, but among other things we are trying to figure out here the question of exactly how many spirits there are in this house has come up. I know your husband passed away some time ago, but we don't know any details. What happened to him? Was it here?"

The frozen look on Gwen's face and the long pause before she finally spoke told Jonathan she was having difficulty with her answer. She chewed her lip briefly for another moment as she began.

"I'm sorry, it was quite traumatic and I know I haven't spoken of it before. The deal to purchase this place had closed and we were now owners, carrying a big mortgage with the bank. It was very stressful and I guess it still bothers me. That's why I left town again and went to stay with my sister for a while, because I just couldn't deal with it right away. But I really think you should look elsewhere if you believe what is happening could be related to him. So, if I got this straight we don't have a plan yet?"

"Hmm," said Miriam, wearing a small frown on her face at not getting a clear answer. "Well, we have some things to do. As I said, we were just discussing how to figure out exactly how many spirits there are in this place, but I think that will have to wait for more information. In any case, Tom and Athena are going to do some digging for us as a start. I'd like to do more research on the internet to see what I can come up with about the whole situation. I didn't have time the other day to really dig in, but there seems to be a ton of information out there."

"Miriam?" said Jonathan. "Aren't there cleansing ceremonies or stuff like that to help deal with these situations?"

"Yes, but I don't know much about them. I've heard of something called a smudge ceremony the indigenous peoples use. Maybe you could do some delving into that?"

Athena gave a small start and looked like she was about to speak, but Dunstan interjected.

"Probably involves smoking some weird shit to make you see things," said Dunstan. "I've heard whatever it is you smoke makes you puke right away before the fun starts, too. You can count me out. I'll stick to my booze."

"For God's sake, Dunstan," said James. "This

may all be nonsense, but these people want to look into the situation and try to do something. If you can't take it seriously or don't want to be involved, maybe you should move on."

The two men glared at each for a long moment, but neither said anything further. Sensing the pause in conversation was verging on getting worse Jonathan spoke up to ease the situation once again.

"I think you might be mixing up smudge ceremonies with something else," said Jonathan to Dunstan, before nodding to Miriam. "Yes, I'll try to look into that."

"Wonderful. I know everyone is busy with getting ready for Christmas, but as Cate said the other day, Christmas may be what this is all about. I just wish we had other options to explore."

"Well, someone could have a look at all the stuff in the basement," said Willie. "What do you think, Gwen? Maybe there's a clue in there."

Gwen shrugged. "Could be. Never thought of that."

"Stuff in the basement? What are you talking about?" asked Tom.

"Well, like I said, this place was an estate sale. It was kind of weird, but the people selling it wanted it sold with the contents intact and I do mean all of the contents. All of the furniture was left, but there was lots of other stuff. The closets were filled with old clothes, shoes, hats, and just about everything else you would find in closets. The dressers in the bedrooms upstairs had old socks and underwear. Some of them had old costume jewelry in them, too, but there was nothing of value. The kitchen was full of dishes and pot and pans. I had to go through it all and haul away a ton of stuff. I'm sure the people selling the place went through it all beforehand and took anything of real value, although I don't know why they were too lazy to clean it all out. But what Willie is referring to are the trunks and boxes in the basement."

"Trunks?" said James. "What's in them?"

"All kinds of stuff. More clothes, letters, pictures, recipe books, photo albums and pretty much anything else you could think of. To be honest, I didn't spend a whole lot of time looking through them. Some of the stuff that was upstairs here I just carted down to the basement and dumped it there to get it out of my way, because I didn't have time to deal with it. It's all still there because that hasn't changed."

Athena sat forward to catch Gwen's attention.

"Gwen? Would you mind giving us a tour of the place? I'm not sure if it will help, but you never know. And while we are in the basement we can have a look at these trunks."

Gwen shrugged. "Sure. If you want a tour just follow me. We'll start at the top and work our way down."

Willie told Gwen he was heading downstairs to his own room, but the rest of them got up and followed Gwen. Leaving the main serving room of the cafe they headed for the hallway leading to the opposite side of the building, passing the washrooms on one side and the entrance to the kitchen on the other. Further along the corridor were two doors they bypassed, coming finally to a staircase leading to the upper floor.

The small hallway they found at the top of the stairs led to four rooms, one larger and the others much smaller. Nothing out of the ordinary could be seen in any of them. All of the rooms had beds in them, with Gwen's cat Shadow fast asleep on one of them, but the smallest room had a desk with a computer set up on it. Strewn about the desk and a side table nearby were various piles of paperwork. Gwen confirmed she was using this as her office, but pointed to the closet filled with her clothes.

"It's kind of a weird configuration up here. You're probably wondering why all my clothes are in here, right? That's because I think what someone did a long time ago was convert a walk in closet that was in the master bedroom to an ensuite bathroom. Come take a look."

Aside from a fascinating old claw foot bathtub and fixtures that looked to be many decades old, there was little of note to see in her room and the ensuite bathroom. Someone asked Gwen where she had experienced the cold spots and she pointed to the entrance to her bedroom.

They made their way downstairs and this time they stopped at one of the doors they had bypassed. This turned out to be another small room, roughly the same size as the office upstairs. Willie was using this as a storeroom for supplies and dry goods for the kitchen. They all stuck their heads into the kitchen and several people commented on how clean Willie kept it. A small walk in fridge at the rear of the kitchen occupied the space on the other side of the storeroom down the hall.

The remaining door in the hallway led to the basement. They all stopped to gather their bearings and look around on reaching the foot of the stairs. A wall that looked fairly recent divided fully half of the basement with a door set in the middle. Old wood panels covered the remaining walls, matching a well-worn hard wood floor in the visible half of the basement. Willie was standing in the doorway of his room and he beckoned them to come and have a look. His simple room was as neatly organized and clean as the kitchen. A bed, a small desk, and an entertainment center filled most of the room along with a small couch to watch TV. A closet covered the space along half of one wall while a small bathroom with a shower took the remainder of it.

They didn't linger in his room long as the rest of the basement was what held promise. Jonathan was bemused at what they found, as Gwen had understated just how much material had been stuffed into the rest of the basement, which was basically just an open area. Stacked up against the side of a wall Jonathan saw what appeared to be at least eight or nine old, large steamer trunks, all closed. Piles of clothing, books, small tools, and an array of hats covered the remainder of the space. A smaller number of boxes were stacked further down the wall. Jonathan was suspicious the piles of stuff hid yet more steamer trunks, but from what he could see all of it looked like junk that would have little value. Despite this it seemed odd it would all be abandoned like this. While it all looked like junk to Jonathan, he was certain someone must have thought it important at some time and he told everyone this.

"Yes, I agree with you," said Athena. "This reminds me of my parents home when I was a child. Everyone accumulates mementos and stuff over the course of their lives and heaven knows my parents did a lot of accumulating."

"Same for me," said Melanie. "So if this was an estate sale, presumably it was family that sold the property. But if they were family, why wouldn't they want to keep at least some of this? Here, look at this."

Stepping forward she went over to a table set against the wall and pulled a large binder off the top of a pile of similar binders, brushing a film of dust off it as she did.

"I knew it," she said, flipping it open to find it was a photo album full of pictures. "These are all photo albums. Why would you leave these behind? Gwen, these aren't yours, are they?"

Gwen shook her head. "So look, that's it for the tour. I'm heading back upstairs, but if any of you want to stick around for a while and look at some of this stuff you are welcome to do so."

"Gwen?" said Jonathan. "What's behind that door in the wall underneath the stairs?"

"Oh, that's just an old storeroom. I don't know why it was put there, but Willie uses it for cold storage when he runs out of room upstairs in the walk in freezer. That's probably what the previous owners wanted it for, too."

Jonathan let his curiosity show on his face and was about to press her for more, but she turned and went back up the stairs. Jonathan shrugged as the others kept talking, flipping through the pages of other photo albums and looking at all the pictures of unfamiliar people. Well over half of the photographs were black and white, while the rest were in color.

Jonathan was standing off to the side, peering into the corners of the room in curiosity, when from the corner of his eye he saw James look around and give a start. His reaction was odd enough that Jonathan turned to focus on him to find out what caused it. James was ignoring him, staring at the stairs leading back to the main floor. Jonathan was puzzled for a moment until it dawned on him that Dunstan was missing from the group. Without saying anything to the rest of them, he had slipped away after Gwen in silence. But even as the realization came he saw James was already halfway up the stairs. Jonathan frowned and hesitated a moment, but decided to follow.

"I'm heading back upstairs, everyone," he said, without waiting to see if anyone was following him. As he got to the top of the stairs he saw James heading into the cafe and heard him call out.

"Do you need a hand here, Gwen?" said James, with an obvious edge to his voice.

Jonathan walked in just in time to find Dunstan had Gwen in a corner of the cafe, his hand on the wall blocking her from getting away while using his body to block the other direction. What wasn't clear was whether she was trying to get away, as she had a hand flat on his chest. Jonathan was puzzled, as it didn't look like she was trying very hard to escape his attention. But James was ignoring that and focusing on Dunstan as he came to a stop right beside them.

"Dunstan, maybe the lady doesn't want the attention you're offering," said James.

"Get off your high horse, Sir Galahad," said Dunstan. "Gwen and I are just having a friendly conversation and reminiscing about old times, aren't we?"

Gwen took her hand off Dunstan's chest and slipped under his arm as she replied.

"Old times are more than a few nights a long time ago, Dunstan. Lets not make it any more than it was."

James was still glaring at Dunstan, though. "That sounds like a good idea to me. I think you should just let it go, Dunstan."

Dunstan scowled at James in a quick aside, but was unwilling to drop it. "Gwen, it was more than that and you know it. I—"

"For God's sake, you two. Would you both please just stop? Both of you had your chance with me a long time ago and it didn't work for reasons both of you don't need me to remind you of."

"Well, I suppose tossing me away and running off after my best friend or, I should say my former best friend, is as good a reason as any, Gwen," said Dunstan, with a laugh. "But hey, I'm not holding grudges. We really had something once and we could again."

"You know it wasn't like that, Dunstan, and I— enough, I'm not interested in discussing this in public any further."

As she finished speaking the voices of the others could be heard, talking as they returned from the basement and came down the hallway. Willie was the first through the doorway and as he saw the tableau before him his eyes narrowed. He walked over and stood protectively by Gwen as he stared at Dunstan and James.

"You okay, Gwen?" said Willie, although his attention remained fixed on the two men.

Although Willie was older, he was the biggest of the three men and Jonathan was certain he was deliberately making himself look even bigger than he was. Gwen reached up and put a hand on his shoulder, giving him a small smile as she did.

"I'm fine, Willie. We were all just having a friendly conversation, weren't we gentlemen?"

"Right," said James.

"Sure," said Dunstan. "Well, I'm out of here for tonight. I'll talk to you tomorrow, Gwen."

"Yeah, but first you pay your bill, Dunstan."

"Of course."

Dunstan pulled out his wallet with deliberate slowness. He pulled a hundred dollar bill out and handed it to Gwen, making certain everyone had a glimpse of the wad of bills stuffed into his wallet.

"Keep the change, Gwen."

"Dunstan, this is far too much."

Dunstan shrugged. "There's plenty more where that came from. And I like the service I get."

Gwen rolled her eyes, but before she could speak Athena interrupted.

"Well, I think most if not all of us have to call it a night, too. We have our tasks, as Miriam put it, and

I'm sure we can get together again at some point once we've got more information to compare notes. Maybe we can meet before the party?"

"Party? What party?" said Jonathan.

"Oh, sorry, Jonathan," said Gwen. "I've been meaning to tell you about that. We've got a little Christmas party happening here on the Saturday night coming up. Nothing fancy. Willie is going to make a whole bunch of different appetizers and people can just graze all night. There are a couple of local musicians coming down to do a few sets, too. Who knows, we may even get people up dancing if the place isn't too crowded. It's by invitation only, but not to worry, I'd already decided to squeeze you onto the guest list."

"You'll come, won't you?" said Melanie, putting a hand briefly on his shoulder and standing close by Jonathan with what looked to be a genuinely hopeful look on her face.

Jonanthan smiled in return at her. "Sure, I'd love to."

As she took her hand away Jonathan couldn't help noticing for the first time that she was no longer wearing a wedding ring. Jonathan was saved from having to explain the sudden puzzled look he knew had flashed on his face as Dunstan spoke up.

"You've put me on your list too, of course."

Gwen gave him an arch look, but nodded. "Yes, against my better judgment. You happy now?"

"Absolutely. See you all soon."

Dunstan shrugged into his coat and was the first to leave, but the others weren't far behind. Tom spoke as he pulled his on, looking around at the remaining people.

"Well, I have a little time right now since school is out for the Christmas break. I'll have a look at that town history book and pop back in here tomorrow afternoon, for any of you that can spare the time."

Both Melanie and Jonathan agreed to be there to work on searching the trunks in the basement while waiting for Tom. As Jonathan parted from them to head back to the hotel he thought about everything he had learned and tried to focus on how he felt about the whole situation, but his mind's eye kept coming back to a vision of Gwen's pretty face and her long blonde hair. Dunstan and James were obviously both interested in her, although she wasn't showing any motivation to return their interest. Crowding into his mind along with all that was the hopeful look on Melanie's face and the mystery of why she wasn't wearing her wedding band anymore.

For a brief moment he felt he was at the bottom of a well of loneliness, with the women's faces on the surface far above peering down at him. The strange image of the sight of the two women framed in the light above him stirred a yearning inside and he permitted himself a small smile at the flicker of hope this was an opportunity to finally climb out and into the light.

Chapter Four

Jonathan was finishing his soup and sandwich lunch when Dunstan walked into the cafe. Jonathan groaned inwardly, as he was hoping the cafe would clear out and he could spend some time alone with Gwen, but he caught Dunstan's eye and waved for him to join him at the table.

As Dunstan slumped into the chair across from Jonathan he captured Gwen's attention and pointed at the coffee pot. She nodded and Dunstan turned his attention back to Jonathan. The two men stared at each other for several seconds before Dunstan spoke.

"You really have become a regular in here, haven't you? So when did you say you're leaving town?"

"I didn't, actually. Thought I'd hang around for a while."

"You still pretending you're sticking around because of this haunted house bullshit? I think the real reason you're still here is you've got your eye on her. So am I right?"

Jonathan was prevented from answering right away as Gwen came over to drop off Dunstan's coffee, picking up the now empty dishes in front of Jonathan before turning to leave.

"Thanks, good looking," said Dunstan. "Hey, Gwen, I saw a real pretty dress in a store in Vegas before I left that you would be stunning in. It would show off that sexy butt of yours enough you'd break hearts everywhere you went."

Gwen was already walking away, but she gave

him a quick glance over her shoulder and rolled her eyes before stopping at the next customer's table to clean up.

"Come on Gwen, I know you still love me," said Dunstan, laughing in her direction loud enough to ensure she would hear him. Gwen continued to ignore him so he turned back to Jonathan.

"Well?"

Jonathan shrugged. "Like I told you, I really am curious about what is going on here, whether you care to believe it or not. I don't have any other place I need to be and I like it here. And as for Gwen, I haven't figured out if she's my type yet. So maybe yes, maybe no. Don't know it would matter to you anyway, because from what I can see she has zero interest in you."

"That just proves how wrong someone can be. Money talks, buddy. I could take her away from this dump and show her some real action. I'll bet she doesn't want to be here anymore than me. Besides, you don't know her like I do. Trust me, there's a bad girl hiding under that perfect exterior."

"Really?" said Jonathan, raising an eyebrow. "Hmm. So you said something the other day that got me curious, if you don't mind my asking. Did I get it straight, she dumped you for your best friend and married him?"

"Pretty much. Yeah, I know, she says we just had a one-night thing, but it was more than that. What I didn't know was she was playing me off against my friend. I suppose its fair, get the best deal you can in life. I understand that. What pissed me off was my friend, because he knew she was mine. Some friend.

They took off and left town, I think the bastard had some kind of scam going somewhere, but it must not have worked out in the end because they came back here. What I didn't know until recently was he died and I'd like to know more about that."

"Why? You think he might be the spirit haunting this place? Gwen seemed pretty adamant it's not him."

"This haunting stuff is all horseshit. But she's being very cagey and I think there is something odd happened with him."

"Huh. So why don't you ask her? Looks like the rush is over and she can maybe join us."

At their urging Gwen came over after pouring a cup of coffee for herself and slumped into a chair.

"I guess I can afford to take a little break. Won't get any one coming in for dinner for a couple of hours now."

"So Gwen," said Jonathan. "We were just carrying on our conversation about the spirit in this place. I don't want to pry, but you seemed real certain the other day it's not your husband. How can you be so sure?"

Gwen sighed and took a sip of coffee. "I don't know, I guess I can't be 100% certain, but it doesn't feel right."

"So what did happen, Gwen?" said Dunstan. "Did you do him in for the insurance money?"

Gwen scowled. "You are such a dick sometimes, but you know that, and no, I did not do him in. Believe what you want."

She took another sip of coffee, before visibly relenting and continuing.

"I suppose maybe it's for the best I tell you, if only to shut everyone up about it. There really isn't much to tell. Yes, he died here in the cafe, right over there by the entrance. It was right after we bought the place. We were both out doing separate chores and he got back here first. He was long gone by the time I came in and found him. They did an autopsy and it turned out he had a heart problem that was undiagnosed. The doctors told me even if he had somehow made it to a hospital in record time it is unlikely he would have survived. I don't know if they just said that to make me feel better."

"So you collected a pile of loot from the insurance company, huh?" said Dunstan.

"No, you idiot, I didn't have insurance on him. We were still in the process of setting ourselves up and hadn't gotten to that yet. You can believe what you want, but ask yourself why I'd be in this place working ridiculously long hours if I'd cashed in big time on some insurance policy."

"I think she's got a point there, Dunstan. So you decided to just carry on, Gwen? It must have been hard."

Gwen sighed. "Well, I took some time off. Went and stayed with friends and family down south. Sat on the beach for a long time. In the end I had no choice but to come back here. Took me forever to get things sorted out and, of course, all the while I had no income. I missed most of the summer tourist season as a result. It was a goddamn mess, because everything we owned was sunk into this place. Not what I wanted to do, but there you have it."

"Not what you wanted? What does that mean?"

said Dunstan.

"It means just that. This was his idea, not mine. I'll be honest, I made it clear I wasn't happy about it, but he really was insistent, so here I am. I know, don't speak ill of the dead, but he was a fool sometimes. I knew how long the hours would be and lets face it, this is basically a tourist town. I think this coming summer will be good, if I can survive that long, but it's when the rains come is the problem. So yeah, it's been hard. Here I am, thirty years old and trapped in this place trying to make a go of it on my own. I had hoped for better in life, but you have to take what comes and deal with it."

"Well, you can deal with this real easy," said Dunstan. "Ditch this place and come with me to Vegas. I've got bags of money."

"Dunstan, last time I checked, you are still a donkey. Why would I go straight from being hitched to a dreamer with no common sense to tagging along with a donkey in a place like Vegas?"

Jonathan cleared his throat to catch their attention.

"So, to be clear, you are absolutely certain the spirit isn't your dead husband?"

Gwen shrugged again after downing the last of her coffee and rising from her seat.

"Well, everyone seems to be focused on how they feel something is going on around here and all I can tell you is what I've felt does not give me any sense of it being my dead husband. Besides, weren't we talking about there being some reason a spirit would be attached to a place? If the spirit is my husband I have no idea what attachment he would have formed to the cafe. We had barely just finished the deal and had only moved our belongings in a few days before it happened. Look, I can't sit here all day. I've got a few things to do, so I'm going to leave you two to speculate away."

She stopped and turned away from them as the cafe door opened.

"Hi Tom" she said. "I wasn't expecting to see you this early."

On seeing them Tom steered his way over to their table and sat down, although he left his coat on. He waved away Gwen's offer of coffee.

"Thanks, but I've already had lots today and I'm not going to stay long anyway. I just dropped in to give you some news, as I'm not sure if I can pop in tonight. I worked my way through that history book I was telling you about and relearned a few things about this place. It seems to have more of a history than most places around here."

"Well, don't keep us in suspense," said Gwen, sitting down on the edge of her chair.

"Bet you never guessed the cafe also had a speakeasy back during prohibition, Gwen," said Tom, laughing as he saw the look on her face. "I'm pretty sure the original owner didn't build the house with that in mind. I suspect the place was sold and someone saw the potential to modify it. The cafe served as a front for the saloon downstairs, of course."

"Wow," said Jonathan. "I guess that would make sense. This place is right in the heart of town and with a cafe upstairs it would lend itself to lots of people coming and going without raising suspicions."

"So what else did the book have to say, Tom?" said Gwen.

"I'm afraid the reference was a little vague, but there was mention of its rather checkered past in this period, including nefarious deeds such as murder. Not sure who was murdered or how many there were. You may be interested to know it also hints at prostitution being another of the various criminal acts the police were paying attention to."

Dunstan burst out laughing and looked around the room. "So this place used to be the town brothel? Hey, Gwen, just imagine all the fun stuff that was probably going on in your bedroom upstairs. I wonder if they had mirrors everywhere? It could have been a real boudoir for the rich boys to play in."

"If you had put your vivid imagination to other purposes I'm quite sure I could have made something more respectable out of you," said Tom, wearing a wry look. "In any case, the last tidbit of interest is a hint there was a secret entrance to the speakeasy, but no indication as to where it was. The reference is rather vague."

"Damn, this is actually getting interesting," said Dunstan. "I don't care about ghosts, but this sounds like my kind of place to hang out in. I wonder where the secret entrance was?"

"Well, it's all news to me," said Gwen. "If there was a secret way in somewhere it must have been renovated out of existence, because I haven't found it."

"Yes, but you haven't been looking for it, Gwen,"

said Jonathan. "I wonder if its still there and maybe has just been walled up?"

Gwen frowned at the thought, but then shrugged and looked around the room. "Maybe. I'm not sure I want to know what may be hiding inside these walls, but I suppose everyone will want to hunt for it."

"Well, Melanie is supposed to be coming by to help us dig through that stuff in the basement soon," replied Jonathan. "Think of looking for a secret passage as part of the mystery and the fun."

"I like your approach, Jonathan," said Tom. "See, this is history, people. Delving into history isn't always boring. Right, Dunstan?"

"Whatever you say, teacher. But I have to point out it really depends on what kind of history you are talking about. I confess having a secret saloon and a brothel in your place is interesting. The rest of this has all been rather boring till now."

"All history is interesting to me. Anyway, I'm off to see Athena before she leaves the office. Now that we have a better sense of the timeframe of these events we can focus our efforts on going through the newspapers better. They should have a lot more details than what was in the book."

As Tom rose to leave so did Gwen, although she forestalled him with one last question.

"Tom? Was that the only reference to this place in the history book?"

"Yes and that is a bit curious given the age of this place, its history during prohibition, and where its located. Whoever bought the place after that ended must have been too boring even for a history book, let alone for Dunstan. Anyway, hopefully we'll have more information soon, although it will still take a while. We've narrowed it down, but there is a lot to cover. The library has scanned the old newspapers, but there's no way to use search terms to find items, which means doing a quick look at each and every day's headlines. Well, I'm off."

"Me too." said Dunstan, rising and putting his coat on. "I can think of better things to do with my time than poke around in a bunch of dusty old trunks in the basement."

"Better things?" said Tom. "Like what?"

"Like going outside for a smoke, old man. Like going to find a proper bar somewhere so I can get on the net with my laptop and make a few bets through my favorite sports book in Vegas. See you around, losers."

As the door closed behind him Tom shook his head and looked at Jonathan.

"I really did try with him. A bright fellow, but he marches to his own beat. I'll maybe see you both tonight, but if not then tomorrow for sure."

The two of them watched him leave too, before turning to look at each other. The only other person in the cafe with them now was Willie, who they could hear bustling about in the kitchen cleaning up and doing preparation work for the dinner rush.

"I should finish cleaning up," said Gwen, but Jonathan forestalled her.

"Why don't you take a little longer break? Have a refill of your coffee and take a load off your feet. Talk to me until Melanie gets here."

Gwen gave him a speculative look, but nodded.

Taking their empty cups over to the counter she refilled them, came back and sat down. Gwen was the first to speak.

"You're still here," she said, in a way that was both a statement and a question.

"I am. I know, what's with that, right? I assured your friend Dunstan that I really am interested in what is going on here and really do have nothing better to do, but he thinks my real purpose is to chase after you."

Gwen laughed. "He would think that, wouldn't he? Well, are you chasing after me?"

"Maybe," said Jonathan, joining her with a laugh of his own. "Maybe not. Don't know yet. Haven't figured out if you are my type or not. Not even sure I want to be involved with anyone anyway. I know, another fuzzy answer, but it's the best I can offer."

"You aren't wearing a ring."

"No. I used to. Not too long ago, in fact."

"I see. Well, God knows I understand sometimes things don't work the way you think they will. Too bad it can take a while to figure that out. I hope it was a friendly split?"

"No, she's being a total bitch. So with all that and other things going on in my life, I just had to take some time off. And here I am."

Gwen stared into her coffee cup for a moment before replying.

"Well, I suppose it's good to be popular, but so you understand I'm not really in the market just now. Don't want to be. Call it what you will, but I really, really want to get my life sorted out on my terms. I confess I feel angry at being in this financial hole I'm in and, you know what? It's my own fault. My husband had this scheme—well, I won't bore you with details, but it was get rich quick and get out. And I went along with it, just plain old greed on my part. Didn't work out, of course, and here I am."

"I understand—" said Jonathan, stopping mid sentence as the cafe door opened and Melanie walked in.

On seeing them alone an uncertain look flashed across her face for the barest second before she smiled and came over to join Jonathan and Gwen.

"Well? Ready to hunt for some ghosts?"

"Ready when you are," said Jonathan.

"I think I'll leave you both to it, at least for now," said Gwen. "I've got a little clean up to do still and some paperwork awaiting me, too. I'll try and join you in a bit."

"You sure you're okay if we poke around on our own?" said Melanie.

"Of course. Just tell Willie you will be down there as you pass the kitchen, so you don't scare the crap out of him if he heads down to the basement unexpectedly."

Jonathan stopped to use the toilet while Melanie talked to Willie. Moments later they were alone in the basement, staring at the trunks. Jonathan was contemplating where to start when Melanie placed a soft hand on his shoulder to catch his attention.

"Well, what do you think?" she said, leaving her hand where it was for a few seconds longer than Jonathan was expecting. "What's the best way to tackle this?"

Jonathan shrugged. "I think we pick a trunk each and get started—oh, I forgot, Tom came by with some interesting information."

Jonathan relayed what he had learned from Tom and Melanie's dark eyes glinted in the light as she listened.

"Well, who knew?" she said as he finished, looking around at the basement walls as if seeing them for the first time. "So there's another interesting job, find a secret door or a passageway. This is getting better by the second. I don't see anything odd in the structure down here that might be hiding a door. But what about that door under the stairs that Gwen said was a store room?"

Jonathan shrugged. "Let's go look."

To accommodate its location the door was almost two feet shorter than standard and they had to duck their heads to look inside as Jonathan opened it. In the gloom of the interior Jonathan made out a bare light bulb off to the side on one of the walls with a chain hanging below the fixture. He pulled it and stark white light flooded the small room. Open shelves were attached to the wood walls on either side of it. A few bags of root vegetables and onions filled the shelves while a pair of large sacks of potatoes lay against the back wall.

"Hmm," said Melanie. "Not much to see here."

Jonathan frowned. On the surface the little storeroom seemed innocuous, but something didn't seem quite right. After a long enough pause for Jonathan to respond passed by Melanie spoke up.

"What is it?"

"Dunno. Something odd here, but I can't place it.

Must be nothing."

Stepping back he closed the door and they both turned back to the task at hand.

"Well, I guess we need to start somewhere," said Jonathan. "For now I suggest we each pick a spot and start working our way through it all. If you start over there, I'll start here and we can work toward each other."

"Any ideas on what to look for?"

Jonathan shrugged. "Anything that talks about who lived here in past, I guess. An old diary, maybe? Anything that hints at bad things happening that might cause a spirit or two to hang around. I expect we'll know it when we see it."

Jonathan went over to his side of the pile and after shoving an old side table out of his way he opened the trunk nearest to him. An overwhelming smell of musty age greeted him as he peered inside. This one held several layers of old blankets and sheets, all of which appeared to be of good quality. After working his way through it to ensure he wasn't missing anything he closed it and opened a second trunk. This one was considerably heavier and he soon realized it was because of several old photo albums filling the entire trunk. Numerous loose photos were haphazardly stuffed inside it, too. Jonathan groaned at the sight.

"My God, it will take forever to go through this trunk."

Melanie looked up from what she was doing. "What?"

Jonathan explained and she laughed. "Nothing of interest over here so far, unless you consider a couple of trunks filled with old paperback books interesting. Maybe what we should do is work our way through all of them quickly first just to organize these so we can find the ones with the most promise. We can focus on those later."

Jonathan nodded. "Good plan, let's do it."

The stairs behind them creaked as someone came down to the basement. Both Jonathan and Melanie looked around as Willie appeared. He stopped to peer at what they had found and sneezed because of the stirred up dust motes floating in the air. Jonathan filled him in on what Tom had told them and what they had found so far.

"Huh. I suppose it's fitting I end up living in a former house of ill repute," said Willie, with an amused look on his face. "Well, I'd love to help, but I don't do so well if I don't get my afternoon nap. See you later."

As the door closed behind him Melanie stared after him, before turning to Jonathan.

"Wonder what he meant by that?"

"Guess we'll have to ask him later," replied Jonathan, turning back to the latest trunk he had found.

This one held more promise. Inside it were numerous old notebooks and papers. Some were old bank checkbooks and financial records, but most were old letters still in their now torn open envelopes. A couple of the small notebooks caught Jonathan's attention, along with one book that seemed to be a diary, and he set these aside to look at in detail. He was so engrossed in what he was doing he didn't immediately recognize someone had just spoken to him. As his conscious mind worked to process what had just happened, he was distracted by a cry of alarm from Melanie.

"Oh—that's cold! Jonathan, your hand is freezing, you—"

With alarm Jonathan turned sharply to look at Melanie, who was still where he had last seen her, working on a trunk on the other side of the room. She stared wildly at Jonathan, as if trying to understand why he wasn't where she thought he was. An instant later she got to her feet fast and in a rush came over to stand beside Jonathan.

"What the hell happened, Melanie?" said Jonathan, as once again she put her hand on his shoulder. This time, she was gripping it hard and she was standing close enough her body was touching his. A second later Willie's door opened and he was standing in the entrance, a look of fear on his face.

"What was that? I heard you call out, Melanie. I—God, it's cold in here. It's back."

As he finished speaking Jonathan felt the faint chill himself, while Melanie clutched him even tighter. Willie stepped back, deeper into his room. The three of them stood in silence for a moment, wondering what would happen next.

"Who are you?" said Jonathan, trying hard to keep the fear he felt out of his voice. "What do you want?"

The three of them remained where they were, but nothing more happened. After almost a minute Jonathan felt the cold dwindle and disappear altogether. He peered at Melanie from the corner of his eye and at the same time she relaxed her grip slightly.

"Whatever that was, I think it's gone," said Jonathan.

"Yes," said Willie. "You both felt that too, right? The chill? That's exactly what happened to me in the kitchen."

Melanie wordlessly nodded agreement before speaking. "I felt the chill, but I also felt—a hand touch the skin on the side of my neck. It was cold as ice. God, I thought it was you, Jonathan. It scared the crap out of me."

"I felt that chill, too, but I didn't feel a touch," said Jonathan. "However, right before you called out I heard a voice. It was weird, because it was like I heard the voice inside my head, although it wasn't by using my ears. Does that make any sense?"

"That makes sense to me," said Willie. "That's also exactly what happened to me in the kitchen."

"So what did the voice say?" asked Melanie.

"I—" said Jonathan, frowning as he focused back on what happened. "I can't be certain, but I think the voice said only one word. I think it said the word 'wrong'. It was like a whisper."

"Wrong? I wonder what that means?" said Melanie.

The three of them stood there for a few more moments in silence, before Willie sighed.

"Well, it doesn't seem to be coming back and I am missing my nap. Don't know if I'm going to get any sleep, but I might as well try. I'll see you later."

As the door closed behind him Jonathan and Melanie turned to look at each other. Almost as one they both realized she was still standing with her body pressed against his side. She gave him a small smile and this time reached around his waist to give him a hug. The feel of her body with one of her breasts crushed to his side was tantalizing, bringing an immediate thought of how long it had been since he had been with a woman. But she stepped back, still smiling.

"Sorry to be draped all over you, but I was scared and you were my refuge, so thank you."

Jonathan smiled. "I enjoyed being of service."

Melanie gave him a speculative look. "You're not married, are you?"

"I was, but now I'm busy dealing with a messy divorce. I saw you were wearing a ring a few days back, so you on the other hand must still be married or attached to someone? Any kids?"

"No. We tried, but I can't have kids. My husband was always away travelling. A lot."

"Was, you say? Of course, you mentioned you are divorced, too."

"Yes, you and I have divorce in common. We just finalized it a while ago. I wear a ring sometimes anyway. It helps to keep unwanted attention away when I'm not in the mood. The boyfriend I'm trying to decide whether I want to dump has a lot to do with my mood. Anyway, let's work our way through the rest of this stuff, shall we? Hopefully the spirit won't be back anytime soon."

They spent the next hour digging through it all, with little more success than they had already realized. Most of the trunks were either empty or filled with worthless junk and clothing. Melanie sneezed as she closed the last of the trunks and shoved it back into its place.

"I don't know about you, but I've had enough of this for one day," she said. "Besides, I think we've got all we're going to get here. So what now?"

"I think I'll take these notebooks and maybe a few of these photo albums and letters to dig into. See what I can find. You want a few to look through?"

"I'll happily delegate that to you. Let's get out of here."

Just as they were leaving Willie came out of his room and joined them heading back upstairs, where they found Gwen preparing for the dinner rush. Her eyes grew wide as they explained what they had found and what had happened. Jonathan showed her what he had and asked if he could bring the notebooks and the diary back to the hotel, along with one of the photo albums he had taken at the last minute to look through. She gave a quick wave of her hand to show her agreement. Pulling their coats on both Melanie and Jonathan left and went their separate ways.

Back in his hotel room Jonathan flipped through the pages of the photo album and the notebooks. Most of the pictures were in color and appeared to be family photos from the fifties and sixties. He pulled out some of the pictures to look for names, but none had any reference to who they were. Jonathan knew the older faces in the pictures would be long gone, but some of the children in the photos could easily still be alive. The notebooks appeared to be scrapbooks of long forgotten camping trips that held nothing promising, but he knew he needed more time to look at them thoroughly. He turned to the diary, but with tired eyes he put it aside and stretched out on the bed.

That his thoughts immediately turned to Melanie and their afternoon together didn't surprise him. She was attractive and seemed to be drawn to him, but the possibility she might have a boyfriend was a problem. He dismissed the notion of pursuing her for the moment and slipped into sleep.

Almost two hours later he woke and groggily looked up at the time before falling back to the bed. He lay there for several long moments before forcing himself to get off the bed and into the shower to freshen up. He knew they would be well into prime dinnertime at the cafe and at least some of the people would be there, wanting to know what they had found in the basement.

He grabbed a coffee to go from the hotel lobby bar as he left and made his way down the street to Gwen's, hunching deeper into his heavy coat to ward off the chill. The sidewalks were busier than normal with people going home for the night, although several carried shopping bags filled with the results of last minute Christmas shopping. Many were huddled into their coats too, showing he wasn't alone in feeling the bite of the weather. The temperature had dropped significantly and it seemed quite cold. The threat of snow hung in the air.

The warmth of the cafe was welcome. Jonathan looked about and saw only two tables of customers who had ordered dinner. Athena, Tom, and Miriam were all sitting at their usual table, so Jonathan went over to join them. After ordering his dinner

Jonathan told them what had happened in the basement and of what they had found. The three of them peppered him with questions they already had in mind, as Gwen had filled them in that another encounter had occurred. When the questions finally dried up he told them of the photos and the notebooks, apologizing he had not found time to work through the diary.

"Hmm," said Miriam. "Well, let's hope there is something to work with in it. But I find it very interesting you think you heard the word 'wrong'. I will have to meditate on what this means. I've never heard of anything quite like that happening before."

"Yes, I'm starting to believe the spirit is clearly trying to communicate with us," said Tom. "I mean, who knows how this works in the world of spirits? Maybe it is limited in what it can or cannot do."

"This is all a question of being attuned to the spiritual world, my friends," said Miriam. "Think about it, if you accept that the spiritual world is real, why would it make any sense that it would be somehow separate from the rest of the world we know with our five senses? I'll say this again, when things we can't explain happen it is because we don't have an good understanding of how it works."

"I guess we just need to pay more attention," said Tom, a small smile on his face. "Kind of like in the classroom, right? Pay attention and maybe we'll learn something. So, turning to other matters, I wasn't going to come down here tonight, but Athena has been teasing me with hints she has more information herself, so here I am. We were just about to get into it when you came in, Jonathan."

"I agree with paying more attention," said Athena. "And I agree something is driving this spirit to connect with us. We just need to keep digging into what this is all about. So yes, I learned a few things of interest today. We delved deep into the town land title records. A rather shady fellow named Daniel Black converted this place to commercial purposes during the prohibition era. I cross-referenced the purchase and ultimate sale dates with the town newspaper files quickly to see if there was anything of consequence. There was no fanfare about the purchase, but the sale was another matter. This was a forced sale by the bank, because our man was in prison for engaging in all manner of illegal activity and couldn't pay the bills. We have to do more digging in the files for details of a murder or murders, but we'll find them."

Tom rubbed his chin in thought. "Okay, that lines up with what I found. It still seems weird to me that we only now have an active spirit in this place after all these years, though. What about other owners?"

Athena frowned, but was forestalled from responding by the arrival of Jonathan's dinner. She waited till he began working on his meal before continuing.

"Not much to tell. The original owner in 1906 was the town mayor here for a long time, but the family sold it when he passed away. Can't see him engaging in anything nefarious. Another fellow named Markleigh, who served as a town councilor, bought the place from the bank after prohibition ended. He seems to have been a fairly upstanding citizen, too, because I know he was involved in a lot of local projects, like raising funds for a new library. The only odd thing is there must have been something going on with his estate, as the courts blocked a subsequent sale when he passed on. Anyway, when the dust settled the name on the title ended up being Rose Markleigh. And in case you are wondering, I have no knowledge of her, but presumably she would be a daughter."

Jonathan let a puzzled look appear on his face in between mouthfuls. "So did the Markleigh family use this place as a cafe, too?"

"Yes, sorry, I forgot to mention that. They did have a cafe here for several years, but once the elder Markleigh died the cafe appears to have shut down. A new business license wasn't granted until Gwen came along."

"Hmm," said Tom. "Well, lots to contemplate. Doesn't sound like the Markleigh family have any potential, but I suppose one never knows. It was the family that sold it when this Rose passed away, right?"

"Correct," said Athena. "I wouldn't mind knowing more about this woman Rose, although how I'm going to learn more is a problem. Hopefully this diary Jonathan has may shed some light. But I am thinking if Gwen is correct that our spirit isn't her dead husband then our best lead is probably whatever happened in the prohibition era."

As the sound of the cafe door opening came they all turned to find Dunstan in the doorway. He stopped at the table, but he left his coat on and made no move to sit down.

"Back talking ghosts again, huh?" he said. "Any

spooky stuff lately?"

Jonathan took a couple of minutes to fill him in on the day's events and on what Tom and Athena had learned. Dunstan frowned at mention of what Jonathan thought he had heard the spirit say to him.

"Wrong? What the hell does that mean? You been smoking some wacky shit with these people, too?"

Jonathan shrugged and shook his head as Miriam groaned and got up.

"Believe what you will, Dunstan. Well, I have to get going soon so I'm going to talk to Gwen for a minute about her party on Saturday night. I think they could use a hand."

"That's who I'm here to see. I didn't come to talk to any of you."

"Well, you can join me talking to her if you must, but I'm first. She looks to be just about done clean up here."

The two of them walked over to Gwen and after a moment they all sat at another table. Gwen went to get a beer for Dunstan and within moments of her return they were all deep in conversation. Jonathan turned away from them and focused his attention on Tom and Athena, who did the same to him. Jonathan concentrated on finishing the remains of his dinner as Athena spoke.

"So Jonathan, we are a little curious about you—"

Jonathan forestalled her from continuing by holding up his hands and laughing. "Let me guess, you are both wondering, like everyone else, why I am still here."

Athena acknowledged he was right with a nod

and Jonathan obliged by giving them the same explanation as he had given everyone else.

"And yes, I confess to having maybe some interest in Gwen, but I swear that isn't the only reason. With my marriage falling apart I can't honestly say my head is on straight yet, so I don't know, we'll see."

"You've certainly got competition for her," said Tom. "Dunstan has obviously set his sights on her and, what you may not realize, is I think James is in the running also."

"Really?"

"He's just being a little more subtle about it. He has a history with her, too, kind of like Dunstan. That was all long ago and it didn't work out, but I do believe he has a desire to rekindle what he had with her."

"Well, thanks for the heads up. So, turnabout is fair play. I confess I'm a little curious about you two as well. Hope I'm not being too forward, but I notice neither of you wear wedding rings either. Did neither of you every marry?"

Athena and Tom remained silent for a long moment, before turning to look at each other. By some unspoken agreement Tom was the one to respond.

"No, neither of us ever married. I guess it's fair to say both of us are married to our work. For me, at least, after my parents were murdered I dedicated myself to achieving what they wanted me to do. That just never seemed to leave room for anything or anyone else. I don't know, sometimes I—no matter, what you need to understand is Athena and I are very good friends and have been for a long time."

"I see. But you say your parents were killed? My God, if you don't mind my asking, what happened?"

"It's okay, it was all a long time ago. My parents and I were refugees. Do you remember mention of the Vietnamese boat people in the news back in the seventies? I was fourteen in 1977 when we left. We were in one of the first few waves of people fleeing the communists. We had no choice, because my father had been a mid ranking officer in the South Vietnamese army. If they had learned of his past he would have been jailed or killed on the spot and there were too many people out there who knew who he was. It was only a matter of time, so we paid a criminal gang to get us away. Of course, criminals can't be trusted."

As Tom paused for a brief second Jonathan grimaced and responded.

"No, they certainly can't."

"They sold us out to pirates who stopped us on the high seas. It seemed to me they were waiting for us. Who knows? They may even have been part of the same gang. In any case, they robbed everyone of what little they had left. One of the pirates took a fancy to my mother and tried to drag her onto their ship. He probably wanted to keep her or sell her for a sex slave. Of course, my father wasn't having any of that. In the ensuing fight he was stabbed and died on the spot. My mother was bumped during the fight and fell overboard. The sharks that were following us were waiting for something exactly like that to happen and they made short work of her.

An Australian Navy ship showed up as this was all happening and the pirates took off. I spent a long time in a refugee camp before I was sponsored as an orphan to come here."

"Good God, I'm sorry. That must have been incredibly traumatic to have your parents die like that in front of you."

"I—yes, the short answer is yes. It's taken me a long time to be comfortable enough to even talk like this about it. I guess it's fair to say it changed the direction of my life. Who knows, my life might have been fuller in many ways, but it's all past now. So there you have it."

"I confess I've always felt blessed to have been born in a country like this, where there is no need to live in fear or to flee from it. I give thanks for that every day. And you, Athena?"

"I married my work. There was someone long ago, but it didn't work out. I'd still like to know more about you, but I'm afraid that will have to be another day. Time to go, Tom."

The two of them rose from the table and pulled on their coats, just as Miriam came back over to rejoin Jonathan. They exchanged goodbyes and left. Jonathan looked over and saw Dunstan was now deep in conversation with Gwen. As he did Dunstan reached over and grasped Gwen's hand. She let him hold it for several long seconds before pulling it away. Jonathan turned to Miriam, who was watching the same scene. They turned and looked at each other.

"Dunstan would probably do better with her if he didn't come across like he was trying to pitch some deal in Vegas. But who knows, maybe he really is pitching a deal."

"Indeed. So that was an interesting conversation I just had with Athena and Tom."

Jonathan summarized what they had told him and Miriam simply nodded before speaking.

"Well, they are interesting people. They both had difficult early lives, so its maybe no surprise they are such close friends and, in all likelihood, much more than just friends."

"Difficult early lives? What kind of life did Athena have that was as harsh as Tom?"

"She was abused as a child. Oh, I'm not telling you anything she hasn't been very up front about, although I think it took her a long time to be public about it. One of her older cousins abused her for a time when she was young and I think she had difficulty with relationships after that. Who wouldn't, I guess. When someone you should be able trust turns out to be the exact opposite and takes advantage of you for their own personal gain, I expect trusting anyone would be a challenge after that. Anyway, her response was to dive into school and her profession. I guess being an engineer is both a blessing and a curse, given it is so male dominated. But as a professional she can maintain a distance."

"Well, that certainly makes their relationship a lot clearer. With shared experiences like that, it makes sense they would find common ground."

"It's odd, you know. I've known both of them for a long time and these things happened many years ago, but I don't know if either of them has truly ever let it all go. When each of them talks about what happened it sounds on the surface like they have, but there is always just a little edge to their voices. Well, heaven knows finding forgiveness in your heart for things like that would be hard."

On the other side of the room Gwen and Dunstan were still deep in conversation, but the tone changed and a hint of an edge crept into it. Jonathan and Miriam both looked over at the two of them and as they did Dunstan once again made to grasp Gwen's hand. This time she didn't pull it back, although the look on her face didn't show any enjoyment of what was happening.

"Well," said Miriam. "It's time I left and headed for home. I'm staying open late tomorrow for the Christmas shoppers. Got to pay the bills. If you find anything of consequence in the diary or those notebooks please do pop in and let me know. I have a coffee pot in my shop and a little table with chairs for anyone who wants to sit and chat."

They both stopped and turned their heads once again to look at Gwen and Dunstan, as the two of them had risen from their seats. As they watched Dunstan pulled Gwen close and kissed her on the cheek, but Gwen looked utterly frozen by his touch. Dunstan let his hands drop away and he stepped back, looking at her in silence for a long moment before grabbing his coat from the chair and pulling it on.

"Think about it, Gwen. That's all I'm asking."

Reaching for his wallet he pulled a fifty-dollar bill out and put it on the table, once again ensuring Gwen had a clear view of just how fat with money his wallet really was.

"That's too much for a beer," she said, her voice wooden.

"See you tomorrow," said Dunstan, leaving the money where it was and turning to head for the door. He didn't break stride as he looked at Jonathan.

"Your turn, spook. Good luck making a better offer to her."

Miriam rolled her eyes and stood up, shrugging into her own coat.

"By the way, did you learn anything about smudge ceremonies?"

"God, sorry, I forgot, Miriam. I promise I shall do some research on that in the next day or two."

"No problem. And in case you are making her a better offer, good luck."

Jonathan waited for the door to close behind her before turning to look at Gwen, who had remained standing where she was, watching them leave too. She sighed and picked up the cups from the table she had been at and took them behind the counter before finally coming over to Jonathan's table.

"Can I get you anything else, Jonathan? And please do me a favor and don't try to make me a better offer."

"No, it's time for me to go, too. You've had a busy day and you were very clear you are not in the market. Anything I really need isn't on the menu, anyway. You ever have the feeling in your life you need to just change everything? Not just your clothes or your hair or whatever. I'm talking about what you do in life and where you live. Find a different purpose to your life and just go after it."

"Yes. This would be one of those times, but the problem is figuring out what the alternative is. And even if I knew what it was, I'm not sure I would have the means to do it."

"You know, when I was younger what I really wanted to do was to explore. Travel the world. Find romance with a fair maiden I could lure away to come with me and explore exotic and far distant lands. Learn the lessons of life by walking streets people have tread on for thousands of years. See the stone of stairs that are so worn from countless feet over the centuries that the stone is worn and grooved. My fantasy always was someday I would reach out a hand and ask my fair maiden to come with me to the Orient or the Holy Land or the depths of Africa. And in my fantasy she would take my hand and feel the romance and believe it could all come true. But somehow, that never happened."

Jonathan paused for a moment and moved his now empty beer bottle across the table to her.

"Instead, I've been learning the lessons of life by riding a commuter train to work every day and paying a mortgage. Staring at spreadsheets all day. Finding myself married to a woman whose only real interest is in money. I don't know how it all went so wrong."

Gwen was silent for a long moment as she stared into his eyes. At last she sighed, looking away before speaking.

"That—that's a wonderful vision, Jonathan. I hope some day you find a way to make that happen for you. It's not the kind of thing I've ever wished for. I don't know, I've just never felt a need to travel that much. I guess I'm just a small town girl."

"I thought you didn't really want to be here?"

"Not true. I like my hometown. It was my husband who wanted to move away and I confess I didn't really like doing that. When we came back here I was ecstatic. It was opening this cafe that I wasn't all that happy about."

"Ah," said Jonathan, allowing a wry look to crease his face. "Well, I know you are probably thinking I'm trying to make you a better offer and, who knows, maybe I am. Or not. I'm going to go and leave you to it for another day. I have some research to do."

Jonathan pulled on his coat as he rose to leave. Gwen forestalled him by sighing and putting a hand on his shoulder briefly.

"I think you really are a good man, Jonathan Thomas. I'm certain you are, because you've fit in with the rest of my friends with ease. But I think it likely you will remain just a friend."

Jonathan smiled. "I'm okay with that. See you tomorrow."

Chapter Five

The bar in the hotel was a welcome sight by the time he got back from the cafe. The clouds steadily rolling in all evening had not brought warmer weather. The heavy marine cloud blanketed everything and a fine mist that was neither rain or even a light shower or snow was everywhere, with minute droplets of moisture giving Jonathan a strange sense they were almost suspended in the air. But the deepening chill meant snow was guaranteed if the clouds let loose any serious moisture. Back in his room he shucked out of his coat, but left his heavy sweater on as he picked up the notebooks and the diary he had taken from the basement before making his way back to the bar.

Jonathan knew the server was waiting for him to settle into his favorite chair. Jonathan made eye contact, gave her an approving nod, and the server headed for the bar to place the order. The glass of cognac they both knew Jonathan wanted appeared two minutes later.

After settling down comfortably he decided to work his way through the three notebooks in detail before tackling the rest. He judged them to be relics of the early nineteen fifties and soon concluded based on the handwriting they belonged to a child, perhaps a pre-teen or someone just reaching that stage. A closer look revealed his first impression was correct, as they proved to be travel scrapbooks from camping trips to nearby locations. The dates of handwritten notes with details of what the author did each day confirmed Jonathan's guess of the age of the notebooks. Whoever they belonged to had been on summer vacation trips over a period of a few years, recording every detail.

After working his way through a random selection of entries it became clear the author was a girl. Sometimes postcards from nearby national parks were pasted into the notebook, while hand drawn scenes of mountains and lakes filled other pages. A few photos were included, too. But there was little of interest for Jonathan, so he turned to the diary.

At first Jonathan feared the diary would also prove to hold little of consequence, but he persevered. He soon realized the diary held entries back to a period somewhat later than the notebooks and he quickly saw the handwriting was very similar, making it certain the same person had owned them all. Jonathan scanned a few of the early entries at random and could see the topics were comparable to the notebooks, as they contained snippets of the girl's daily life. The entries were made on an irregular basis, with gaps of several weeks between them at times. But gradually he noticed some of the entries seemed odd, as they talked about having disputes with other people.

Jonathan flipped ahead through the pages, stopping at an entry dated 1959 that caught his eye because of a noticeable, distinct change in the writing style. Prior entries were made in a steady, recognizable hand, but this one stood out because the writer had pressed her pen to the page hard. Jonathan could see the writer was angry enough at the time for the pen to cut through the page at one point near the beginning.

The anger was directed at her two sisters, one named Beatrice and the other Agnes. The entries weren't explicit as to exactly what was happening, but it seemed clear a boyfriend was involved and the author of the diary felt very wronged. As Jonathan read further he realized the strange tone of the diary grew exponentially from that point on. Jonathan continued flipping through the pages of the diary, quickly scanning each of the entries to maintain a sense of what was happening. Jonathan could see that although the diary had moved into a period of years after the initial sudden change, the tone remained consistently harsh when the subject of the sisters came up. Further on Jonathan frowned to discover some of the pages in the diary had been ripped out with out explanation.

Toward the end of the diary he found the entries were now regular, bitter diatribes against the other sisters, the common theme being accusations of seeking to undermine her in her father's eyes. The diary insinuated the goal of it all was to steal her share of a future inheritance from their father, who by 1965 had become gravely ill. The last entry in the diary told of an attempt by the sisters to take control of the old man's affairs in the courts, but to no avail.

The anger of the author at this point seemed overwhelming and it was here where Jonathan finally confirmed who he suspected the author of the diary was. The diary ended with a written vow to fight Beatrice and Agnes with every means at her disposal, signed with the name Rose Markleigh. Yet more pages had been ripped out after the last entry and none were left.

Jonathan put the diary down and took a generous sip of the cognac in his glass. He stared into the fire contemplating what he had read and realized he was disturbed by it all. A sense the pages weren't telling the whole story was firm in his mind, but there was more to it. A question of whether this woman was unstable formed in his mind, but he had nothing he could point directly to as confirmation he was right. But most of all what permeated the latter entries of the diary was a sense of dark, unfettered greed and anger dominating the relationships of the three women. Whether it was because of the behavior of one or of all of them he couldn't say.

The question of whether any of this was relevant to the situation at hand in the cafe appeared next in his mind, but he had no clear answer to that either. Jonathan knew the possibility was there, acknowledging he was all too familiar with the power of greed and money to warp people's lives.

While contemplating this his mind shifted to the dynamic he had witnessed earlier between Gwen and Dunstan. On the surface Gwen was pushing back at Dunstan's advances, but Jonathan sensed there was more to it than what he was seeing on the surface. In reality she seemed both attracted and repelled by him and Jonathan sensed her need for financial security was one element in the larger picture.

That thought led to the question of what it all meant for himself, as he sat staring at the amber liquid swirling in his glass. Once again, the question of why he was still hanging around and involving himself with these strangers appeared, but as before, no clear answer came. Gwen had made it evident she didn't want anyone's attention, but whether there was still a chance to change her mind was no more obvious than whether he even wanted her to change it. And flitting in the back of his mind was an image of Melanie's dark eyes.

The possibility of simply getting in his car and heading much further south to find some sunshine and a warm beach to sit on for Christmas was still there. As tempting as the thought seemed, it was balanced by an odd sense he needed to see this through. Jonathan realized he had a feeling there were yet more undercurrents at play in the lives of these people and perhaps it was not just the spirit haunting the cafe in need of help. He marveled at the notion, not knowing how or why it had come, but there was a firm certainty to it that left him no doubt it was true.

He was sitting and shaking his head at the thought when someone abruptly draped their coat over the back of the chair beside him. Jonathan turned and saw Dunstan sit down, waving at the server as he did. As the server came over Dunstan looked at Jonathan.

"You want some more of that fancy shit you're drinking or would you prefer a real drink, like the scotch I'm going to order? It's on me."

Jonathan shrugged. "I should probably stick with the cognac, although I really hadn't planned on having another. But what the hell, if you're buying, I'm drinking."

"That's the spirit," said Dunstan, giving the server their order. "Drinking alone is supposed to be bad for you. Of course, I've been doing that for years and look at me, I'm just fine."

"I'll take your word for that. So what brings you out on a night like this? Judging by what I see outside the window I'd say we will have snow before the night is out."

This time it was Dunstan that shrugged and he picked up the diary off the table in front of them.

"Didn't feel like sitting around. Felt like getting out and doing something. Felt a little restless. So what's this stuff you're reading?"

Jonathan told him what the books were and gave him a brief summary of what they contained. A bored look crossed Dunstan's face as he put them back on the table.

"I don't know why any of this shit is of interest. Dead is dead, right? I'd rather spend my time living life, not worrying about why someone is dead and, allegedly, going around haunting the place. But I suppose if somebody is going to haunt somebody, then stealing an inheritance and fighting over money would be a good reason to do it. Money is what it's all about, man."

Jonathan stared at Dunstan for a few moments, waiting before speaking as their drinks appeared before them. Dunstan proceeded to down half of his glass of scotch on the rocks before Jonathan even had his own glass at his lips. The two men eyed each other in silence before Jonathan finally spoke.

"So I'm curious about you. I have some familiarity with Las Vegas and I can certainly understand how difficult it would be to succeed in that environment. So what exactly is your line of business, if you don't mind my asking?"

"Gonna look me up when you get back to spook central, are you?"

"You have that much to hide it would be worth my while?"

Dunstan laughed. "Damn, you're pretty smooth, you know? I'll bet you're a cop or something similar, which means I am a lunatic for even talking to you. Whatever, I don't give a damn. But if you must know, yes, I am a businessman. I specialize in dealing with all the shit other people don't want to. That includes dealing with people that are shit. Didn't always do that. I think I mentioned I came close to declaring bankruptcy and had dig my way out a couple of times from other ventures. Serves me right for trusting the people I did. That's an important lesson, by the way. If you're ever thinking of starting a business remember to trust no one."

"I'll try to remember that. But now I'm really interested. Not everyone goes down twice and finds a way to claw their way back up, especially in Vegas. How did you manage that?"

"Ah, well, I always kept a grubstake for myself stashed away in the eventuality something went south. Made sure I siphoned enough out of the company I'd have a fallback. What the bankruptcy trustees don't know won't hurt them, will it? No point throwing a bunch of perfectly good money down the toilet."

"Enough to start a new business, eh? Hmm, it's not easy to hide that much. I'm impressed."

"Ah, well, it wasn't that much. I had a harder time hiding money from my bitch ex-wife than from them. What was more important was to know the right people. In Vegas, it's always about who you know."

"Ah, this would be the dealing with people that are shit part, would it?"

Dunstan shrugged. "There are plenty of people who fit the description and also have stupid amounts of money, more than they know what to do with. Anyway, what happened is this guy I know who was aware of my situation and my, uh, various skills, pointed me in the right direction. This wasn't because he was a friend, you understand. Everyone around here keeps telling me I'm an asshole, but they haven't seen anything. Look in a dictionary for the word asshole and all it will show you is a picture of this guy's face."

"That wouldn't surprise me. But why was he good enough to put you onto something? Did he owe you big time for some reason? Or maybe it was the other way around?"

"Neither. It was all about his needs and nothing to do with me personally. He had a need for a particular kind of service and the guy that had been doing it for him pissed him off. Bad idea. Well, I confess I kind of helped get the goods on this fool. I suppose you could argue I stepped on this guy to get him out of my way and you wouldn't be far from the truth. But that's the nature of the business. If you can't take a punch you should get out of the boxing ring. Don't know what happened in the end to my predecessor, but it can't have been a happy outcome."

"Well, don't keep me in any more suspense," said Jonathan, swirling the cognac in his glass and taking another sip. "What exactly have you ended up doing that is making you filthy rich?"

Dunstan smiled. "The thing about Vegas is for every winner there are thousands of losers. It's a tough place. So I do bad debt collection mostly, along with evictions if necessary. I prefer dealing with businesses, but there's money to be made no matter whom I deal with. A lot of the time I help the businesses in particular with some creative ways to, hmm, organize things so they stay in business. That is actually the preferred solution, since having them pay their bill makes my client a lot happier than if they don't. So it doesn't matter what the debt is or why it's there, I'm just the guy cleaning things up and putting it all right."

"I see. So these are all clients of your friend that really isn't a friend, are they?"

"Oh, I'll deal with anyone, but a lot of my work does come through him. I make a point of not asking a lot of questions about what is behind any of the deals he has on his plate that aren't working out."

"Bet there's lots of actual cash moving around, eh?"

Dunstan raised an eyebrow as he looked at Jonathan. "There can be, on occasion. You did confess you're a cop, right?"

"Did I? Don't remember. So you said you're divorced? My sympathy, I'm working on that myself."

"God, that was a mistake," said Dunstan with a scowl, as he paused to shoot the rest of his drink down and order another. After catching the server's eye and signaling for more he continued.

"The marriage barely lasted a year. Serves me right for letting the brain in my pants lead me into trouble. But that's what happens when you're young and stupid. The problem was she went and got pregnant before we split. She's been a bitch ever since and takes every opportunity to poison the kid's mind against me. The kid's just turned eleven years old now and he loathes me. I have the right to see him more often, but he's such a little bastard it's a waste of time. Well, I won't be making that mistake again. So you're in the process too, huh? Any kids?"

"No, thank God. We talked about it, but she decided I was working far too much and not paying enough attention to her, so she had an affair. She's set to marry this shithead, who also happens to have a swimming pool filled with money. That isn't stopping her from trying to soak me out of everything I have. Claims I'm the one at fault for the break up. Apparently trying to do your job and make money for our future was actually a character flaw."

Dunstan gave a small grunt of laughter. "If making money is a character flaw then I'm as imperfect as it gets."

"So why'd you go to Vegas in the first place? Lots of other places to make money in the world."

"Had to get out of this town. Family was a pain in the ass and Vegas is where the bucks are, man."

"So only one of your parents is still around?"

"My mom died giving birth to my younger sister. The old man—well, let's just say things didn't go well with him running the family. Hey, you think I'm an asshole? At least I don't pretend to be something other than what I am. He wanted me to be something I wasn't interested in and when I didn't cooperate, he turfed me out without any help. You having another drink?"

Jonathan stared at the almost empty cognac glass before responding.

"No, I'll hate myself tomorrow morning if I do that. So what did the old man want you to be?"

Dunstan downed the rest of his drink and flagged the server for yet another, telling her to make it a double this time. Jonathan raised an eyebrow, but said nothing.

"He wanted me to be someone noble, which is something I certainly am not. Maybe it was to make up for his own character flaws because he for sure isn't noble, although he likes to pretend otherwise. No, I wanted to be an accountant, believe it or not. Yeah, I know, that sounds stupid. The thing is accountants know where all the money is to be made and I'm all about money. But my dear father cut me off and I had to pay my own way. But that's enough about me. So, you still chasing after Gwen, spook?"

Jonathan shrugged. "Dunno. She doesn't seem much interested, so I don't think so. Not sure I'm at a stage where it would be a good idea for me anyway. I like her, though. And you? Doesn't seem a whole lot interested in you, either."

Dunstan grabbed the fresh glass of scotch as it

appeared in front of him and downed more before responding.

"Maybe. We'll see if she comes around. I don't know why she's wasting her time in this dump. It's nickel and dime stuff here. I've got a big condo in Vegas with a layout and a view that would blow her away. Not the penthouse, I grant you, but I'll get there. If she'd just come and check it out she'd never come back here."

"Maybe it's not about the money."

Dunstan turned and gave Jonathan a look of disbelief. "Not about money? Why wouldn't it be about the money? I don't know what the hell would be more important."

"Well, maybe having someone she can care about and even love, who knows? Maybe a little romance?"

Dunstan gave a snort of disbelief. "Love and romance? Well, there are enough people out there that believe in that nonsense to keep the Elvis impersonators busy officiating at weddings in Vegas. Listen, spook, it's always about money. It doesn't matter what subject we are talking about, money is involved in everything. There is nothing more important."

"So what about when making money shifts from being just a tool to achieve a goal to becoming an end in itself? That sounds like pure, unadulterated greed to me."

"You some kind of philosopher in addition to being a spook? Look, I don't know what your world looks like, but in mine it's all about winning. I'm going to be a really big dog in Vegas some day, maybe sooner rather than later. And to be the biggest winner of all, you need money. Piles of it. So if you want to call that greed, go right ahead."

"Dumb question, but if you have all this money, why are you chasing Gwen? We both know money talks in Vegas and there's plenty of new talent coming through there every day that would be more than happy to help you spend your money. You don't even have to marry anyone, since money will buy you anything you want in that town. And I guess since I'm asking dumb questions, here's another for you. If your old man is such an asshole, why are you here spending time with him?"

"Ah, but I'm not spending time with him. I'm sitting here drinking with you, aren't I? And Gwen, well, it's up to her. You may not believe it, but there's a part of her that has more in common with me than you think."

"I'll have to take your word for it as to what she was like when you were both younger, but don't you think she may have changed in the years since?"

"Not in her case, man. Winning is never easy, but she'll come back to me eventually. Money talks."

Jonathan stared at his now empty glass and wrestled in silence with the temptation to have another drink. Outside the window he could see the snow had finally arrived, coming in huge, crystalline flakes that didn't melt on hitting the ground. The initial flurry was so thick with flakes it was impossible to see anything beyond the pool of light spilling out of the windows to the patio in front of the hotel. The snow brought a deadening lassitude and Jonathan had the crazed thought it would permeate everyone and everything, never to stop, and he would never see sunshine or warmth again. Jonathan shook his head and got up from his chair.

"Not going to have another and keep me company, spook?"

"Tomorrow is another day."

Jonathan left money on the table for his tab and picked up the books from the table. He turned to look back as he left the lounge and saw Duncan was ordering yet another scotch.

After sleeping late and indulging in a big breakfast the next morning Jonathan went back through the diary one more time, in the hope that with fresh eyes he might find a clue he missed from the night before. No new insight presented itself, so he turned to the internet to do the research he had promised he would do.

Two hours later Jonathan realized his eyes were tired and he desperately needed a break, so he went for a long walk along the beach in a different direction than he had gone before. Despite how heavy it had seemed to be snowing the night before the accumulation was only a few inches deep, so he had no difficulty navigating the pristine white carpet before him. He was glad he had bundled up with warm clothes before he set out, as it was just cold enough outside that the snow was dry and crunchy, like the snow back east. The soft, wet snow he knew was the norm along the west coast had not materialized.

After returning to the hotel to pick up the diary he made his way to the cafe toward the end of the dinner hour, but as he approached the entrance he stopped in his tracks as a sudden curiosity took hold of him. Instead of going inside he made his way around the side of the building, leaving tracks in the virgin snow as he went. The odd storage room in the basement had been nagging all day at his mind in the background, but he had been unable to put his finger on why. The idea of looking at the puzzle from another angle was what made him approach the problem differently, although he didn't know where the thought had come from or exactly why it could be important.

Walking past the snow covered verandah he made his way to the beachfront side of the house and over to the unplowed beach path that meandered along parallel to the shoreline. A few animal tracks crisscrossed the white carpet of snow that was otherwise untouched.

Looking back at the house he studied the west-facing facade and was immediately struck by the difference between it and other structures along the waterfront. Although the house had two windows on the west side, they were both small and on the upper floor of the building. All of the other nearby structures had some sort of picture window of various sizes affording an opportunity to look out at the ocean. Recalling the house had been converted to a cafe Jonathan surmised there had perhaps been a window at one point in the wall when it was originally a private home.

Removing the window seemed odd, though. Jonathan was puzzled at the thought, as taking out a feature that people might enjoy seemed strange, until with a rush of insight the pieces fell together in his mind.

The key was in thinking his way into the interior layout of the house and the realization the odd little storage room under the stairs lay on the west side of the building. He smiled, feeling certain the secret entrance to the speakeasy had been through the little storage room. Renovating the west window out of existence and adding the big verandah along the south side of the building on the surface would have made sense, as there wasn't enough room for one between the beach path and the house. Doing so would also have given cover for something that could be made to look innocuous enough for the purpose of an entrance. People using the beach entrance in the dark of night would be hidden from the street.

As he stood staring at the wall, certain he was correct, he realized he could just make out a slight dip in the ground at the exact spot where he judged the storeroom to be. With the ground covered by snow it was just possible to see the dip, which would likely be harder to see if covered by grass. He smiled once again at his detective work and vowed to have another look at the storeroom.

Making his way back to the entrance of the cafe he came in to find it less than half full. With the exception of Dunstan, most of the others were already there, seated at the largest of the tables. For the first time Gwen now had a music player set up and Christmas carols could be heard in the background. As everyone greeted him the door to the cafe opened once again and the gathering was complete as Dunstan walked in, pulling up a chair as he came over.

Gwen was busy finishing up with other patrons, but she soon appeared to take their orders and get them drinks. The others had already finished and were nursing their own beverages. As Gwen finally made her way over and sat down Jonathan took time to tell them about what he saw outside the house. The possibility the storage room was actually the secret entrance elicited interest from everyone.

"I think you're on to something there, Jonathan," said Tom. "I have news, too. I worked my way through a whole pile of newspapers at the library today. Turns out there was indeed not one, but two murders here. Both were linked to the speakeasy. It seems there was a gang fight that started inside and may have moved outside to the beach, where two men were found dead of gunshot wounds by the police. That they were found on the beach side of the house would align with where you think the entrance once was. The interesting part is there was reference in the story to the scene appearing staged. It was a few days later the police came with a warrant and found the speakeasy. Obviously they either already had their suspicions or there was something about the scene that led them to the house."

"So it's possible they could have been killed in the basement and dumped outside?" said James.

"Exactly. And the other possibly interesting tidbit is this all happened in mid December back in the late nineteen twenties. Don't know if it's a coincidence or not that our spirit or spirits are being active now at the same time of year."

Everyone turned to look at Miriam, who frowned and took a long moment before she spoke.

"I don't know. I suppose that could be possible, but I simply don't know. This somehow doesn't feel right, because it's such a huge gap in time. But I admit this might hold some promise. I will have to meditate on this further."

"Look, I don't know much about all this stuff, but I have to agree it doesn't feel right," said Willie, who had also quietly joined the group at the start of the conversation. "I've had some experience with bad people, and this just doesn't feel the same."

A few of them wore puzzled looks, appearing torn as to whether to ask him for more explanation. Jonathan rubbed his chin in thought for a moment and broke the silence.

"Well, maybe the best way to answer this is to explore that storeroom. Gwen, could I poke around in it? Maybe tear out a board or two and see what is behind it?"

Gwen shrugged. "Sure, why not? When you're done just put it together again more or less the way you found it if possible. Maybe Willie could supervise so you don't mess up his storeroom too much?"

"I could help you, but I've got a pretty busy day tomorrow getting ready for the party," said Willie. "Maybe when I'm done we could tackle it?"

"Could you use an extra hand in the kitchen? If you're going to feed me at this party the least I can do is help out."

Willie smiled. "I can always use another hand.

I've got tons of preparation work to do. You're on. Anyone else want to help us?"

The rest of them begged off, announcing they were too busy with Christmas preparations, but Miriam spoke up once again.

"I promise I will take some time to meditate on this tonight and hopefully it will help to answer whether those murders are involved. What about that diary, Jonathan? Did you have any luck with it?"

Jonathan explained what he had gleaned from it, which garnered several thoughtful looks on the faces around the table. This time it was Athena that broke the silence.

"Well, this sounds like it has promise, too. I hadn't thought to look at court records involving this building, but I shall now that I know about this."

"So we still have three possibilities," said Tom. "The murders in the basement, this strange situation with the daughters of the owner, and Gwen's husband. We're further ahead, though."

Gwen cleared her throat to speak. "Look, folks, I know you are all interested in my former spouse, but I remain convinced this is not him. I wasn't going to mention this, but like Willie I too had a strange dream. I—I don't know how to explain it well enough. It was like I was having a normal kind of dream when it changed. I knew something was in the room with me and as that notion came to me I woke up. I really had no real intense interaction like Willie and I never felt threatened. But I'm telling you this because when I awoke I could have sworn there was a faint scent in the room."

"A scent?" said Miriam. "What was it?"

"It was very, very faint, but I could have sworn it was the smell of flowers. It faded away within a minute or maybe less of my waking up. But look, my point is if this really was the spirit of my dead husband, I am absolutely certain he wouldn't be manifesting himself with the smell of flowers. He would be far more likely to have the smell of stale beer following him around. So look, it's true he left me in the lurch and I suppose that could be motivation for a spirit to hang around, but I recommend we look elsewhere."

"God, I can't believe you people are still obsessed with this," said Dunstan, speaking for the first time since coming in. As he finished he threw a small bag he had brought with him onto the center of table.

"Since you're all persisting with this annoying search why don't you just get on with it and try talking to your friendly spirit? That's what this is for. The sooner you really get going the sooner you can all figure out how this will resolve itself, because I have no idea how you are going to bring some closure to this endless chase after nothing."

Athena reached over and opened the bag, pulling out a board with the letters of the alphabet and numbers on it, along with a little triangular piece of wood with small legs.

"It's one of those children's toys for pretending to talk to spirits."

"Hang on, that's not what the internet says. I read mediums use these to talk to spooks, so that's why I brought it from that secondhand store down the street."

"Just because it says that on the net doesn't mean it really is useful or even good to use," said Miriam. "There may well be some people out there that would consider using one of these, but I'm not one of them. In fact, I've read this can be quite the opposite. I think I'll pass on that."

"So I think he's really just laughing at us with this stunt and we should ignore him," said Gwen.

Dunstan laughed. "Maybe, or maybe not. Whatever, I was just trying to be helpful. I think this is all utter crap, of course."

"Well, I may not agree with his methods, but Dunstan may have a point about how to resolve this," said Tom. "I confess I'm not real clear myself on what we're going to do once we sort out who or what we are dealing with. I know the plan is to try and help, but how?"

"Well, unless some other option presents itself, I thought we were going to look into a smudge ceremony," said Miriam, turning to Jonathan. "You were going to do some digging on that?"

"I did. There are all kinds of references on the net about this. If I have this straight, at a fundamental level a smudge ceremony is basically about cleansing and purification. There seems to be a plenty of different reasons to do one, like purifying oneself or to place a blessing on a particular place. It can also be about healing or seeking renewal if you will. The problem is there seems to be a ton of different ways and approaches to doing them and not all are specific to indigenous people. There are many different kinds of prayers that can be used and I have no idea what would be best. We would also need to find some of the herbs to burn and do a proper smudge if we were going to try it. I think you can get smudge sticks with the herbs bundled together, but I have no idea where we would find them around here."

Dunstan laughed. "Why not try that shop selling dope that's just down the street? If they don't have exactly what the recipe calls for I'm sure they'll have something to give us all some kind of a buzz."

Melanie turned along with several others to scowl at Dunstan. "I thought you were trying to be helpful? Didn't take long to fail at that, did it?"

"Hey, I made my suggestion. I just don't think waving a bunch of burning sticks around is going to get you anywhere."

Athena cleared her throat to catch everyone's attention before she spoke.

"It might not be a problem to get a smudge. I'm pretty sure I know where I can get one, if we are actually going to do a ceremony. As for a prayer, I will have to give thought to that and maybe talk to some friends. I wouldn't feel confident enough to do it myself, but finding someone to do something appropriate may be possible."

Several of the people around the table showed surprise on their faces at her revelation. After a long moment where no one spoke Paula finally broke the silence.

"Well, that's good Athena. I can't help being curious, how is it you are so familiar with the subject?"

Athena shrugged and sighed. "My mother. She was from the local band here, but she married a white man. I've never felt a need to advertise my origins, but I'm proud of both of my parents and the heritage I have from them. But as I said, I am definitely not familiar with this subject, although I know people I can consult. I have a question for all of you, though. Is everyone comfortable doing this?"

Once again a brief silence descended as everyone took time to process that thought, but Dunstan didn't need long to speak his mind.

"What's the problem? So we all sit around while someone prances about chanting some mumbo jumbo and blowing smoke in our faces. Aside from the fact I think its all nonsense I have no problem with it. I'll just make sure to bring a bottle of scotch with me to help enjoy the show."

"Hmm, well, sorry Dunstan, but that is exactly what we don't need," replied Athena. "It is never a good idea to make light of approaching the Spirit for help, at least not if you want success. Look, all of you, the reason I ask is there are many different faiths and beliefs out there. I am not familiar with the personal beliefs of all of you. I recognize some of you may not wish to participate in a ceremony such as this for reasons of faith. I already know what Tom thinks and he is fine with the idea, but what about the rest of you?"

Dunstan groaned and got up from his seat. "I need another beer. Time to go for a smoke, too."

Gwen waved at the beer fridge for him to help himself, which he did. After popping the bottle open he went outside.

"I'm okay with this, Athena, but I expect you already knew that," said Miriam. "What about the rest of you?"

Gwen was the first to respond. "I was raised in the church. I consider myself a Christian, but I confess I don't attend church unless it's a wedding or a funeral. I guess I'm okay with this, though."

James echoed her comments, as did Paula. As she finished everyone turned to Melanie, who was the next person in line to respond.

"You all know my Dad was from India and yes, I do respect Hindu beliefs, as I do my mother's Christian background. I think there's room for everyone's beliefs, so I am fine with this."

"How about you, Willie?" said Miriam.

Willie sighed and rubbed his chin before speaking. "I'm from a part of the country where religion is everything, so although I was never real keen I was brought up in the church. I won't lie that there have been times in my life where I doubted and wavered in my faith, but yes, I still do at heart believe in Christ. I don't have any experience with anything else. But people around the world area all so very different, so I guess I'm not surprised what everyone believes is different, too. I'm okay with this."

Jonathan was the last to speak. "I'm like Willie, I guess. I consider myself a Christian, but I don't go to church. Don't feel a need to, because I try to make every day, all day, a day in church. I say a prayer every day, sometimes more than once. But like Willie, there have been times where I have doubted. Probably will be in future, too. But I firmly believe we are all God's children and, like Melanie, I think there is room for everyone to be different out there. I like the concept of the Great Spirit and the thought there have been many who served as the voice of the Spirit throughout time and across cultures. So count me in."

"Well, I guess that's settled," said Tom. "But I still think it would be useful to understand what we are dealing with here. Some of us seem a little more attuned to the spiritual world. I wonder if there is anything else we could look at doing?"

The door to the verandah opened and Dunstan came in. As he dropped his coat on the back of his chair, everyone could see the questioning look on his face that stopped anyone from responding. He looked around at everyone before he spoke.

"So are we still talking ghosts here? Ah, I see from the look on your faces you are. Bah! You know, if I were putting up a Christmas tree the ornament I'd put at the top would be a big, bright dollar bill sign. Something with lots of glitz to it. Come to think of it, I'll bet I could sell a ton of those in Vegas. May have to look into that when I get back. I need to make a pit stop."

As Dunstan headed in the direction of the washroom James called after him.

"Hey, Dunstan, you forgot to add a 'Humbug!' for us."

Dunstan stopped and turned around. "Yeah, you all think I don't like Christmas, but I do. Listen, the amount of money spent on Christmas every year just warms my heart. People pretend otherwise, but it's all about spending a ton of dough."

As Dunstan disappeared around the corner everyone turned to look at each other and Tom finally spoke up.

"Somehow, I think he slept through the lesson on what Christmas is really all about."

"Does anyone need anything else?" said Gwen. "More wine or coffee or something else? I replenished my secret stock of liquor."

A few asked for top ups to their various drinks and she bustled about taking care of them with Willie's help. As she was sitting down Miriam spoke up once again.

"So before Dunstan interrupted you were about to suggest we try other approaches, Tom? What did you—oh!"

Paula's dog had lifted his head from the floor where he had been sleeping and uttered a low, guttural growl. Everyone craned their heads around to look under the table at the dog, who was sitting head erect and staring transfixed in the direction of the washroom. Jonathan saw fearful looks appear on some of their faces as the dog growled a second time, moments before the crash of a door hard against a wall in the back of the house startled everyone. They were all mesmerized, staring in the same direction as the dog and waiting to see what would happen.

A bare second later Dunstan appeared in a rush from around the corner. His appearance was disheveled, with one of his shirttails still hanging outside his jeans. For a millisecond he stared back the direction he had just come from before turning and rushing over to the chair where his coat was hanging. He pulled out his wallet in a rush, threw some bills on the table without looking, and shoved his wallet back into his pocket. Grabbing his coat, he began struggling into it as he headed for the door.

"Dunstan?" called James. "God Almighty, are you all right? What happened?"

Dunstan looked back over his shoulder for a quick moment to respond.

"Ah—nothing. I'm fine. I just remembered I have to do something. See you later."

Jonathan could see everyone was stunned as they watched the door close behind Dunstan. As it did Joker gave a low whine. Without a word James, Jonathan, and Willie all rose from their chairs at the same time and headed for the washroom. Dunstan had left the light on and the door was ajar, but there was nothing to be seen. The three men milled about and explored the surrounding rooms, including the kitchen, but they found nothing. Willie went to check the basement while Jonathan and James went upstairs for a quick look about, but they all came back empty handed to meet again in the hall outside the washroom.

"Either of you sense anything?" said Jonathan, but both men shook their heads and shrugged. "Well, neither do I. Let's go back and rejoin the others."

As they returned Jonathan looked down at Joker and saw the dog had returned to sleeping peacefully at Paula's feet. The others gave them questioning looks and Jonathan shook his head.

"Nothing. We saw nothing and felt nothing."

"My God," said Gwen. "Did you all see how pale he looked? I've never seen him look so rattled."

"I'm no expert, but he looked like someone in shock," said Athena.

"I don't know what happened there, but my bet is our spirit or spirits decided to pay a personal visit to him," said Miriam. "And you know what, I'm not surprised. Is it so strange the one among us who has no belief was in for some special attention from this spirit? I think there is purpose behind this."

Tom frowned. "Perhaps, or maybe perhaps not. I would caution against reading too much into this."

"I don't think it's a case of reading, Tom," said Paula. "This is all about feelings and I feel she is right."

"I agree, Mom," said Cate.

"I agree, too," said Melanie. "This feels like it was a message to get with the program, whatever it may be."

"Well, whatever it was, it will be interesting to see if he does or if he even shows up again," said Jonathan. "So Tom, back to what we were talking about before all this. Do you have something else in mind?"

"I think we need to redouble our efforts to find the time to research this. I will help Athena and maybe Paula can help us do more digging for clues in the town records. But I was also wondering if a sleep over might help? I suggest that because for whatever reason this spirit or spirits seems to be more active when there are more of us around. I don't know, just an idea. I know everyone is pretty busy getting ready for Christmas."

A few faces crinkled in thought as they contemplated the suggestion, but no one responded immediately. Jonathan frowned and finally spoke up.

"So your idea is the more contact with this spirit we have, the better chance we have of understanding why this is happening. Is that about it?"

"Exactly," said Tom. "If we accept Miriam's thinking that this is happening for a reason and we want to help it sort out what is needed, it only makes sense we should do what we can to give the spirit opportunity. Of course, that all depends on whether Gwen is interested in having something like that happen."

Gwen rubbed her face in thought before shrugging and responding.

"I suppose. I haven't had any dreams quite like Willie did and personally don't fancy having any. If some of you want to stay here one night and are willing to risk that, then you are welcome to do so. Those of you that went on the tour know what the accommodation looks like. I have three extra bedrooms upstairs, so I can fit a few of you in. I don't know when we would do it, though. I'd kind of prefer it was after the party tomorrow, as I have plenty to do between now and then."

"Well, Tom's suggestion could be a good one," said James, although a doubtful look remained on his face. "Remember what Cate said a few days back? I was thinking about it and it feels to me like this really is somehow connected to Christmas.

Maybe we could do it on the twenty-first, the night after the party? I think I could be available. How about the rest of you?"

Jonathan smiled. "Well, you all know I have nothing else to keep me occupied, so I'm willing to take advantage of one of the extra rooms and see what happens."

Melanie shrugged. "I'm on my own. My boyfriend that really isn't a boyfriend won't be back till Christmas Eve. I can just as easily sleep alone here as I can at home, so I suppose you can count me in, too."

"Well, this may be a good idea, but I'm not sure if it's really necessary," said Miriam. "Why don't we just do a meditation here in the cafe? We can see how it goes and if it seems like staying a night would help, then we can do that too."

Everyone looked at each other and acknowledged they were game for attempting it. Miriam added she could lead the meditation the next night after the party if they were all available.

"Sure, let's give it a try," said Athena. "Gwen, you said you have plenty to do before the party. Do you need a hand with anything?"

Gwen rubbed her face again and Jonathan could see she was tired. She managed a tiny smile for everyone, though.

"Well, yes. Willie has his hands full in the kitchen, but with Jonathan helping him tomorrow that will go a long way to making this easier. But I haven't even had time to put up the real Christmas tree I bought yet, let alone get out the decorations for it. This little artificial tree I have over there is okay, but I'd rather have the real thing in here. I still have other decorations I'd like to add around here, too, and I need to set up the room to accommodate our musicians. That means I have to take some of these tables downstairs and store them to make more room."

"Gwen? How many people are you expecting?" asked Athena.

"Hard to say. There's a total of about thirty or so people I've told to drop by, but whether they will all show up, well, who knows?"

"Wow," said Jonathan, looking around the room. "This could be standing room only. Where are the musicians going and how many how there?"

Gwen pointed to the far corner of the room. "They don't need much space, because there's only two of them. One of them plays guitar and the other has a fiddle. They aren't bringing any other equipment or anything other than their instruments and themselves."

"Well, what are we all sitting here for?" said Cate. "Mom is going to make me go to bed soon and I'd like to help adding decorations to the Christmas tree."

Paula laughed. "Hmm, you're done with school now so I guess I can let you stay up a bit later than usual, if that is what everyone wants to do."

"If we get going on this we've got enough hands here to get this done sooner rather than later," said James. "I could be wrong, but Gwen looks tired as hell and she needs our help."

Gwen brushed a stray strand of hair from her face and gave James a grateful look. Jonathan agreed with him and told everyone so. Within moments they had organized themselves into working parties to get the various tasks done. Jonathan and James began hauling the extra tables down to the basement, while Tom and Willie went outside to bring in the Christmas tree Gwen had bought to put up. By the time Jonathan and James finished moving the last of the tables downstairs the others had decided on a spot for the tree and were just finishing erecting it in a stand off in another corner of the room.

The fresh scent of the tree filled the room and brought smiles to the faces of everyone. To their amusement Gwen brought several boxes of decorations out of storage and put Cate in charge of picking out the decorations for the tree. The girl fell to the task with glee as Gwen continued pulling numerous other decorations and garlands out of the boxes and handing them to the others. The room was soon festooned with a host of decorations, while the tree itself steadily became draped with a riot of bells, balls, assorted decorations, and a huge strand of colorful LED lights.

Gwen had James rearranging the remaining chairs and furniture around the perimeter of the room to create a space for dancing in the middle as the rest of them continued focusing on the tree. A couple of small tables would still have to be moved to the basement the next day, but most of the work was now done. While James was doing that Gwen had Jonathan bring a huge wreath for the door to the cafe in from where she had stored it outside and she delegated Melanie to help him with it.

When they finished hanging that Gwen handed them a large piece of mistletoe and told them to find a place to hang it. The obvious location was to put it on a light fixture hanging from the ceiling near the entrance to the cafe. Jonathan got up on a chair while Melanie held it until he was ready to tie it on. As he got down off the chair Melanie's dark eyes twinkled as she grinned and looked up at him.

"So this was a lot of effort to put all that up. I think we deserve some kind of reward for our efforts. Since we're standing under the mistletoe, why don't we be the first to take advantage of it?"

Jonathan laughed and made to give her a peck on the cheek, but she wasn't having anything so simple. She gave a quick look around to see if anyone was watching and saw everyone else was paying attention to final touches being put on the Christmas tree decorations. Melanie put her arms around his neck and pulled him close, giving him a long kiss full on the mouth. The firmness of her body crushed against him was electric, but she didn't linger with her embrace. As she stepped back she stared into his eyes to gauge his reaction. Jonathan sucked in his breath and smiled, laughing softly as he did.

"Well, that's the kind of reward I like."

"Me too," said Melanie, before turning away to rejoin the others.

As he watched her walk away Jonathan couldn't help pursing his lips in wonder. The kiss would probably have seemed innocuous enough to anyone that had seen it, but Jonathan knew better. This had been a sensuous, burning kiss that conveyed an enormous desire, bordering on a sense of greed for the contact.

Jonathan shook his head, knowing she had an undeniable attraction and he was facing a decision. She had sent enough signals that her current boyfriend wasn't an issue, so the only question remaining was whether he wanted to do something about her. But with enough problems on the other side of the country still to face, being involved here would add a new wrinkle to his situation.

"What a lovely tree," said Athena, as the last decoration being put up was the star at the top. The strand of colored lights made of LED's wrapped about the tree contrasted with the star that had its own old fashioned, incandescent bulb of white light behind it to give it illumination.

"That star is my favorite decoration," said Gwen.

"A symbol of purity," said Miriam. "Something we all want and somehow seem to lack."

"Yes, but isn't this what Christmas is all about?" said Tom. "Christmas is an opportunity to renew our faith and to find redemption."

"Tom?" said Cate. "What is redemption? I don't know that word."

"Ah, it means to be saved from sin or evil. Have you ever done something you knew could be wrong, but did it anyway? That would be something you might need redemption for. Many people believe God will save them. It boils down to seeking forgiveness."

Cate was silent for a long moment before she turned and looked at the star once more.

"I like the star, too. It feels—good. I hope I can be forgiven."

Paula placed her hand on her daughter's shoulder and smiled.

"I have no doubt you are, my love."

In the silence that followed as she finished speaking an old, classic Christmas carol began playing on Gwen's music player. For a few moments no one spoke, but the song was a favorite of Jonathan's and he felt an irresistible urge to sing along with the song. He began softly singing and within moments everyone had joined in.

Chapter Six

Jonathan found himself getting up a lot earlier than he was used to in order to join Willie and help him out in the kitchen. Despite having snatched a quick coffee and breakfast sandwich at the hotel to consume on the way he was still stifling a yawn as Willie let him into the closed for business cafe. Willie seemed amused the shock of a brisk walk through the chill morning air to the cafe hadn't been enough to get Jonathan going. For his part Willie had a big pot of coffee brewed and was already hard at work by the time Jonathan showed up. After gratefully accepting another cup of coffee and downing a few sips Jonathan asked Willie what his first task would be. Willie handed him a peeler and pointed at a mostly full sack of potatoes sitting beside a pair of huge empty pots.

"When you've filled those up I have other stuff for you, but this'll do to start."

Jonathan realized his facial expression must have betrayed his thoughts as Willie laughed.

"Hey, man, you didn't think you were going to get the sexy jobs to do, did you? I'm the high priced help around here, so the fancy stuff is mine. Your only perk is you can bring that chair over from the corner to sit on."

Jonathan laughed as he settled in and began peeling, while Willie went back to the job he had been working on when Jonathan showed up. Jonathan could see Willie was working on wrapping a pile of tiny sausages with his own pastry and putting them on trays for baking later. As Jonathan finished peeling his first potato he gauged how many it would take to fill the two pots and realized it was a lot.

"A question for you, Willie? I don't mind peeling spuds, but I am curious. I thought you were just doing a whole bunch of appetizers for tonight. What are you going to do with this mountain of potatoes?"

"Make tomorrow night's dinner, of course. Doing all these appetizers is finicky and time consuming, but with all those peeled it saves me a huge amount of prep time. Cooking is all about preparation and being organized, my man. I do appreciate your help, even if I don't know why you're being so generous. Must be all this Christmas spirit in the air. You okay with listening to some Christmas music?"

"Sure. Some people get a little tired of it, but I don't."

"I never get tired of it. It made a huge difference and turned my life around."

"Oh? How so?"

Willie took a moment to finish what he was doing before he replied.

"I like listening to music and when you're doing hard time, some days there isn't a lot else to do. I always liked Christmas music when I was a kid and so did my Mom. So with plenty of time to really listen and understand the songs, that's what I did. They helped give me back a little of the innocence and maybe the faith I lost a long time ago, I think."

"Hard time, Willie?" said Jonathan, pausing a moment to look over at the cook. "My God, if you don't mind my asking, what's your story?"

"I don't mind. I don't talk much about my background, but I don't keep it a secret either. My Mom was a single parent and she died when I was thirteen. Dad had left us and disappeared long before that. I ended up in foster care and it all went downhill from there. I got in with some bad dudes and drifted. Drank too much and flirted with some badass drugs. Found out I liked coke and that was a problem, because coke is expensive. So you steal shit from people to pay for it and keep yourself going. When you can't get your hands on as much money as you need or as much cocaine as you need, you try other shit like meth. That stuff is bad news. Anyway, I was in and out of jail for small property crimes more than a few times. I spent three or four years out living on the street before I finally woke up and realized I was killing myself and had to change."

"So what did you do? Is that how you ended up as a cook?"

"Yeah, but I had a little detour before that. I was trying to line myself up with one of these deals where to help you get off the street they train you, right? The caseworker I connected with was pointing me in the direction of being a cook because I really like food and I had just gotten into a course, but one of my bad dude friends from my past came back into my life."

Willie stopped what he was doing for a moment, leaning on the counter with both hands and looking over at Jonathan.

"Yeah, I know. What the hell was I thinking, right? I kind of owed him, you see? He had stuck up for me and helped get me out of a bind with some really major assholes before I began trying to turn my life around. He wanted me to do one last big job and he needed a hand. Well, God knows why, but it seemed like a good idea at the time. I won't bore you with details, but suffice to say we got caught in progress. Worse, in the process the owner we were robbing saw our faces. My buddy lost it and beat him up badly, who knows why. I think he'd done a little something to get his courage up beforehand without my knowledge and his thinking was muddled. And naturally, the cops showed up. I got time as accessory to it all, with no sympathy from the judge. Being black didn't help matters. Ten years is a long time."

"It is. So you learned to cook in prison?"

"Would have been a lot simpler if I had just figured out I love to cook back when I was thirteen, but I'm not that smart. Yeah, I dove into the courses they offered. The guy teaching us saw I was keen and apparently thought I had some actual talent for being more than just a basic short order cook."

Willie paused and laughed, looking over at Jonathan.

"Man, that was weird. First time someone actually paid real attention to me. I got permission to spend extra time with him because I had committed to good behavior and he taught me a lot, way beyond what he was contracted to do. Of course, finding someone willing to hire you when you're fresh out of the joint, let alone do something other than fry eggs for people's breakfast, is easier said than done. And being black still wasn't helping.

But I've hung in there."

"So how did you end up here?"

"I had met her husband, friend of a friend kind of thing. Don't tell Gwen I said this, but he was a bit of an asshole. Anyway, he was the one recruited me for this, which all went south when he died. I was surprised as hell when Gwen got in touch and said she still wanted me, but I wasn't complaining since I liked her. I've come to learn over the years you can't assume someone is an idiot just because they hang around with idiots. It's funny, you know. Our relationship has really sort of evolved. I don't know what having a daughter would be like, but she feels like the daughter I never had. She's given me a free hand in the kitchen, way more than I've ever had before. So I'm happy here. I just wish all that other bad shit hadn't happened first."

Jonathan nodded and the two men fell into silence as they went back to their work. Fifteen minutes later he finished peeling the last potato and filled the second pot. Willie saw he was done and cleared a spot on a different counter, pointing at a small bag of onions.

"You can hack up those onions and put them in this pot over here. Dice them fine. When you finish that I have a big bag of carrots you can peel, too."

Jonathan laughed. "Wow, I am getting all the primo jobs. So if I got this straight, Gwen is basically your family now?"

Willie looked up from what he was doing and gave Jonathan a contemplative look.

"Yeah, I guess so. Well, she doesn't have much in the way of family herself around here. They are all kind of distant cousins and she isn't close with them. We're doing Christmas dinner here in the diner, just the two of us. We weren't planning to open, but if you want to I'm sure she'd be happy to have you join us."

"That's kind of you, Willie. Have to confess I hadn't thought that far ahead, but I'd love to join you. Got no place better to be."

"Way I figure it we all got regrets in life, man, some of us more than others. Can't do anything to change the past, though. So I carry on. Which I assume is what you are doing, although you seem to be taking a time out from that by hanging around here."

"More or less. Not much to tell, Willie. The wife is divorcing me and angling for everything I own. Work sucks big time, too. You know, I've had times where my personal life has problems and other times where work is full of those too, but never at the same time. It all became rather overwhelming, so I just took off. And here I am."

Willie grunted in response. "Hope you get it sorted, man."

The two men went on with their tasks in silence, spending the rest of the morning working steadily. Gwen appeared and opened the cafe. A small group of customers came in and sat at the few tables left, forcing Willie to focus on his orders while continuing to work on the appetizers for that night. But the last lunch customer finally left and Gwen hung a sign on the door to tell everyone the cafe was closed until the party set to start later that evening.

Gwen finished cleaning up just as the two men were doing the same in the kitchen. They had done everything Willie needed to finish and were now making time to eat some lunch themselves. She came into the kitchen with her coat on and announced she was going shopping for an hour. Willie gave her a paternal smile and waved.

"Enjoy yourself, Gwen. We're going ghost hunting downstairs now. Wish us luck."

"If you find some vintage booze stashed away somewhere save a drink for me," said Gwen with a laugh before disappearing.

Willie wiped his hands on a towel, looked around to make sure there was nothing else to do, and let out a big sigh.

"Okay, man, can't put this off any longer. Let's go do this."

"You don't sound real enthusiastic about it," said Jonathan, a wary tone in his voice.

"I'm not. To be honest I've been kicking myself ever since I volunteered to help you, but I'll stick to my promise. None of this is right and it shouldn't be happening. Look, I don't know about you, but I do believe this is real. I also believe ghosts aren't supposed to hang around and when they do, it can't be good. What about you? You believe there really is a spirit here too, don't you? Doesn't this scare you at least a little?"

Jonathan shrugged. "I'd be a liar if I said no. I guess we all fear the unknown. And yes, I do believe there is a spirit or maybe two here. But I was thinking about it and it seems to me this is a pretty benign spirit, if it is one. It hasn't hurt anyone, despite having a bunch of encounters with us now. The worst it has done is to scare some of us a little."

"What about Dunstan yesterday? I don't know what happened there, but he looked like something nasty from the depths of hell was after him as he ran out the door. And the night I got a visit in my sleep a while back wasn't real pleasant either."

"Yeah, we need to find out what really happened to him for certain. But that dream or whatever it was you had? I got the sense it wasn't really hurting you. Was it more the fear of the unknown?"

Willie paused a moment with his chin sunk to his chest in thought.

"Hmm. I suppose you could be right. But it's not an experience I want to repeat any time soon. Well, let's get on with it."

Downstairs the two men stood staring at the storeroom after Willie opened the door and turned on the light. This time Jonathan focused his attention on the ceiling of the storeroom and after a few moments thought he turned to Willie.

"You got a flashlight by any chance? A few tools would be good, too. Maybe a hammer or a screwdriver would help. Whatever you got that can pry open one of these boards."

Willie grunted and went into his room as Jonathan stared at the storeroom in thought, realizing he understood now why the room had seemed odd the first time he saw it. On the first occasion he had seen the door it was obvious it's height was two feet shorter than standard, but what hadn't been clear is why the ceiling inside the storeroom was the same height, as there was no apparent reason for it. The possibility it was hiding a secret entrance provided the likely answer, while the real question was what else might be hiding in the walls and ceiling. His musings were interrupted as Willie reappeared at his side with a handful of tools and a flashlight. Jonathan smiled as he saw one of them was a small crowbar.

"Perfect," said Jonathan, taking the crowbar in hand and using it as a pointer, explaining his thinking that something was behind the ceiling.

Willie rubbed his chin in thought. "Yes, I agree. That also probably explains why the light bulb is set off to the side on the wall here instead of in the ceiling. Well, I've got a hammer and nails, so if you're going to pull a few boards off we can put them back on. Let's go for it. Try not to damage the boards too much if you can, so we can put them back."

Jonathan used the flashlight to peer at whatever might be behind the ceiling as the boards weren't set tight against each other, but the cracks between were too small. However, they did afford enough room for the crowbar to do its work and after a little steady effort the first board was off. A small cloud of dust motes were set free to float in the air, making both Jonathan and Willie sneeze. After recovering himself Jonathan took the flashlight and shone it in the cavity.

"Huh. What the heck is—ah, I should have guessed that. Not sure, but this looks like a set of stairs."

"Stairs?"

"Yeah. Here, take the flashlight and have a look. I think this may be a little staircase that could be dropped down and pulled up whenever you wanted. It's obviously latched in place somehow."

Willie peered into the gap in the boards with the light and grunted.

"Yeah, I think you're right, but why does it look like the staircase goes beyond the back wall? I think there's something there, but I can't make out what it is."

After looking again Jonathan agreed. The two men peered at each other to see if the other had an answer to no avail. Jonathan shrugged.

"Well, I guess I should take a few more boards off."

Working steadily Jonathan removed a few more of the ceiling boards and then did the same with two of the boards along the back wall after moving the sacks of potatoes out of the way. By the time he had the second board off the rear wall enough had been uncovered to reveal the truth of what was hidden away for so long.

The staircase still worked. A simple latch hook on either side of it held the structure in place. As they unlatched it the narrow staircase dropped down with a loud groan of protest and the squeal of metal hinges that had not seen use for a long time. Behind it was a hatch cover that Jonathan was certain would be in the spot he had seen from the outside. With the boards gone it became clear the entire room was supported by bricks mortared in place to support the space from caving in. Both men agreed this had to be the rumored secret entrance to the speakeasy. But the strange part was the cavity in the rear wall that Willie had found. As Willie shone the flashlight inside both men laughed.

Reaching inside, Jonathan brushed aside the cobwebs to pull out a small, clear glass bottle that had been sitting on a small shelf set into the top of the cavity. To their surprise it was a third full of a dark amber liquid. The cork looked brittle with age and the bottle had a heavy feel to it, coming from a time when glass bottles were made much thicker than now.

"Looks like Gwen got her wish," said Willie. "What else is back there?"

Jonathan shone the light around but the lower space of the cavity was empty. He poked further around the shelf area and pulled a couple of fragile looking old newspapers out. They looked to be the local newspaper and both were dated 1930. The only remaining find on the shelf was a two-foot long cudgel, with a leather thong threaded through a hole in the handle. Jonathan slipped it around his wrist and tapped his other palm with it.

"Not much doubt what this was for, I'd say. What do you think, did they have a guard posted here and this belonged to him?"

"Has to be. If I were running a secret gin joint I wouldn't be letting just anybody in here. And, I'd want to make sure anyone that did come in was behaving. I'll bet they had some muscle stationed here. Maybe they'd sit on a stool in the corner. This hole in the wall was a place they could keep some food or drink or newspapers to amuse themselves with when they weren't busy. Who knows?"

"Yeah, that makes sense. What I can't figure out is how they would keep this staircase a secret if the cops showed up? These boards we pulled off weren't in place back when the booze was flowing here. There had to be some—ah, I wonder."

Jonathan pointed at the wall near the ceiling in a corner on one side and reached up to grasp the head of what turned out to be a small metal pin sticking out. Similar metal pins were on the other three corners of the little room. Jonathan grinned at Willie.

"There you have it. I'll bet they had some sort of a wood panel handy. If the alarm were sounded they would close the hatch, put the staircase up, and cover it all up with the panel supported by these four pins. You'd never notice it unless you looked real close. Clever bastards, weren't they? I guess they had to be. But what about the other side of the entrance hatch? They must have had some way to cover it up."

"Bushes and shrubs," said Willie. "There must have been some thick brush planted along the wall of the house at some point and its just been taken out. I'll bet they've put some kind of big metal cover over this wood hatch outside once the speakeasy was shut down. Cover it all up with dirt and unless you were looking for it, like you did, no one would know this was here."

Jonathan nodded. "Makes sense. And I suppose this empty space in the back wall is where they stashed at least some of the booze when they had to. I'll bet they had some kind of panel they could cover it with in short order, too. Well, mystery solved, wouldn't you agree? You want to board this back up?"

"Nah, not yet," said Willie, looking at his watch. "Gwen will probably want to have a look. I'll take care of putting it back together. Besides, it's getting late and I need my nap. Going to be a busy night."

Jonathan laughed. "Yes, I know. Naps are important. I should get back to the hotel and clean up."

Willie closed the door and turned the light off as Jonathan brushed the dust off his clothes and went to make his way back upstairs. A sudden realization came and he stopped half way up the stairs. Looking back he called after Willie, who paused on his way to his room.

"You know what, Willie? It just dawned on me we haven't encountered our friendly spirit in all of this. We found some interesting stuff, but nothing spooky. I wonder what that means?"

Willie's face crinkled as the implication of what Jonathan said sunk in, before he shrugged in response.

"Well, maybe it means we're barking up the wrong tree in thinking these old murders have something to do with what is happening around here. I suggest you ask the rest of them that tonight."

Jonathan nodded and after one last look around he left the basement. Gwen had still not returned so he made his way back to the hotel, still musing about why the spirit had not made its presence felt the entire time the two men had been in the basement. After taking his own short nap he showered and changed for the party, making his way back to the cafe two hours later.

Most of the regulars were already there, along with a few people Jonathan didn't know. Miriam and the others pulled him away from the strangers and asked him what they had found in the basement. Tom was fascinated by the story and immediately wanted to see it all. Gwen had already been shown everything, but Jonathan got permission from her to take the rest of them downstairs. After examining it all in detail they unanimously agreed with the conclusions Jonathan and Willie had arrived at. The fact nothing unusual happened during their explorations got the most debate.

"Well, I'll have to contemplate this more, but I think Willie is right," said Tom. "This may be a sign to us this has nothing to do with what is going on here."

"Perhaps, but I don't think we're going to answer that tonight," said Melanie. "And we're missing the party."

They all went back upstairs to find even more people had arrived and were mingling about. Dunstan had joined the crowd and looked surprised when they all appeared from the basement. After they explained what happened he grunted noncommittally and tried to step away to get a drink, but Miriam stopped him.

"Dunstan? I have to ask about yesterday. You looked awful when you left abruptly. Did you see something or did something happen to you? We were concerned."

Duncan wore a cornered look, but he finally

grimaced in response.

"Look, I'm fine today. I—I think my mind was playing tricks on me with all this stupid talk of ghosts. If you must know I suddenly felt cold and kind of nauseous. It wouldn't go away so I just left, because I figured if I was going to be sick I should do it at home and not infect everyone. But it must have just been something I ate. Something I didn't digest properly, I suppose."

"What do you mean when you say you think your mind was playing tricks on you?"

Dunstan shook his head firmly side to side. "There's no ghost story here, sorry. It was all nothing. And now, if you'll excuse me, I'm thirsty and need a beer."

Miriam stared after him for a few moments before turning to look at Jonathan, a quizzical look on her face.

"He's hiding something," said Jonathan.

"I agree. But if he isn't going to tell us about it, there isn't much we can do. Well, I see Willie is putting out some appetizers. Let's go check them out. I'm starving."

While they were talking to Dunstan even more people had come in and Jonathan estimated the crowd had grown to about thirty people or more. He recognized many of the faces as semi regular customers. One of them was the man who had come in several days before dressed as Santa, who was now reprising his role. Gwen had set up a drinks station near the fridge and was selling beer and wine at a steady pace. Willie had taken over the diner service counter and was covering it with an appealing array of cold food trays.

The first dishes on offer were a variety of different cheeses and crackers, followed by a fresh raw vegetable tray filled with sliced carrots, peppers, celery, and cucumber. A variety of savory looking dips for it all was on the side. A tray of cold cut meats with yet more crackers appeared along with a huge tray of egg salad sandwiches cut into tiny triangles. A big bowl of fresh potato salad covered the only remaining space on the counter.

By the time the last of the trays of food were in place a crowd had formed and people were lining up to fill up paper plates. But before anyone could get started Gwen called for attention and began distributing Christmas crackers. The air was soon filled with the sound of people pulling at the crackers and laughing at the cheap prizes and the jokes they contained. Several people took to wearing the paper hats that came with them. Jonathan joined with Melanie to open theirs. He donned the pink hat that came out of his cracker and traded his plastic diamond ring prize for Melanie's spinning top as she laughed in amusement.

The line up for food soon formed itself once again. Jonathan realized he was hungry, but decided to wait until the line dwindled. As he stood waiting the door to the cafe opened and two young people came in, a man and woman. Both were carrying instrument cases and on seeing Gwen they waved to catch her attention. She came over and gave them both a hug before pointing to a corner of the cafe where two chairs were reserved for them. A fiddle and a guitar appeared from the cases they brought and were set beside the chairs with care before the two came back to join the hungry crowd and get their own plates.

Jonathan knew the food on display was only the beginning of what Willie had prepared and wasn't surprised when Cate came out of the kitchen carrying a tray of steaming hot chicken wings, followed by Tom with a plate of equally hot stuffed mushroom caps. Athena appeared moments later with the tiny sausages Jonathan had seen Willie working on that morning. As those were consumed a variety of even more hot appetizers kept coming in a steady parade of food.

Tom made certain everyone knew Willie had even made rice and pork dumplings in a homemade wrapping based on one of Tom's favorite Vietnamese recipes. Jonathan tried one and realized they were delicious. As others did the same they disappeared fast. But Willie had something for everyone that night, with even a small plate of fresh cut and peeled carrots for the dog Joker. Jonathan laughed at the sight, but Paula assured him Joker loved to eat fresh carrots.

The crowd grew more raucous as the beer and wine kept coming along with the food. Jonathan mingled with some of the people he didn't know and discovered they were as friendly as those he already knew in the cafe. He spent several minutes in conversation with the old man in the Santa suit, who like Jonathan had worked back east for many years before retiring to his hometown.

The flow of food from the kitchen eventually stopped as Willie gauged the crowd's appetite was finally being sated. Several people helped him with clean up in order to let him join the party and as they did the musicians made their way over to their instruments. On seeing this people began taking seats around the perimeter of the room to leave space for dancing.

Within minutes the musicians were ready and they began playing. Jonathan soon realized the two young people had talent and knew their instruments well. Neither of them sang to the music, but Jonathan recognized the first few songs with ease.

By the time the third song was well underway there was still no one dancing. Letting mock frustration appear on his face, Willie took off his apron and went to stand in the middle of the dance floor. He put his hands on his hips and glared about the room.

"Well, what's with you people? Is this a party or what? Gwen!"

Gwen looked up and saw Willie was crooking his finger at her to have her join him. She grinned and handed the beer she had just opened to one of her customers before joining him just as the song ended. Willie looked over at the two musicians.

"Something with a little jump to it, please? Come on people, let's go!"

The two musicians laughed and immediately launched into another song. Willie and Gwen began dancing about the floor in what looked like a polka, but they were soon forced to make room for others as the crowd finally followed their lead. Jonathan was standing and clapping in time with the music when a soft hand on his shoulder got his attention.

He turned to find Melanie grinning up at him before pointing to the dance floor.

'I think there's room for a couple more, don't you?"

Jonathan smiled and led her out onto the dance floor. Two hours later the party was still going strong as Jonathan took a break, having danced with several of the women in the room. Gwen was still doing a brisk business selling beer and wine, and the crowd was even noisier as a result. Jonathan realized he was a little tipsy after his fourth beer, but having spent most of the last two hours dancing he wasn't feeling it as much as he otherwise would. As he made his way over to Gwen for another he realized Dunstan was coming over from a different direction for the same reason, laughing at something someone had said as he came.

"Having a good time, man?" said Jonathan, as Gwen reached into the fridge for yet another beer.

"I am. Hey, I'm used to parties almost every night of the week and we certainly haven't had much of that around here lately, have we? And everyone else seems to be having a great time, too. Good job, Gwen, you must be making a killing on the booze here tonight. But say, I keep forgetting to ask, what's the tab for the food? I haven't paid you anything for it."

Gwen stared at him in puzzlement for a moment until understanding dawned on her face.

"There's no charge, Dunstan. The food is on the house."

"No charge? My God, are you crazy? This must have cost a bag full of money. You've been complaining money is tight and you could be making a ton of money here."

Gwen grimaced, allowing a hint of exasperation to appear on her face.

"Yes, I suppose I could, but I'm not. I'm doing well enough selling booze. The food is to reward my loyal customers. Think of it as a gift, Dunstan. You know, it's called Christmas, remember? This is what one does this time of year. I'm thankful for the people that have supported me."

"God Almighty, you're never going to get anywhere doing that. People are all too happy to take advantage of things like this. And if you think loyalty will get you somewhere you really need to have your head examined. Loyalty doesn't put food on the table."

"Well, I'm not sure about that, Dunstan," said Jonathan. "I think this is called building brand loyalty, is it not? It's a well-established marketing approach. But I don't think you've quite got what she's talking about. Besides, how much would something like this really cost? I'll bet Gwen will at least break even when the dust settles."

Dunstan rolled his eyes and shook his head. "I suppose breaking even is better than breaking your bank account and going under, but not by much. I'll go back to my swimming pool filled with money now, thank you."

Gwen and Jonathan watched him walk away before turning to look at each other and shaking their heads in dismay as one. As more customers appeared looking to refresh their drinks Jonathan elicited a promise for at least one dance with her before the night was out.

Two hours later the party was slowly starting to wind down, but Jonathan barely noticed. As the evening had worn on Melanie spent more and more time with him, including dancing with him every time the musicians played a slow dance tune.

The first time it happened the crowd on the dance floor forced them into a close embrace and as Melanie was obviously enjoying herself Jonathan thought little of it. He enjoyed the sensation of her full breasts mashed into his chest as they danced slowly about the room. She had been drinking wine all night and Jonathan knew she was likely as tipsy as he was. But Willie had brewed some decaffeinated coffee and they had drunk a cup each, so they were both still holding their own.

By the time almost half the people had left the musicians announced they would be doing their last song of the night, finishing with one final slow dance. Melanie grabbed his hand and pulled him into the crowd forming on the dance floor. As they began to dance Melanie made no effort to maintain any distance, effectively molding herself to his body. She stumbled a couple of times, inadvertently stepping on his foot and grinning at her mistake each time.

As the song ended everyone reached for their coats and made their goodbyes to Gwen and Willie, thanking them effusively for what a good time it had been. They helped put some of the furniture back in place before Gwen finally refused any more aid, adamant she would finish clean up the next day. Jonathan stepped outside with Melanie and she grasped his arm, slipping just a little on a small patch of ice.

"Walk me home, Jonathan? I'm afraid I've had a bit much and don't want to fall. My place isn't far."

Jonathan sucked in his breath for a moment as he thought about it. The possibility this was leading to something a lot more intimate than a close, slow dance was obvious. But the alcohol made thinking about it difficult so he decided to simply go wherever the situation led him.

"Can't say no to a lady, now can I?"

Her home was only three blocks away, but they had to take it slow, as more little patches of ice were everywhere. When they finally got there Jonathan made to leave her at the door, but she pleaded with him to come in.

"I'll make a little decaffeinated coffee and we can have one last nightcap. Pour a drop of liqueur or brandy in it? Please? I need to sober up just a bit before I go to bed. Besides, its cold out here and you need to warm up before you leave."

Once again, Jonathan saw no way to refuse her so he went inside, although he was certain she was still more inebriated than he was. He resolved to leave at the first opportunity, not wanting to take advantage of her.

As he woke the next morning to the feel of an unfamiliar bed the same thought came to mind and he rubbed his face in rueful dismay over his lack of willpower. He looked over and was unsurprised to find Melanie lay asleep beside him, although she stirred slightly and shuffled her position. Jonathan reached over to glance at his watch and saw it was almost ten in the morning. The late hour wasn't a surprise either because he remembered it was past one in the morning by the time they arrived at her home.

Getting out of bed he made his way to the bathroom, picking his way through the bits of clothing strewn about the room. He couldn't remember exactly how it started, but within ten minutes of their arrival at her home the two of them were tearing at each other's clothes while making their way directly to her bed. Jonathan wasn't certain what time they had finally fallen asleep, but he knew it was a lot later than when they had got to her place.

By the time he came out of the bathroom she was awake and when she saw him coming she threw off the covers with a small groan. She came over, rubbing her face, and gave him a quick hug and kiss before disappearing into the bathroom herself. Jonathan felt his body stir at the feel of her, but he walked into the kitchen to make some coffee. He was still working on it when she came around the corner and grinned.

"Now this is what I like to see, a naked man working in the kitchen. What could be better? Are you going to cook me breakfast naked, too?"

Jonathan smiled. "I had rather thought we could have some coffee and then get in the shower first. I will happily fix you breakfast afterwards, but I think it'll be while I'm wearing clothes to stay warm."

Melanie gave him a mock pouting look, but wrapped an arm around his waist. She stared blankly at the coffee pot that was finishing the brew cycle. Jonathan poured two cups the second it was ready and they both sipped at the hot coffees. Melanie murmured her appreciation between sips.

"Ah, that's good," said Jonathan, feeling his own gratitude at the simple pleasure. "Have you ever noticed how that first cup of coffee is like a wave washing over your brain, washing away all the debris you left behind on the beach the night before?"

Melanie laughed. "Is that what last night was? A bunch of debris?"

Jonathan grinned. "Well, I was going to say cobwebs, but that would be mixing my images up, wouldn't it? And no, it was not debris. How about that shower?"

The shower ended up taking longer than normal, as the process of soaping each other down led to more than a simple desire to get clean. By the time they were both back in the kitchen the smell of the scrambled eggs, bacon and toast he was cooking for them made his stomach rumble in anticipation several times. As Melanie sat at the table watching him she was uncharacteristically silent for a long time, until she finally broke the silence.

"I just want to say I'm sorry if I've led you astray, Jonathan. I wasn't real sure if you wanted this to happen. But I had a few too many last night and when that happens I sometimes cave in."

Jonathan looked over at her in curiosity. He stared back down at the food he was cooking before responding.

"No need to apologize, I was a willing participant last night. I had a few too many drinks as well. But I expect this isn't the first time something like this has happened to either of us at various times in our lives."

"No, it's not," said Melanie, a penitent look on her face. "I guess I'm not afraid of the truth, which is that, yes, I have done this with other men before a few times. I keep telling myself I shouldn't, but I do. And you?"

"First time having a fling with a woman who in theory already has a boyfriend, I'm afraid, and I'm sorry. I guess it's because I had a need for someone. The wife I'm divorcing hasn't been close to me for quite some time and it has been a while. Can't keep the beast under control forever and it got the better of me."

"Well, I liked the beast," said Melanie, with a laugh and an impish look on her face. "But listen, I'm the one that lured you here last night. Yes, I was giving in to my weakness, but you have no need to apologize for anything either."

"I guess you're not real close to your boyfriend? And what about your ex husband?" said Jonathan, portioning the now cooked food out onto two plates and bringing them over to the table.

Melanie gave him a small grimace as she picked up her knife and fork.

"I'm not close to either of them. I know that sounds weird, but it's true. My ex spouse and I were married very young. I had just turned eighteen and he was only a month older than me. It was our parents, of course. They wanted a fairy tale match made in heaven. We tried to keep it going for a long time and we worked on having a child, too. I lost one to a miscarriage and we found out afterwards I'm not capable of bearing children. It also turns out we both like each other as people, but we've realized we actually aren't each other's type, if that is making sense. I see him once in a while, but he travels a lot for business now."

Melanie took a few bites before continuing. "As for the boyfriend he travels a lot too, maybe more than he needs to. The truth is he really is just a friend who happens to come over and have a good time once in a while. For all I know he has women in other places and it wouldn't surprise me to learn he does. I don't ask or complain about it. Don't know if any of that makes sense."

"It is making sense. At least you've managed to stay friends with your ex. My soon to be ex wife and I are not friends, in addition to very much not being each other's type. Well, I don't think we're alone in making mistakes. I figure it's one of the great mysteries of life, how some people can marry and live happily together for decades while other people end up with exactly the wrong partners."

Melanie worked her way through her breakfast for a few moments before responding again.

"Yes, that would be a mystery and it's one I'm not likely to ever understand. I wouldn't say my husband was wrong for me, though. We do like each other. As for my friend, he's an old shoe I put on when he's around. He's comfortable and he fits, but I don't want to spend the rest of my life with him. Sometimes I want to try a shoe that is new and different, because I want passion and I want to feel alive. I'd like to be swept away. I want to feel like I have purpose and I'm the most important person in someone's life. He just doesn't inspire that kind of feeling. So is it so wrong to want that and find someone else's arms to fall into? I struggle with it every time this happens. I feel like I'm in a wrestling match with myself."

Jonathan shrugged as he finished his breakfast and took their dishes over to the sink to clean up.

"Not for me to say whether it's wrong or right. I guess we all struggle with sorting our lives out. If doing what we did is wrong, I'm in good company with a lot of other people in the world and not alone."

"Well, that's true. You don't have to look any further than at my friends."

"Really?"

"Oh, yes. Take our man James, for instance. You've noticed he has an interest in Gwen, right? Well, that isn't new because they were sweethearts back in high school. Engaged to be married, too. But that only lasted till he met another blonde equally as good looking as Gwen. That was the first one he married. This survived all of a couple of years before he did it again. And what a surprise, he went three for three with blondes. The difference with her was she had a bunch of money. The thing is, I think he may have made another pitch for Gwen somewhere along the way, and it had to be while she was married. She's never said much, but there always seems to be an edge to their conversations."

"Sounds like his problem is he loses his mind every time a blonde walks by and he starts thinking with something other than his brain."

"Yes, indeed. But Gwen isn't an angel herself or, if she were, she would be a fallen angel. I'm pretty sure she jumped into bed with James in the interlude between wife number one and wife number two. I was meeting someone for coffee at the hotel and guess who I found checking out together. They made up some feeble story, but we all knew what was going on. Of course, who am I to look down on them? Anyway, I expect she got seriously pissed off at him when he dumped her a second time."

Jonathan folded his arms and sat back in thought, nursing the remaining dregs of his second cup of coffee.

"Huh. But I think they still have a thing for each other, right?"

"Absolutely. And then there is Paula. She's a lovely person and so very quiet and unassuming, right? You'd never guess she was involved with a married man, too, would you? But that's where the kid came from."

"Damn," said Jonathan, shaking his head. "You're right, I wouldn't have guessed that at all. Wow, this town is getting more interesting by the second."

"I don't know what happened with her, but she did confess who the father was to me and he was definitely married the whole time. Still is. She never said much else, but I expect she just had a desire, too, and had to do something about it. And then there's Miriam."

"Good Lord, her too? What's her story?"

"Not sure, but I'm almost positive she has a bit of

a shady past. I've never talked to her about it, but I've picked up hints from others she wasn't as angelic and spiritual in past as she is now. But if you want to know more you'll have to ask her yourself."

"Well, maybe I will. I've been meaning to pop into her shop and have a look around. She did invite me in for a coffee. Anyway, I should get going. Somewhere in the dim past of last night I think I offered to help Willie with anything left to clean up this morning, although I don't think there's much left of the morning to do that."

Jonathan pulled out his phone and turned it on as the two of them stood up. She followed him to the door and watched in silence as he pulled on his coat and shoes. He was about to say goodbye when his phone pinged to announce a text message had come in and he automatically glanced at it. He stiffened when he saw whom it was from and swore under his breath.

"Bad news?" said Melanie.

Jonathan paused as he shoved the phone back into his pocket. With a grimace he looked down at her and grunted out a response.

"A message from someone at work. Usually, anything coming from this asshole is guaranteed to ruin my day. Since I've been enjoying my day until now I'll keep it that way and look at it later. I'm off to help Willie."

They stood looking at each other for a second before folding into each other in a long hug. She looked up at him and gave him a lingering kiss, before finally stepping back.

"I enjoyed last night and today."

"I did too."

As he began trudging back to the cafe he resisted the urge to pull out his phone and read the text, knowing it really was likely to ruin his day. The brilliant sunshine of the late morning left the air clear and cool. Snow crunched under his feet on the few sidewalks that hadn't been cleared.

The warmth inside the cafe was welcome. Gwen smiled as she walked by to deliver an early lunch to a few customers and Jonathan stuck his head in the kitchen where Willie was bustling about. Willie waved off his offer of help, having finished the remaining clean up hours ago. Jonathan apologized with a remorseful smile, explaining he had slept in. Willie just grinned and winked at him in response.

Jonathan was about to leave and return to the hotel, but the temptation to read the text was too great. As he sat at a table and pulled out his phone Gwen came by with a menu, but he waved her away and said he was only staying a minute. His focus wasn't on her, though, as he sat frozen faced, reading the text at the same time as he was speaking. Jonathan knew his reaction to the contents must have been all over his face, as Gwen had been about to turn away, but stopped in her tracks.

"Are you all right?" said Gwen, a look of concern on her face.

"Ah—yes, yes, I'm fine," said Jonathan, pulling his attention away from his phone. "I must be off."

"Okay. Sorry, you looked unhappy about whatever that is. See you later?"

"Not to worry, I'll be fine. Thank you for your

concern. I'll be back at—at some point."

As he was speaking the phone he still held in his hand pinged with another text and they both looked at it. Jonathan was debating looking at the screen again when another text came in, followed in rapid succession by two more. With a quick glance he saw they were all from different people and what he was expecting to happen was now becoming a reality.

"You sure seem to be popular at the moment. If you change your mind about leaving, I've got some fresh brewed coffee if you want to hang around and read all of that."

"Um—sure. I'll have just one cup."

Jonathan shrugged out of his coat and sat down. He was so deep into reading the messages he barely noticed when Gwen placed a cup in front of him and poured it full from the pot of coffee in her hand. When he finally finished reading them all he went back and read them a second time. He toyed with the thought of doing responses, but he restrained himself, as he knew doing so would be a bad idea. Another maxim he had learned the hard way was that writing messages to people when you were seriously pissed off would only serve to make matters worse.

The problem was the way he felt. Describing it in his mind as simply being pissed off somehow didn't do justice to the seething rage boiling inside. Struggling to keep his face bland he downed his coffee, stood up, and pulled on his coat once again. Throwing some money on the table he waved goodbye to Gwen and left the cafe, striking out for the beach path he was coming to know so well, as Jonathan couldn't think of anything better than a long walk to work off his anger.

The town had finally cleared the path of snow, but as he trudged along it he was forced to pay attention to the icy patches of black ice that still remained. Focusing on where he was putting his feet helped restore a measure of composure, although it did little to improve his mood. As the rage dissipated he found himself slowly shifting to a deep despair. A feeling of lassitude stole over him as the question of why he was letting any of it affect him kept coming to mind. Adding to his weariness and indecision was the nagging uncertainty of why he was still hanging around in this town, leaving him feeling rudderless.

But as he kept walking he realized the reason the situation was affecting him was the sense it mattered. The problem was whether he could untangle it all and do something about it, along with the nagging question of why he had to be the one to do it. And strangely, through it all from the recesses of his mind a vision of Melanie's face kept coming to the surface to intrude on his thoughts. As he marveled at why that was happening, a clear explanation came to him. He was truly enjoying being with her.

He came to a big dock that stretched two hundred feet out into the water and instead of passing it by as he had done in past this time he walked out onto its icy, slippery planks. As it was high tide a couple of people were fishing for crabs in one spot, while another man had a fishing line in the water on the other side. Jonathan made his way to a spot in between them and stood staring out into the ocean for a long time as he focused once again on the ramifications of the texts he had received.

After standing there long enough to get thoroughly chilled a flash of insight finally came to him and he turned away from the vista before him to begin walking toward the hotel. Although a host of questions still swirled in his mind, he felt certain he had found the key to unravel the morass of conflicting interests and motivations of the corporations, criminals, and worst of all, his own superiors that were all party to the situation. Acting in the way they now had was damning proof, or at least it was in his mind. Whether he could convince anyone else of this was another matter, as was the question of whether he even wanted to convince anybody.

But this question belonged to another day for answer. With his initial burning rage gone and his mind now much clearer, an equally feverish desire to simply put all the pieces together and paint a clear picture of the situation came over him. Jonathan knew his outrage at the situation needed expression and having at least some sense of his way forward helped.

Jonathan permitted a grim smile to appear on his face at the irony of finally realizing all he needed for motivation was to be seriously and justifiably pissed off. He quickened his pace back to the hotel, for he had work to do.

Chapter Seven

As he opened the door to the shop it triggered a tiny bell to emit a soft tinkle, not enough to be jarring, but enough to make Miriam glance up and look to the entrance.

"Jonathan! I was wondering when you would get around to coming in."

Jonathan shrugged and gave her a small smile as his nose twitched at the faint smell of some exotic scent that permeated the shop.

"Well, you did invite me for a coffee. And here I am."

Miriam pointed to a little table in the rear corner of the shop with two chairs beside it as she pulled a bag of coffee from a small nearby cupboard.

"I'll throw on a fresh pot. Make yourself comfortable. Say, you weren't at the cafe last night."

Jonathan rubbed his face and hands after shrugging out of his coat, grateful for the warmth of the shop. He used it as opportunity to consider his response, as he actually had met Melanie at the cafe early before leaving soon after, only to end up returning and spending the night with her once again.

"Ah, the truth is I was there early, but I had some—pressing business to deal with that evening. Kept me going rather later than I thought and by the time I got there Gwen and Willie were almost ready to pack up. I gather I jut missed you. But they fixed me dinner and Melanie kept me company. Melanie tells me I didn't miss anything of consequence last night anyway. So this morning I looked at the stuff I was working on with fresh eyes and I think the effort was worth it, though. And now my brain needs to focus on something completely different or it might just explode, hence the reason for my visit. And the fact is I wanted to pop by regardless."

"Well, I'm glad you have. The rest of them never stop by much to see me. Everyone is rather busy with Christmas, of course."

Jonathan waved a hand around the shop. "You don't seem very busy. Is business bad?"

"It's okay. Clients tend to come in a bit later and they aren't necessarily buying my wares as Christmas gifts for people anyway, although some do. The crystals in particular are a personal item, one where it's best if the owner to be is the one who choses it. If you're interested in something in here do let me know. I give friends a discount."

Jonathan laughed. "Well, I might be. I confess I don't know much about all of this. You seem to have a range of interesting stuff."

"All kinds of mystic crystals, lovely jewelry and stones, body oils, sacred dream catchers from the local indigenous people, and plenty of books on just about everything. If you need an astrology chart done I can arrange for that to happen. I have lots of Buddhist materials, too. You name it."

"I promise I shall have a look around before I leave, because I'm starting to think I'm at a point in my life where I need a better understanding of the spiritual world. But I'm more interested in you, to be honest. I'm curious to know how you came to be an expert in all of this?"

Miriam frowned for a brief second. "Well,

everyone thinks I'm an expert, but I'm not. I don't think anyone really is. The fascinating truth, I believe, is that the spiritual world is so vast and so all encompassing that it's impossible for anyone to comprehend the entirety of God. And that maybe explains why there are so many different religions and beliefs out there. Each of us is given something appropriate for us and our job is to learn and grow."

"Many paths leading to the same place, huh? I think I can buy that. So each of us is on a path and our task, as you referred to it somewhere in the dim past, is to learn."

"Exactly! Hey, you've been paying attention," said Miriam, laughing as noticed the coffee was now ready. She got up and poured them both coffees before sitting down again.

"But I'm still curious about you. How did you find your way onto this particular path?" said Jonathan, waving a hand at the shop around him. "Was this something you always wanted to do?"

"Oh, my God, no. It's only in the last few years I came to understand this was what I should be doing. I—well, why not. I'll tell you. I haven't broadcast my background and I'm not proud of it, but I'm not hiding from any of it. I was bad when I was younger. Really bad."

"Bad? What does that mean?"

"It means I was into doing some heavy drugs and living on the edge. I took off from home and headed to the big city and bright lights, because I wanted it all. I hung out with a bunch of people where the party was on all the time, every day. Cocaine and all that other heavy stuff is bad news, though. I ended up doing massage parlor stuff because the money was good. Providing the occasional happy ending for a client, if you know what I mean, was even more lucrative."

Miriam paused to grimace briefly. "And yes, I got raped once. Along the way I got pregnant too, God knows how. I guess I forgot to take my pills because I was so stoned or drunk all the time. When I found out I was pregnant it was a massive wake up call. I struggled with the idea of staying clean for the sake of the child, but I was in the grip of the swamp I'd been living in. I made the decision to have an abortion, because by then I realized I was a total wreck and my doctor warned me the child could be severely damaged."

"My God, I'm sorry to pry. I had no idea you've been through all of this. It must be difficult just talking about it."

Miriam shrugged. "The truth is sometimes people have to learn their lessons the hard way. But I'm okay with talking about it all. It's all in my past now. While knowing how you got somewhere is useful, the really, really important thing is what you are doing right here, right now. Anyway, as I was struggling with what to do with myself I met a woman who had been through similar trials. She became a wonderful friend and she saw me through the worst of it. And I'm sure you've guessed by now she was very much into the spiritual world. I learned—"

The soft sound of the bell signaled the arrival of a customer and Miriam's face lit as she recognized the woman that walked in the door.

"Oh, Mary, how nice to see you. I have those stones you were looking for. Excuse me for a moment, Jonathan."

As the two women met over by a glass case filled with crystals and jewelry Jonathan rose from his seat to explore the shop. Miriam's boast that she had a wide range of products proved correct. Jonathan spent the next ten minutes wandering about looking at everything, but most of his time was spent marveling at the wide range of books on a host of subjects. Some of them seemed so esoteric as to be beyond belief, but most were not.

He found his attention drawn to a small self-help book on the basic principles and benefits of meditation. He put it away on the shelf after skimming through it and moved on, but found himself coming back to it two more times. On the third occasion he took it back to the table and sat down to look closer at it. He was still doing so when the bell tinkled once again and the customer left.

"Ah, you've found a book you like. Or more likely, the vibrations of the book attracted you," said Miriam, as she brought over the coffee pot to refill their cups.

"Come again? The book attracted me?"

"Sure. Remember, this is the spiritual world we're talking about. That happens to be a very good book, too. I've read that many times and found much wisdom in it, to a point where I no longer see a distinction between meditation and any other task. All of life is meditation. I suppose that may not make sense to you now, but maybe some day it will. Anyway, it may just be your task to read it and see if it becomes as dear to you as it is to me."

"Okay, I'm sold."

Jonathan flipped the book over and after looking at the price tag pulled a few bills from his wallet to pay for it. Miriam made to give him some of it back, protesting he was entitled to a discount in addition to change from the bills, but he demurred.

"Merry Christmas, Miriam. I doubt your business has you swimming in money like Dunstan and I'm sure you have bills to pay. So, you were telling me your story."

"Ah, right. Well, thank you for this," she said, putting the book in a paper bag for him. "Anyway, there's not much else to tell. My friend met a man and left for another city, but I was well on my way by then. Not much money in my pocket though, and the material world runs on it, so I came home."

She paused a moment to sip her coffee before continuing.

"My Dad passed away long ago, but my Mom was still around and she helped me. She passed away a few years ago too, and with a tiny inheritance from her I set up this shop. By that time I had dove in deep to the spiritual world, you see? I felt the need to pay back the help I had found in my hour of need, so I opened this shop and here I am. I suppose you could say doing this has become my personal task and purpose. You're right about there being bills to pay, though. I do well enough in the tourist season, but the winter months are a bit leaner. I guess my only regret is missing my child growing up."

"That has to be hard."

Miriam shrugged. "Yes, I sometimes still struggle with who I was and what I did, but I cannot change it. What I really wrestle with is whether destiny was a part of that."

"How so?"

"Well—"

Once again the door opened and this time two customers came into the shop, looking around before beginning to browse about. Miriam looked back at Jonathan and gave him a rueful look.

"Any conversation about destiny would be a much longer one and I'm afraid things are going to start getting busier in here from this point on."

She went over to the customers to see if they needed any help, but they were both just browsing and she came back to sit down. Jonathan downed the remnants of his coffee and made to pull on his coat to leave.

"You don't need to leave just yet, do you?"

Jonathan shrugged, as the bell tinkled and another customer walked in.

"Your prediction about getting busier seems to be on the mark and you need to get some sales, so I should go."

"Sadly, I do. You know, there's a paradox there and it's something else I struggle with. I really want to grow and learn and help other people, but the mundane need to pay bills and keep my head above water keeps dragging me down. But maybe that's the lesson I'm tasked with learning, is to find the balance I didn't have earlier in my life."

"What do you mean?"

Miriam shrugged. "Well, if I hadn't been so

focused on my bad desires and greed for more of everything, maybe I'd have had my child. No one wants regrets in life, but the truth is that's mine. I live with it constantly. But here you are, ready to leave and all I've done is talk about me. We're all curious about you, you know. Here we have a mysterious, handsome man who drifts into town and decides to hang around. Half of us are leaning to Dunstan's idea that you're a government spy, maybe hiding out or something. The other half of us think there's some other romantic and fascinating reason, like you've stolen an art masterpiece and you're on the lam with it."

Jonathan laughed. "I'm afraid the truth isn't mysterious, romantic, or fascinating at all, although I do work for the government. I suppose a case could be made I'm on the run from my own life. And as for the handsome part, I'll have to let the ladies decide that. And now I really should go, as I can see one of your customers hovering over by the till for your help."

Miriam called over to the customer she would be right there before turning back to Jonathan.

"Ah, I forgot to mention, since its Sunday night the cafe won't be busy tonight. We can do the meditation at the cafe we were talking about the other day to see if we can get the spirit's attention. Are you in for that?"

"Uh, sure, I suppose. I'll be there for dinner and will see you then."

On leaving the shop Jonathan decided to head back to the hotel for a quick lunch and an afternoon nap. As he was about to walk into the hotel lobby he saw James coming toward him from the direction of the cafe. Jonathan waved hello and decided to wait for him, but as James got closer Jonathan sensed a tension on his face.

"Afternoon," said Jonathan. "Just coming from the cafe?"

"Yeah," said James. "Had lunch with Gwen and just heading back to my parent's place. You?"

"Going for a quick bite and a nap. I was just visiting Miriam."

"What, chasing her too, are you?"

Jonathan laughed. "Well, actually, no. Don't think she's really my type, but she is an interesting person."

"Good thing you're not after her, because it would be a waste of time. Rumor has it she's gay."

"Really? Huh, I hadn't realized that. But then, it's not always obvious who's straight and who's gay out there, is it?"

"No, it isn't, and I'm certainly not an expert on sorting it out. Frankly, I couldn't care less what people do in the bedroom if everyone involved is happy to be doing it. But to be clear, her taste may actually lean to both men and women, since I hear she's been known to be in the company of both. But then, who knows, especially when it comes to women?"

Jonathan stared for a moment at the glum look on James's face as he finished speaking and decided to risk asking about it.

"I agree with all of that. Hmm, it's not my business, you understand, but you don't look real happy at the moment. You okay? It's a little early, but you want to join me for a beer? I can have some lunch while we're at it," said Jonathan, jerking a thumb in the direction of the hotel bar.

"Sure, why not. It would beat standing around freezing out here. God knows I do enough of that at work and I don't need to do it in my spare time."

The two men went into the warmth of the hotel and were soon seated in the bar with a view seat looking out over the beach. Clouds had begun to move in and the bright sunshine of earlier in the day had disappeared. Jonathan ordered a sandwich and both men ordered beers. As they settled in to wait for their drinks James pointed at the bag with the book that Jonathan had placed on the table.

"You buy something from Miriam?"

"Yeah. Here, have a look."

Jonathan pulled the book out of the bag and passed it over to James, who stared at both sides of the cover and passed it back with out opening it.

"Doesn't interest you?" said Jonathan.

James shrugged. "Don't know much about all that stuff. We keep getting told these ideas of employing mindfulness and doing meditation are good ways to help keep some of the bad stuff in our line of work from getting to us, but I've never tried it. I've never been big on religion either, and as for all that mystical stuff Miriam believes in, well, it's all a bit too far out there for me. I'm a pretty simple guy when it comes to it."

"I suppose after you've had to deal with some of the things you have in your line of work, keeping it simple is maybe a good plan."

James grimaced. "It's about all you can do. I've

been on the scene of enough fatalities for various reasons, some of them real unpleasant, that I'd be happy to have a chunk of my brain cut out to make the memories go away. But that's not going to happen, of course, so you compartmentalize it and make a point of not remembering as best you can. You go for beer with the boys at the fire hall every so often and decompress. Go fishing. Go home and take the dog out to the park. The fact I love my job and I love to help people in need keeps me going. I'm just trying to make a difference, right? But going to church or getting into some of this flaky shit Miriam is into has never interested me."

"So you think all this stuff about a spirit in the cafe is bullshit, I take it?"

James grimaced a second time, but as he did their beer arrived and both men reached for their glasses after the waiter left.

"I don't know. I guess I believe in what I can see and hear and feel. I acknowledge there may be something to this, but I'm not the guy that's going to sort it all out. Look, I guess it's fair to say I'm a bit of a skeptic. If someone can stick proof in front of me that there's a ghost hanging around then I'm prepared to believe it. I do think God exists somewhere and there is some kind of reason to all of this, but what it is, well, who knows? Not me. I'm just trying to be the best I can be and I hope it will meet with God's approval when the time comes. But what about you? You believe there's a ghost?"

"Actually, I think I do. Never really thought much about it, but that day in the basement I felt something that I had no other explanation for. But the larger question of why it's all happening? I agree with you. Who knows?"

"So, changing the subject here. If you don't mind my asking, are you still chasing Gwen?" said James, blurting out the question in a rush as if he had been holding it back for a long time.

Jonathan was a little surprised at the intensity that came through in James's voice, but kept his face bland.

"No, James, I think it's safe to say I am not. I'd be a liar if I said I hadn't been interested in her, because I was. But she's made it pretty clear she's not interested in me, so there you go. I've moved on."

James stared at him for a long moment before sighing and downing more of his beer, wearing a morose look once again.

"Well, at least that's one less obstacle in my way."

"Hmm. This is none of my business, like I said when I invited you in here. I can't resist asking why you're so glum, though? Gwen, is it?"

James threw his hands wide. "What else? Had a long conversation with her again today, but I'm not sure if I'm making any headway."

"But you two have history, right?"

James turned to look sharp at Jonathan, before hanging his head and staring at his beer.

"Yeah. Obviously someone has been filling you in, which I guess is no surprise. It's not like I was being subtle about being an idiot. I can't blame her or anyone else for thinking that about me, because I haven't treated her right and I see it now. Women are my downfall, especially good looking ones. I kept seeing her as just another in a series of conquests, right?"

"I hardly think you're alone here, James. People break up and make up all the time. Just about nobody finds the mate of their dreams right off the bat."

"True, but cheating on people is another matter. It always seemed like a good idea at the time. I just couldn't resist the women, like somehow someone else would be infinitely better than what I already had. Maybe it was the thrill of it all. I don't know. And it's cold comfort to acknowledge I'm not alone. I know more than a few guys I've worked with over the years who have fallen into the same trap."

"I gather you were married twice, is it? And you were involved with Gwen more than once but never married her?"

James sighed. "Yeah. Both of those marriages were mistakes and so was dumping Gwen."

"So this may be a dumb question, but why Gwen again? Lots of fish in the ocean, right?"

James was silent for a few long seconds before he finally nodded agreement.

"Yeah, that's true and the thought has crossed my mind. I suppose I will have to do that if she doesn't come around, but for now the focus is on her. And as for the reason? Look, I turned thirty a little while back and, I don't know why, but it was like someone dumped me into the deep end of an ice cold swimming pool and I've been struggling to get out ever since. I gave a lot of thought to what I've done and how I got to where I am and came to a real simple conclusion. I have to grow up now. I look around at a lot of the guys I work with and they're all stand up guys, you know? Most of them have been married for several years and have kids and have their lives together. So here I am, thirty years old, looking in the mirror and seeing a complete fool."

Jonathan's sandwich arrived and he saw both their glasses were now almost empty. With a nod of agreement from James, Jonathan ordered two more from the server.

"Funny you should mention looking in the mirror and seeing what you do, as I've been wondering if that's what I've been seeing lately, too. But back to Gwen?"

Jonathan took a deep swig from his glass and put it back down before continuing.

"In the process of trying to sort my head out on this it finally dawned on me that I keep coming back to her for a reason. We're alike in so many ways and we always had fun when we were together. Even when I ran off with other women I always kept in touch with her. I care about her, a lot. When she took off with that dick she married it was like, my God, how could she hook up with a loser like him? But then, as she has pointed out on more than one occasion, I wasn't exactly behaving like Prince Charming myself. So I guess what I'm saying is I've finally come to understand she is the one for me. She's my destiny if you will. Ten years or more too late maybe, but there you have it. So what do you think? Am I screwed here?"

Jonathan shrugged as he swallowed another

mouthful of his sandwich and more beer appeared on their table.

"Dunno. What about Dunstan?"

James sighed. "Yeah, he's a problem. Gwen has a bit of a wild child in her heart, you see. Not much different than me, I suppose. He's a big city guy with a ton of money and can offer her a grand time of it, while I'm just a small town, blue-collar guy. I don't know how to compete with that."

Jonathan gave James a sharp look as he finished speaking, but with a mouthful of sandwich couldn't speak until he washed it down with more beer. James had noticed the look, though.

"What? Did I say something important there?"

"Maybe," said Jonathan, wiping his mouth with a napkin as he finally finished his sandwich. "It's funny you mentioned being a small town guy, because that's exactly what Gwen said to me."

"Really?"

"Yeah. Look, I sort of made an effort to catch her attention, right? You know, I was still trying to sort out whether or not the two of us could make a go of it. Anyway, one of the things she came back at me with was the thought she likes it here, that she's a small town girl. So maybe that's the key for you."

"How so?"

"Well, maybe what she's looking for is someone who will give her what she wants. I would think that might include things like being swept off her feet with a little romance. Tell her you've been a fool and promise to make it up to her every day for the rest of your life. Buy her flowers every day. Tell her you love her, because it sounds to me like you do. Tell her you want to build a home and a life with her in a small town like this. Kids maybe? Look, I may be talking shit here. I'm hardly the one to be offering advice. Hell, maybe I should be taking my own advice."

James was silent as he stared out into the distance at a freighter passing offshore. He reached over and picked up his glass, tipping it briefly in the direction of the ship.

"Must be a lonely life sailing on those ships, huh? Long days and weeks at sea, going from one port to another. I don't envy them. And you know what, I don't want to be lonely anymore. I've been lonely for a long while now. That's of my own making, but I think I can do something about that."

James downed the last of his drink and glanced at his watch before turning to Jonathan, reaching out his hand as he did. Jonathan did the same and the two men shook hands.

"I think that's good advice and I'm going to take it. I'm glad we ran into each other. I'd like to stay and talk more, but I have to get back to check on my folks. Mom's health has been going downhill and my Dad isn't coping real well with that, which is why I've been coming to town a lot over the last year."

The two men both stood up and James made to pull some money out of his wallet for the beer, but Jonathan forestalled him.

"It's on me. You can buy next time."

James hesitated a moment and then nodded.

"Thank you and yes, there should be a next time, so that's a deal. You know, when you first showed up I wasn't at all sure about you, but I am now. I'm usually pretty good at detecting people that are full of crap, but you haven't rung any of my bullshit alarm bells. You're a good guy, aren't you?"

"I like to think so. I try to make a difference in my own way, like you. I guess maybe you and I aren't so different from each other."

"Maybe. Next time I'll do the listening and you talk."

Jonathan laughed and drained the last dregs of beer from his glass as James turned and left. Jonathan paid the bill and went up to his room. The early afternoon beer had made him drowsy and the thought of checking his messages gave way to the urge for a nap.

As he made his way to the cafe for dinner late that evening the conversation with James kept coming to his mind. The turmoil James was in seemed uncomfortably close to Jonathan's own feelings over the nights he had spent with Melanie. The image of a freighter filled with lonely souls kept coming to mind, too. The thought of taking his own advice, of leaving and simply getting on with his life, and finding someone new seemed appealing. He tried to put it all aside for another day as he walked into the cafe, although somehow Melanie's dark eyes kept appearing in his mind.

No one he knew was there, but it was a little busier than he thought it might be. Gwen came and took his order before bustling off, leaving him on his own. Jonathan was reluctantly checking his messages again when the door opened and both Tom and Melanie came in at the same time, joining him at the table. Tom ordered a coffee and said he couldn't stay long, while Melanie did the same. Tom eyed the phone Jonathan was just putting away.

"Busy checking all your social media accounts?"

Jonathan was unable to hold in his laughter at the thought.

"Ah, no, I don't do that stuff. Because I work for the government I have to be careful about it, but even if that weren't necessary I wouldn't use it anyway. It's all nonsense as far as I'm concerned. But the real problem is the phone itself. It's nothing more than a fancy electronic dog leash. Even though I'm on leave at the moment I kind of have to stay connected, which is both a blessing and a curse."

"Ah, a young man after my own heart," said Tom, laughing. "I'm an old fart, of course, but I just feel humans are wired to connect with each other in person, not through this impersonal machine. And as for the security of my personal information, well, I have difficulty trusting it all."

"I like social media, or at least, some of it," said Melanie. "I have relatives I like to connect with. I can see pictures of what they are up to and stuff. But I get it, not everyone is into this. I know for a fact James thinks its all crap and I'm pretty sure Miriam is just glad she wasn't using it in her younger days. Paula doesn't use it and she makes a point of ensuring Cate is totally offline."

Gwen came by and dropped their coffees on the table along with Jonathan's meal and Melanie asked her if she used social media. Gwen rolled her eyes.

"A little, but not much. Too busy around here. I keep telling myself I've got to get a website for the cafe though. The problem is Willie and I don't know anything about how to do that. Hell, I think Willie doesn't even have a cell phone, let alone a social media presence."

The door opened once again and this time Dunstan came in, while right behind him was Miriam. Dunstan was engrossed with his phone, which pinged with a message as he slumped into a chair at the table. He offered a grunt of acknowledgement to those already there in response to Tom saying hello. He surfaced once more long enough to order a beer and whatever Willie had on special for dinner from Gwen, while Miriam opted for a coffee herself.

After studying the message for a few more moments Dunstan muttered what sounded like a curse under his breath and began typing a message on his phone, tapping at the phone keyboard hard enough to make it clear he wasn't happy about something. Miriam looked at the rest of them and shrugged to show she had no idea what was going on with him before she spoke.

"So, are the rest of you all here to try a meditation with me?"

Tom begged off, as he had to leave, but both Melanie and Jonathan nodded and Miriam smiled.

"Well, let's see how it goes. I talked to Gwen and Willie yesterday and they are both still game for trying a meditation."

"Well, let me know the outcome," said Tom, looking directly at Miriam. "The reason I came by was to tell you Athena is working on something about the previous owners of this place and no, she didn't tell me what. We'll be by in the morning to fill you in, though. We would have done it tonight, but I've got a commitment with Athena to stuff bags of toys and food for the needy."

As he walked out the door Dunstan's phone pinged with a text once again. He took a quick look at the screen and cursed, this time loud enough for everyone to hear him. He sat back and took a long pull at the beer in front of him, shaking his head. Frustration was evident on his face. Miriam raised an eyebrow at him as she finally spoke.

"Bad news, Dunstan?"

"It's always bad news when you have to deal with the kind of shitheads I do," he replied, staring at his beer and downing a second, even bigger mouthful of the beer. He waved the now almost empty bottle at Gwen, who detoured over from the table she was about to clean up to get him another.

"My sympathies," said Miriam. "So, are you here for the meditation tonight, too?"

"Meditation? What are you meditating for?"

"You know what. We want to learn more about the spirit here and to try to help it," she replied, showing exasperation on her face. "Like, what we've been talking about for the last several days."

"Christ, no, unless it involves drinking I'm not joining you tonight. I'll meditate on what my next drink will be, eat my dinner, and be on my way."

"So Miriam?" said Melanie. "I confess I know very little about this. What do I need to know?"

"It's really very straightforward. Meditation is all

about working toward being still, in order to quietly observe and feel your inner world. First, we will all sit straight, but comfortable in our chairs. You close your eyes and focus on your breathing. You'll find your thoughts will wander and this is normal. This may sound odd, but what you want to do is observe the thoughts, letting them pass through your mind without becoming fixed on them. When you realize you are becoming fixed on a thought, you simply bring your attention back to your breathing. So really, the key is to just keep focused on your breath. If you are successful you may feel a flow through your body linked with your breathing and if so, focus on that."

"Okay," said Jonathan. "How is this going to help with contacting the spirit?"

"Meditation is a powerful tool to raise awareness of the Universal Spirit that fills all of us on this planet. It is even more powerful when a group of people comes together to meditate. When such a group has a specific purpose, especially a purpose that involves helping others, much can be achieved. So, I will say a brief prayer at the beginning of the meditation and we will see what happens."

Gwen appeared with the meals for both Dunstan and Jonathan at the same time, and both men set to with gusto. Dunstan was just finishing his meal when his phone rang. He glanced down at the device and swore, as he wiped his lips with a napkin and stood up. Grabbing the phone and his beer he made for the door to the verandah, answering the phone as he went.

"Jack, what the fuck are you calling me for? You

know—"

Silence descended as the door closed behind him, although Dunstan was talking loud enough his muffled voice could still be heard inside.

"Given the kind of day he appears to be having, I'd say it's a good thing he doesn't intend to join us tonight," said Miriam.

Ten minutes later he was still outside, but the cafe had finally cleared out of the other remaining customers. Gwen finished cleaning the tables and Willie made an appearance, stacking the now clean dishes for the next day. They had just finished their remaining chores and sat down at the table, each of them giving a tired sigh, when Dunstan came back inside. His face was still dark with anger as he pulled a wad of money from his wallet, dropping it in front of Gwen. James came walking in the door of the cafe as Dunstan turned to leave.

"Got to go," said Dunstan, barely acknowledging James as they passed at the entrance. "Have fun with your séance. I'll be back tomorrow when I'm in a better mood."

As the door slammed shut behind him Melanie was the first to speak.

"God, let's hope he is."

"Damn, what's his problem?" said James.

The others could only shrug, so James grunted acknowledgement and sat down. In response to questions from Gwen and Willie about what to expect in the meditation, Miriam explained everything she had told the others. Gwen cleared away the remaining dishes and returned to sit at the table, but Miriam stood up.

"No, no, we don't sit at the table. We should sit in a circle."

Miriam moved a table out of the way and began seating chairs in a circle, roughly equidistant from each other. Jonathan looked at Melanie, who shrugged, so Jonathan looked back at Miriam and spoke up.

"Ah, a dumb question for you, but why a circle?"

"Circles are powerful. I—trust me, this is the way to do it."

Jonathan nodded and they all took a chair. As they settled in Gwen's cat appeared and sat beside her chair, peering up at her.

"Hello, Shadow. Guess I left the door open again. I haven't seen you all day, but you couldn't wait and you've come to see me."

For answer the cat jumped onto her lap and began to settle down.

Willie laughed. "He's been hanging out with me in the kitchen, but it looks like Shadow wants to meditate with us."

"Uh, am I okay to have Shadow on my lap?" said Gwen, a wry look on her face.

Miriam shrugged. "I don't see why not. He may be a distraction, but there's no harm in trying it with him present. Is everyone ready?"

On seeing nods all around the circle Miriam pulled a watch from her bag and worked at the mechanism for a few moments.

"Right, cell phones off, everyone. I've set the alarm on this watch for thirty minutes. You can begin now. I'll be saying my little prayer and join you."

Jonathan closed his eyes along with everyone else as Miriam launched into a brief prayer to the Spirit for guidance and help. As silence descended on the room Jonathan focused on his breathing as best he could, but he immediately found his mind wandering. He persisted, though, and gradually he settled into a gentler, steady rhythm of breathing in and out. He focused for a moment on the faint sound of the others breathing steadily around him and realized to his chagrin this was actually a distraction from keeping focus on his own breath. He made himself focus once more on his breathing, but as Gwen was sitting beside him he realized he could hear the cat gently purring as he sat on her lap. Jonathan smiled to himself as the thought came Shadow was indulging in a meditation with them.

The problem was the cat's rhythmic purr became hypnotic and Jonathan realized he was becoming drowsy listening to it. Jonathan tried to keep his focus, but it was a struggle and by now he had lost all sense of time. He strayed away from attention to his breathing several times, but he made himself come back to it each time. The effort finally began to pay off as in time an understanding came that he had somehow reached the beginning of a peaceful sensation of flow and connection. The feeling was wonderful.

When the change came it was slow and subtle, so it took a while to realize something he couldn't identify was intruding on his consciousness. His mind registered a faint scent had somehow appeared in the room and as he struggled to identify it an understanding came it was the smell of roses. Along with the scent came a faint chill in the air. He could hear a few of the others in the room stirring in their seats and it came to him that he was not alone in sensing the change.

But the scent wasn't the only sign something was happening. With a small start he knew a presence was trying to touch his mind, as it had several days before in the basement. The contact was so strange and so ephemeral he couldn't help recoiling from it. He was still trying to process what was going on when several things happened at once. Gwen cried out in pain, which drew his attention immediately.

"Oww—Shadow!"

Jonathan opened his eyes in time to see Shadow had dug his claws into her legs and was staring off toward the kitchen area, but even as Gwen made to shove him off her lap the cat leapt away, disappearing under the tables in the far corner of the cafe.

Melanie was sitting in the chair on the other side of him. To Jonathan's surprise she knocked it over in a rush as she stood and took two rapid steps backwards, her hand covering her mouth. On the far side of the circle both James and Willie had risen from their seats and were looking wildly about. Miriam, however, was staring hard in the direction of the kitchen and the adjoining hallway. As Jonathan's attention turned to her she raised an arm and pointed at it.

"There it is, I see it!"

Everyone's heads turned, looking in the direction she was pointing. Jonathan could see nothing and he told them that. Slowly, the rest of them turned back to Miriam and told her the same thing. As they finished Miriam dropped her hand to her side and tore her gaze away from the hallway to look at each of them.

"It's left. The smell is gone, too. Right?"

With a start Jonathan sniffed the air and knew she was right. He could see the others doing the same and slowly, each of them nodded agreement. As they all stood looking at each other in wonder at what had just happened, the silence was broken by the watch alarm Miriam had set chirping for attention. As Miriam turned it off Jonathan mustered his courage and went toward the hallway where she had pointed. James joined him, but they both soon returned from their search. Jonathan shook his head on seeing the question on their faces.

"Nothing."

"Miriam," said Gwen, giving James a sidelong glance with a curious look on her face. "What just happened here? I felt—you know, I don't know what I felt, but I'm not sure I like it."

"Me, too," said Willie.

Melanie hesitated a moment before she spoke. "I felt like it was trying to communicate with me. I don't know why. It was so strange it scared me at first, which is why I was jumpy there. Miriam?"

"Yes, I think it was trying to do the same with me. I don't know. I need to process this a bit and contemplate what happened. Is what happened to Melanie the same for everyone else?"

Everyone slowly nodded once again, so she continued.

"Okay, so does anyone have an idea of what it

was trying to communicate to us? And I'm just going to check one more time. You really are all certain none of you saw it? It was just me that did?"

Melanie, Gwen, James, and Willie said nothing. Two of them gave tiny shakes of their heads before looking away without saying anything. Jonathan shrugged noncommittally and changed the subject.

"Everyone? What about that scent? Did you all smell it?"

Everyone had, and they all agreed it was the faint smell of roses. A silence descended on the room once again as Miriam sat, eyes unfocused and staring into space.

"Uh, Miriam?" said Gwen. "Anything you can tell us here?"

Miriam gave a small start and with an effort refocused her attention on them.

"I—sorry, I was trying to gain understanding of what I felt. I don't think the spirit was trying to hurt us at all. Notice I said spirit in the singular, because I am now becoming convinced there is only one spirit haunting this place. I think it or something was trying to communicate to us and we were all so surprised that it backed off. And yes, it definitely had a message for me. I—I think I need to contemplate this in private."

"Good idea," said Willie. "I think I've had enough of this for one night."

"I agree," said Melanie, turning to look for her coat. "I think I'll just go home."

"Miriam?" said Jonathan. "What do you mean when you say 'it or something' was trying to communicate? If it wasn't the spirit, what was it?"

Miriam shook her head. "I need to contemplate this. Ask me that tomorrow."

Jonathan could see everyone's eyes narrow as they considered her response. He considered pressing her on it, but decided to wait.

"Uh, there was talk some of you might want to do a sleepover here?" said Gwen.

Gwen continued giving everyone a questioning look, but no one spoke up. Miriam was already standing and reaching for her own coat to leave, but turned to respond.

"I think everyone is going to pass on that idea. Let's all contemplate this and meet here in the morning. Hopefully we can put it together with whatever Athena has and move forward."

The look on Gwen's face made it plain she was relieved at the thought no one was staying. Jonathan paid for his meal and pulled his coat on, too. Gwen asked James if he wanted to stay for a drink, but he looked away and muttered about having to leave. As they all exited the cafe both Miriam and James left to go their separate ways, leaving Melanie and Jonathan on their own. Jonathan was struggling with whether to head to his hotel when Melanie put a hand on his arm to gain his attention. Jonathan looked at her hand and then up at her face, which seemed to bear a curious mix of fear and hesitation. What wasn't certain was whether desire was in the mix.

"Jonathan? Walk me home, please?"

"I—all right. Yes, I would like that. Let's go."

Taking her arm in his they walked to her home in silence. Jonathan was still trying to process what had happened and he suspected she was, too. But soon enough they were at her doorstep and they both turned to look at each other. Jonathan could see she was in as much turmoil as him, as she bit her lip softly before finally speaking.

"That spirit was trying to tell me something, Jonathan. It did the same to you, right?"

"Yes, but I'm not certain what came to me was complete. Look, I don't know what happened to anyone else, but it was like I got a series of—almost thoughts, I guess. It was all very ephemeral. They just appeared in my mind and all I know is they weren't mine."

"One of the thoughts was about me."

Jonathan was surprised at her certainty and, even more so, was surprised to realize she was right.

"I think maybe yes, you are right."

She nodded her head and in the dim light of a nearby streetlight her eyes glittered briefly as she responded.

"I think I had something similar happen to me," she replied, pausing for a long moment with a dreamy look on her face. "A part of me wants to ask you to come in and stay with me tonight, but somehow I don't think we should do that. At least not tonight we shouldn't. And I don't understand how or why or what is going on, but it may have to do with what happened at the cafe."

"I agree, I think I should go back to the hotel. Let's take this one step at a time. I need to process what happened in the meditation in the cafe. How about I swing by and pick you up after breakfast? We can go for a little walk and then go to the cafe."

"I'd like that."

The two of them stood still for a moment staring into each other's eyes before falling into each other's arms, each clutching the other as if it was the last time they would see each other. Melanie forestalled him as he finally made to step back and gave him a kiss that melted his insides, before she turned and disappeared into her home.

Jonathan stood alone in the darkness for a few seconds before retracing his steps to the sidewalk and heading back toward the hotel. His thoughts were a jumble, but he could only marvel at the possibility a spirit had somehow sent the two of them the same message at the same time. Jonathan wasn't certain what had happened with Melanie, but the message appearing in his mind was the flash of an image of her, along with only one word associated with it. Given that the word love was what had appeared and her reaction moments before, Jonathan felt certain he was right. He resolved to delve into it more with her first thing in the morning.

But the problem was this wasn't all that had come to him in the brief flash of the spirit's interaction with him. As he finished making his resolution to talk to Melanie in the morning he knew he wanted to force his mind to continue ignoring the rest of what had come to him. He instead tried to focus on the double shot he knew he was going to order once he gained the company of others in the lobby bar in the hotel, but his route took him past the cemetery. The bleak scene of tombstones in the dim light and the ground covered with the skiff of cold snow still remaining made his steps falter and he stopped.

The tears came unbidden and ran in streams down both sides of his face as he stood looking around him. In the distance he could hear the endless, rhythmic crash of the waves on the shoreline. And in his heart he wrestled with the understanding which had come to him, for something had laid him bare to its scrutiny and stared into his soul.

Chapter Eight

Two cups of coffee served to sweep away most of the fog filling his mind the next morning, but he ordered a third one to go, as he knew it was later than he had planned in going to see Melanie. The second double shot of scotch he ordered in the bar the night before hadn't helped and his sleep had been fitful.

But the crisp air of the morning and steady breeze helped Jonathan focus even more as he made his way out of the hotel. The clouds were moving fast high in the sky and with the wind coming from the southwest Jonathan knew a change was coming.

Despite the early hour the street was filled with more people about on their business than Jonathan had seen to date. He was surprised to see several parents walking about with their children, but he realized the reason was obvious, as he glanced at his phone and saw the date was December twenty-second.

He passed a park with a playground and saw that with school now out for the Christmas break the children were making the most of it. Others were stopping their parents to take time to peer into storefront windows at the wares on offer. The energy of the children brought back long buried memories of the joy Christmas day would bring. This and the bustle of people with their shopping bags and the decorations that festooned the streetlights combined to leave Jonathan feeling lonely, but he was at Melanie's door soon enough.

She met him at the door with a kiss and had him come in while she donned her boots and coat. As they made their way to the sidewalk in front of her house she gave him a questioning look.

"Walk for a bit?" said Jonathan, gesturing in the direction of the waterfront path. She took his arm and they walked on in silence for a minute before Jonathan finally spoke.

"Sorry I'm a bit later than planned. I confess I was a bit shaken by what happened last night. The scotch I drank in the bar didn't help as much as I wanted it to."

Melanie gave a soft laugh. "The rather large glass of wine I drank didn't make sleep any better for me either."

Jonathan gave her a wry smile. "There are never any answers in the booze bottle, much as we all would wish there to be. So in the hard light of day I find myself wondering whether any of that happened, but I know it did. And yes, the sense remains I was given a kind of message, if you will, that dallying with you as I have is something I should be continuing to do. Can I assume that is more or less the gist of the thought or message you received, too?"

"You can, although I don't understand how any of this is possible."

As they reached the beach path Jonathan stopped and shrugged as he looked down at her. He looked around and pointed in a direction toward the cafe.

"If we walk down here a ways we can detour through that little park and then head for the cafe."

She nodded and they resumed walking, both

huddling closer together as the breeze off the water was cold, biting into the crevices of their clothes to find exposed flesh.

"So I don't understand it either, but I think we have to accept this is real," said Jonathan. "The spiritual world has always seemed intangible and hard to grasp for me, but let's face it. For something intangible, it did a pretty good job of reaching out and making us pay attention, whether we wanted it to or not."

"Yes, it did and I think we need to have a conversation with Miriam about it. I'd prefer that to be in private, but I guess we should just see what happens. But you know, what I find interesting is I had no sense of—well, of detail in the thought that came to me. It was just a simple message that you are—important and I should pay attention."

Jonathan was silent for a moment before responding.

"You're right, that is also pretty much what I got, among other things. I don't know about you, but I was given more than just that one thought. I won't bore you with the details, but I was in need of that scotch last night. Did you get more, too?"

"Yes. And I think the thoughts I was given were just for me, as yours likely were just for you, too, so I won't be sharing them with anyone. But the other interesting point is that if this is what happened to us, what about the others? Were they given some kind of thoughts or messages, too?"

"I expect so," said Jonathan. "And yes, this notion crossed my mind. I guess we'll just have to see what Miriam and the others say when we get there. But you know what?"

Jonathan stopped and looked at her, taking her in his arms as he did.

"I think we both have to figure out what we are going to do about each other. It isn't every day I get a message from a spirit telling me to pay attention to a woman. I have this feeling that if I let you slip away it will eat at me and be a problem for the rest of my life. I know that maybe sounds strange, because I've never had that kind of a thought before, but it feels right."

Melanie slowly nodded. "What you are saying feels right and I agree. Somehow it feels as if my life before now has all been leading to this moment. I don't know why it was so hard to see how lonely I was, but it feels like a veil has been lifted from my eyes. I don't know where we go from here, Jonathan. Can we maybe just take this one day at a time?"

Melanie gave him a hug and a smile as Jonathan nodded, before they both turned and began walking arm in arm once more toward the cafe. As they got closer to the cafe they heard a familiar voice behind them.

"Well, isn't this interesting," said Dunstan. "It's not spring yet, people. Can't explain this as just young lust since neither of you is young anymore. Just getting a head start on some spring time hanky panky, are we?"

Melanie looked at Jonathan and rolled her eyes before turning to give Dunstan a mild glare of exasperation.

"I expect you find yourself amusing and that's

good, because just about no one else I know thinks you are. Have you never seen two good friends out walking arm in arm? Honestly."

"Friends, is it? Call me crazy, but if I were in Vegas I'd be putting my money on this being friends with benefits, since I'm just a nasty, suspicious person. You can't fool me, Melanie. I've seen people with the hots for each other in action plenty of times."

"I expect you have, but it's none of your business, now is it? Think what you like. I assume you're heading for the cafe?"

"Yeah, I like hanging out in ghost central. No dull moments. I—get out of my way, asshole."

Melanie and Jonathan turned to find Dunstan had stumbled on the foot of a street beggar sitting slumped against a wall. Jonathan saw he was a relatively young man, but he didn't look well. His clothes were unkempt and his hair matted with knots. A mongrel dog lay curled on the sidewalk beside him and both of them looked as if they were struggling to stay warm.

"Get a job, for God's sake," said Dunstan over his shoulder as he made to move on. "Christ, the world is going for shit if these scum are out panhandling even in places like this."

Melanie scowled at him. "There's no call for that, Dunstan. Leave him alone."

Jonathan paused a moment and then turned back, pulling out his wallet as he made his way to the beggar. He wordlessly dropped a few bills into the coffee cup and went to rejoin Dunstan and Melanie, who had stopped to wait for him.

"You know, that's called pissing your money away, man," said Dunstan, as they resumed walking to the cafe. "He's just going to go get hammered and he'll be back here tomorrow looking for more. You'd be better off buying us a round of drinks, because then we could all piss your money away and at least we'd be drunk enough to have something to show for you spending your hard earned cash."

Melanie shook her head. "Dunstan, you don't know his story. Has it occurred to you that maybe he's suffering from a mental illness? Maybe he's been abused and ran away from home?"

"So what about it? Life's a bitch, ain't it? Some people are winners and some aren't. Besides, my money says it's a scam, just like all the low lifes working the same con on the streets in Vegas."

"Merry Christmas, Dunstan," said Jonathan.

As they walked into the cafe they saw the only people there were Miriam, Athena, Tom, and Paula with her daughter. Jonathan pulled another table with chairs over to join the group. Gwen appeared from the kitchen and called a greeting, asking if they wanted anything. The three newcomers all asked for coffee, although Dunstan ordered breakfast for himself.

"I slept in today and I'm starving. So what's new, spooky people? Any ghosts around today?"

Miriam rolled her eyes and shook her head, before turning to Jonathan and Melanie.

"Good timing, I was just about to fill the others here in on what happened last night, so you can add your story to it all. Athena says she has some news, too."

Miriam launched into a summary of what happened as Gwen appeared, dropping the coffees on the table for everyone. With no one else to serve, Gwen joined them at the table. Athena in particular seemed fascinated by the scent they had noticed. Jonathan noticed Miriam seemed to gloss over the sense they had all received mysterious messages, but he could see Athena and Tom both pick up on the hint as they turned and looked aside for a brief second at each other. But Miriam was already moving on with her story.

"So I had a little time this morning to contemplate this and I'm feeling confident now of a couple of things. First, I'm very sure now this is only one spirit we are dealing with. The second is I had a definite sense this is the spirit of a woman. It's more than just the hint of flowers, in case you are wondering. I spent a bunch of time considering this and my heart is clear on it. It feels right."

"Well, to my mind this all fits with what I've learned," said Athena. "It was nagging at me that there had been a dispute over this place and when Jonathan told us what he found in the diary it prompted me to dig further into it. There was indeed a court case and at the heart of it was a disputed, handwritten will done shortly before the father died. You all remember the diary seemed to belong to Rose Markleigh and that she had two sisters, Beatrice and Agnes, right?"

As everyone nodded Athena smiled for effect.

"What wasn't made clear in the diary is the daughter Rose didn't have the same mother as the other two. I don't know if that had something to do with the disputes the sisters had, but I suspect it is possible. The court case revolved around what was to be done with the cafe, which was the primary asset in the estate. The earlier will specified everything the old man owned was to be divided equally between the three daughters, as would be normal for most people. The more recent will stuck to that, except that Rose was given sole right to live in the building for the rest of her life. Only then could it be sold."

"Huh," grunted Jonathan, as he watched understanding dawn on the faces of everyone at the table. "Not hard to see this would be contentious."

"Exactly," said Athena. "The court case revolved around the argument the old man wasn't in his right mind when he did the updated will. There were also allegations he had been coerced. I had a quick read through the details and it looks to me like there was fairly strong evidence to support those allegations, but the court in the end deemed it all circumstantial. So Rose Markleigh got what she appears to have wanted."

"So this explains why we were dealing with the estate for the purchase," said Gwen.

"Exactly. So as I said, I think the pieces may all be starting to fit together. We have a difficult family situation, which obviously became hostile. The diary Jonathan found appears to hint at the workings of a disordered mind. We have Miriam here, who seems certain we have a feminine presence here and this mysterious, flowery scent you all experienced. I know, this is all pretty circumstantial, but I don't know if we are going to get much better to work with. We have nothing else pointing at the prohibition era murders or at this being anything to do with Gwen's husband, so I'm really thinking this is the spirit of Rose Markleigh we are dealing with. The good news is I have one more angle for us to check."

"For my part I'm hoping that will involve bringing in a crystal ball," said Dunstan. "While you're staring into it could you do me a favor and find out who's going to win the Super Bowl? It's a tough call this year and I'd like to win back what I lost last year."

Athena grimaced, but decided to ignore Dunstan as she continued.

"I've made contact with the Markleigh family. Beatrice Markleigh is still alive, although her sister Agnes is not. She doesn't live in town, but she does live nearby and I've sent her a message. I'm hoping she would be willing to come and talk to us, maybe shed more light on this situation. She said she would be back to me with an answer before the day is out."

"Excellent," said Miriam, making to rise from her chair. "Let's all meet tonight, then. I have to go open my shop soon."

"Miriam?" said Tom. "Could we go back to what happened last night for a moment? I couldn't help noticing earlier you implied some kind of contact between you and the spirit. What happened?"

Miriam paused and sat down again, although the expression on her face was guarded. She pressed her lips together and frowned, making it clear she was struggling with how to respond.

"Well, yes. I did sense—contact. It was contact with something, but whether it was the spirit I don't know. To be honest I haven't fully digested it, let alone sorted out what really happened or what it all means. I know this sounds strange, but the contact was—personal. I don't know if I can tell you any more than that."

"God, just get the crystal ball and be done with it. I'm going out for a smoke," said Dunstan, rising from his chair. As he did, his phone pinged to announce arrival of a text message. Dunstan glanced at it for a moment before cursing aloud and stalking out the door.

"Dunstan, I have a child here, you know," said Paula, but Jonathan doubted he had heard or even paid attention.

Athena, Tom, and Paula all looked at each other, wearing puzzled looks. Tom turned to Melanie, Jonathan, and Gwen with a question.

"What about you folks? Did you get some contact or messages too?"

Melanie simply nodded in response. Gwen looked uncomfortable, but folded her arms and answered.

"Yes. But as Miriam says, it was personal. And in case you are wondering, Willie told me his experience was like mine."

Jonathan nodded, too. "It was the same for me. What came to me was kind of like—like guidance, and that is probably the best I can give you. I don't know how else to explain it without giving you details, and I'd rather not do that."

Tom frowned. "What about James? Gwen told me he was here, too. Did he sense anything?"

Miriam shrugged and turned to Gwen, who did the same, but responded to the question.

"Possibly. He didn't say much afterwards, but I think he did."

This time Athena frowned, still clearly puzzled at what she was hearing.

"I don't get any of this. The whole premise of what we are doing here is based on the idea the spirit needs help and we are trying to sort out what is happening, with an eye to helping it. So how is it the tables seem to be turned here? Let's face it, we've all heard ghost stories and what not, but I've got to say this is the first time I've come across one where it's a helpful ghost. Miriam, any help here?"

"I—I agree this is odd. Like I said, I need to spend a bunch of time in quiet contemplation of what is going on here. I promise I will do so, but I really must go open my shop now. I promise that if I come up with something I will let you all know."

This time she rose from her chair and began putting her coat on in a clear signal she wasn't going to offer anything further. But Cate spoke up for the first time, forestalling her with one last question.

"Miriam? Maybe it was God talking to all of you?"

Miriam stopped what she was doing and remained frozen for a long moment, as she stared with unfocused eyes off into nothing. When she finally recalled herself she looked at Cate with a tiny smile.

"Maybe so. I'll give that some thought," she said,

before turning away to leave.

The door to the cafe opened and two customers walked in, taking a table over by the windows. As Gwen went over to serve them Jonathan got up from his chair to follow Miriam while the others at the table resumed the conversation. The door to the verandah opened as he did and Dunstan came back in. He was cursing to himself once again and wearing a dark look on his face to match his obvious frustration. Jonathan was grateful for the distraction and as Miriam was about to walk out the door Jonathan stopped her. She gave him a questioning look as he glanced around with care to ensure no one was listening to them talking before he began. Melanie saw what he was doing and came over to join them.

"Miriam? Just one thing I want to mention to you, in case this might help? Melanie and I were comparing notes about what came to us. The two of us were, uh—Melanie, am I okay to talk about this?"

Melanie glanced around the room herself before nodding agreement.

"Right, so Melanie and I are—involved, you see? The messages that came to us covered more than one subject, but the one in common for the two of us dealt with our involvement and we were given advice to just— well, to pay more attention to each other. A lot more. I don't know about you, but I don't understand how it's possible we could both get the same message. As well, I don't know about Melanie here, but among other things I got the sense I was being told to forgive myself for—certain things. Anyway, look, I know you have to go, but we both wanted to mention this to you. If you have any wisdom for us we'd sure appreciate it."

Miriam was silent for a long few seconds before responding. A tiny smile appeared on her face for a moment as she did.

"Well, first of all I don't think you'll find anyone around here real surprised the two of you are having a good time together. You were both enjoying each other's company the night of the party to a point it was obvious. And second, I'm glad you mentioned this to me because what I got involved an element of forgiveness, too. So there is a common denominator here, but the only way I'm going to understand this is if I spend some time in quiet contemplation of it all. I think I'm beginning to gain the understanding, but I really, really must go. Bills to pay, right?"

As the door closed behind her Melanie and Jonathan turned to each other. Jonathan looked over to see the others were listening to Dunstan, who was clearly still not happy. Jonathan glanced at Melanie, who looked as chagrined as Jonathan by what Miriam had said.

"Well, so much for trying to be discreet," said Jonathan. "Hope you're okay I mentioned that to her."

"I am, but this is starting to make my head spin. I don't get this, although we don't have any answers right now. Well, let's go join the others before they start thinking we're going to run away with each other."

As they rejoined the group it was obvious

Dunstan had not let go of whatever was frustrating him.

"Bastards. The curse I live with is I can't trust any of the people I deal with. I do the best I can to fence these devious shitheads in and just when you think you've succeeded, they throw something new at you and sneak around the fence. And here I am, stuck in sleepytown. It'd be a whole lot easier to rein them in and get the deal done if I was in Vegas."

"So Dunstan?" said Paula. "First, can I remind you one more time that there is a child present here? For God's sake, please keep the language under control. And second, if this is that important, why are you still here? Why don't you just go back to Vegas?"

"Ah, right. Sorry. Yes, I need to control myself and I will. And no, I can't—ah, I'll be going back to Vegas at some point, but not yet."

He paused and looked over to the kitchen, where Gwen had just appeared with the food orders for the other two customers.

"Gwen, can I order some lunch?"

Both Tom and Athena looked at each other and shrugged, seeing Dunstan wasn't going to be more forthcoming. They rose from their seats and put their coats on. After assuring everyone they would return that evening, they made their way to the door and left. When Gwen came over the others also placed lunch orders. But Dunstan didn't seem ready to drop his frustration and he kept grumbling until Melanie interrupted him.

"Dunstan, can you give it a rest? We get that you're not happy about something, but it's only money, right? What does that compare with the problems others face in life?"

"Only money? Money is everything in my world."

"What about Paula here? Do you seriously think your problems are on par or worse than hers? She's losing what little sight she has, while trying to make a living and being a single parent at the same time. I can't even begin to imagine how hard it must be to function in the workplace with a disability like that."

"Joker and all the technology makes it a whole lot easier to function, Melanie," said Paula, putting her hand on Cate's shoulder. "I get by, and my wonderful daughter makes it all worth the effort."

"I'm sure it all helps, but I'll be honest. I'd be going crazy if I knew I was going to lose my sight. Never to see a sunrise again? Never to enjoy a fine painting or sculpture, or even to just watch a television show? Maybe some day Cate here will get married, but you won't be able to see it. I guess I just don't see how the impact of that could be outweighed by the problems associated with grubbing for more money."

Paula took a sip of her coffee before responding.

"I guess it's true I have days where I feel bitter about it all. I confess some of those days I practically don't get out of bed. Is that so wrong? I suppose that just makes me human. But I've been trying to come to grips with it all each and every day. In all honesty, I'm grateful for everything I have and I try not to pay attention to what I don't have. I don't need much for myself, but it's Cate I'm concerned about."

As she finished speaking a tear appeared in the corner of one of her eyes and coursed down the side of her face. Cate wordlessly reached into her mother's purse and pulled out a tissue, placing it in her mother's hand. As Paula wiped away the tear Melanie's face took on a worried cast.

"Paula? What's wrong with Cate? What's happened?"

Paula snuffled for a moment, but composed herself and replied in a flat, dispirited tone.

"We just found out for certain Cate has the same thing I have. She's a long way from losing her sight, but it's coming some day unless I can figure out how to do something about it."

"My God, Paula, I'm sorry to have upset you and I'm very sorry to hear this. But what do you mean by that? I thought there wasn't anything that could be done about your condition. Isn't it the same for Cate?"

"You're right about me, at least for now. I've been told there is nothing to be done for me, but who knows, maybe in the future some new medical breakthrough will happen. I keep hoping, because that's all I can do. But for Cate, it's different. There is a new treatment they are optimistic will work on someone young enough, as she is still developing. I don't know all the details of it, but we need to learn more. The problem is its hideously expensive and there is no way it would be covered by our medical plan. We're talking many thousands of dollars and I just don't know how I could find that kind of money on my tiny salary. We make ends meet with not much left over as it is."

Paula paused to use a second tissue on her eyes before continuing.

"But I know what I have to do. I can't be bitter about this. I can only try to accept this is my lot and deal with it. We won't let this beat us, will we, Cate?"

"No, we won't, mom," said Cate, pulling close to her mother.

"I'm going for a smoke," said Dunstan, rising abruptly from his seat and heading outside. Jonathan caught sight of Dunstan's face out of the corner of his eye and although Jonathan wasn't certain, Dunstan seemed to be struggling to hide a troubled look.

Paula was still hugging her daughter close and more tears appeared.

"God, I love you, Cate. I couldn't believe it when I realized I had slipped up and was pregnant. I was weak and I agonized for a long time about it because I didn't want my child to face the same thing I am. I'm so sorry it has worked out this way."

"I'm glad you had me, mom. Don't worry, I'll be fine."

Jonathan didn't know what to say, but felt he should say something. He was saved from having to do so by the arrival of their food. Dunstan had been watching from outside through the window so he came back in. As Paula wiped away the last of her tears once again they all began eating in silence. More customers arrived and the cafe became busier.

As the last of them finished eating Gwen came over and cleared away the dishes, returning moments later with the coffee pot to do refills. Everyone saw Paula had been about to speak, but she waited for Gwen to finish. As Gwen stepped away Paula began.

"So I just want to say I'm sorry to be bringing all this up about our problems. You people don't need to be burdened with any of it. I get emotional because I learned I had this condition when I was about Cate's age and I still remember what it was like. One moment I was expecting a bright future and seeing endless possibility in life, and in the next I had nothing but darkness to look forward to. It felt like my childhood ended that day, because I knew I would have to find a way to be strong and deal with it. The one positive thing about it is I have my experience to fall back on and help Cate when the time comes. Anyway, I really am sorry. Can we talk about something else now?"

Melanie reached across the table and took Paula's hand.

"Don't worry about it, Paula. We're your friends. Remember? Friends listen to each other, even if there isn't anything we can do about it. It always helps to talk about our problems."

"Maybe the cost of this treatment will come down over time?" said Jonathan.

"Maybe," said Paula. "I can only hope. The window to try this on her will grow smaller as she gets older. Our Christmas next year would be a whole lot better if it did."

"I'm going to use the washroom and hit the road," said Dunstan, standing up and pulling a wad of money from his wallet to drop on the table for his meal. He waved at Gwen and pointed to the cash, before disappearing into the back of the cafe.

Jonathan was about to speak when Joker let out a whine from his spot on the floor beside Paula. A second later Dunstan reappeared, walking backwards while staring hard in the direction of the hallway. Jonathan saw the look on his face was one of shock. Paula stirred in her seat.

"Oh!" she said. "I can feel it. The spirit is back. And there is the scent, too. It smells like roses."

Dunstan continued backing up, stumbling into tables and chairs in the process before coming to a stop beside their table. With a wild look on his face he mumbled something before turning away and heading out the door in a rush. The other patrons in the cafe turned to look at where the commotion was coming from, but on seeing nothing they went back to their meal.

Jonathan got up and went into the hallway to see what he could find, but he came back empty handed once again. This time, though, he could sense a faint scent hanging in the air and he told Paula she was right about it. As he finished speaking Gwen came over wearing a puzzled look on her face.

"What happened to Dunstan? He practically ran out the door."

Jonathan explained and then looked at Melanie, who had been closest in proximity to Dunstan before he ran out.

"Melanie? Dunstan said something there? Did you hear him?"

"Barely, but I think he said he could see the spirit. I wonder if it was waiting for one of us. But you know, that's twice he's done that now. Maybe it was waiting just for him? The rest of us have all gone to use the washroom at some point in the last few days, but that hasn't happened to any of us."

"I don't think he understands what Christmas is all about," said Cate. "You all received messages, so maybe God has a message for him, too. I'll bet his was about Christmas."

A soft sob from Paula made everyone turn to look at her and Jonathan was shocked to see this time it wasn't merely a few tears coursing down her face. She had a hand on the side of her head while a strange, small smile of disbelief played across her face.

"My God, Paula, what's wrong?" said Gwen, coming over and putting her arms around her shoulders to comfort her.

"I—I got some thoughts or messages or whatever it is just like the rest of you. I got one big message in particular, I think."

"Are you all right?" said Jonathan.

Paula nodded as she wiped away the tears and began apologizing once again. As she finally mastered herself Melanie took her hand to catch her attention.

"Paula, I can't wait any longer. Why are you smiling?"

Paula gave her a small laugh in response, before laughing even louder and longer. She finally brought herself under control and, still shaking her head in apparent disbelief, answered Melanie's question.

"This is going to sound crazy, but the big thought

was very simple. I was told I shouldn't worry and to be happy. But it was the feeling that came with it that really set me off. I felt—filled with peace and happiness, with a sense that things would work out. Like the future for Cate and I is positive. My God, I hope so."

Paula turned to Cate and they hugged each other for a long moment, while the others stared at each other in wonder.

"This is getting more interesting by the moment," said Jonathan, rising from his chair and pulling out his wallet. "But I think its time I got back to the hotel. I have a bit more work to do, but I'll be back tonight. I'm curious to know what Athena and Tom have come up with."

The others did the same and they all left. As Jonathan walked back to the hotel alone he couldn't help wondering about what was happening to them all. That Paula had been given such a positive message was good, but to him the question was whether it would really work that way. But even as that thought came to him, he knew with certainty he believed and had faith. Somehow, Paula would find her positive future.

Jonathan spent the afternoon reviewing with fresh eyes the work he had done a few days before, knowing that coming back to it after some time passed was always good for finding flaws that weren't obvious at the time. He made several corrections to his work and by the end of the afternoon was satisfied with what he had done. Whether he would put his work to use was another matter. After another long walk to clear his mind he eventually made his way back to the cafe for dinner.

Inside he found most of the group was already there, with only two exceptions. The cafe was once again quiet, with only a couple of other tables of customers. Dunstan had already come and gone, having apparently spent some time in earnest conversation with Gwen yet again. James had not made an appearance at all, but the night was not over and Gwen hinted she was watching for him to arrive. Melanie, Paula and Cate, Miriam, Athena, and Tom were all there and had already ordered meals. As Jonathan joined them he found they were all deep in excited discussion over the events of the afternoon.

Jonathan ordered dinner too, and did his best to keep his stomach from rumbling as he watched the others being served and working on their meals. Willie had made a batch of seafood lasagna as the meal special, which most everyone was eating with gusto together with the fresh French bread he had baked. By the time they were finishing their meals Jonathan's arrived and he dug in as Athena shifted the conversation to the sister of Rose Markleigh.

"So the good news is we've been successful in arranging a meeting with Beatrice Markleigh. She's going to meet us here in the cafe tomorrow afternoon around three o'clock. I assume everyone wants to be here for it?"

As everyone nodded Melanie asked whether Beatrice would be surprised to be meeting so many people, but Athena dismissed her concern.

"I've been very clear with her that there's a number of us interested in what is happening. She is actually the one who said it would be simpler to just come and talk to us, as opposed to answering my endless questions on the phone. She kind of hinted she wouldn't mind seeing the cafe once more. So I'm hopeful we'll get a much better sense of what is behind all of this once we meet her."

"Good work, Athena," said Jonathan. "I agree with you, this is progress."

"I wonder about James, though. I had thought he would be here by now, but he's not. I'm fairly sure he would want to hear what she has to say."

Athena called Gwen over from where she was clearing a table and asked her about him. Gwen pressed her lips together and shook her head in response.

"I don't know. I was expecting him. Maybe he'll show up tomorrow"

"What about Dunstan, dare I ask?" said Jonathan.

Athena grimaced. "I told him about it before he left, but he seemed a little—unfocused. I don't know why. I'm not sure he would be a big help or whether he even has any real interest, but he keeps coming back, so I guess we'll see what he does."

"Tell them your other news, Athena," said Tom.

"Ah, yes, I've done some digging into the possibility of doing a smudge ceremony. I had a conversation with a friend who is an Elder about what is happening. Unfortunately, the Elder is not available to help us in person and wouldn't be for a while. Having said that we did talk about the situation. The Elder understood there seems to be a need to move forward sooner than later. I was given assurance that if we approach the Creator for help in a respectful way we will likely be given what we need. I am confident if we keep it simple we can get it done."

"What do we need to do, Athena? How long would it take?" said Miriam.

"It need not be long. Think of it as a meditation that has a very specific purpose, if you will. We begin with a prayer for help and cleansing and go from there."

"Athena, I'm going to come back to Dunstan here. I'm really not certain how helpful he will be if he is present for this. What do you think?"

Athena pursed her lips for a moment before speaking.

"Well, that is a valid concern. I'm no expert, but as I said my understanding is that participants in something like this should certainly be approaching it with respect. Of course, that could be said about any approach to the Creator for help. I mean, really, if you aren't serious about what you are doing, then why are you involving yourself in it? So I think if he is willing to participate in a positive way and be respectful, I am fine with it. I will speak to him about this if he shows up for it."

"That's good enough for me," said Miriam, looking relieved.

"Actually, come to think of it, this applies to everyone. I think perhaps I'll have a general discussion about why we all need to take this seriously before we get going."

"Even better. So when do we do this?"

"I'm busy tomorrow earlier in the day and besides, I'd rather hear what Beatrice Markleigh has to say. Miriam, perhaps you and I could have a separate chat about what we want to say in the prayers?"

"Absolutely," said Miriam.

"Okay, well, that means it will have to be Christmas Eve, I guess. Not great timing, since I know everyone is pretty busy, but that's the best we can do at the moment. Mind you, Gwen has already told me she wasn't planning to open the cafe for business anyway, so it certainly works from that perspective."

"Maybe that's the best timing of all," said Cate.

Everyone turned in surprise to Cate as she grinned at each of the people around the table with an air of complete confidence.

"It's Christmas, don't you see? Anything is possible at Christmas if it involves giving to others."

The adults all looked around the table and stared at each other and, as Jonathan watched, slow smiles appeared on their faces.

"I hope you're right, Cate. In fact, I know you are," said Athena.

Chapter Nine

The dusting of snow that had fallen overnight was minimal enough, but it still filled the already existing imprints of boots from the first snowfall and returned the landscape to a smooth, glistening white carpet. Jonathan and Melanie enjoyed the hint of sunshine trying to escape from the dark grey clouds, but they both knew it wasn't going to last. The far western horizon was filled with an even darker mass of clouds coming toward them, leaving only the question of whether it would come as rain or result in even more snow when the system arrived.

The night before Jonathan told Melanie he wanted to stay with her that night and she had given him a broad smile. Jonathan realized she had likely been wondering what his reaction would be to everything that had happened and with a wry smile to himself he knew he was wondering the same about her. Melanie slipped out of her coat and wrapped herself around him seconds after stepping into the warmth of her home. They were soon in her bedroom once again and they both had all the answers they needed. The next morning she agreed without hesitation to his suggestion they go for a morning walk and then have breakfast in the cafe.

They walked along the beach path with coffees Jonathan had made before leaving her house. As they walked Jonathan asked when her boyfriend was going to arrive home and she frowned.

"He was supposed to be home tonight, but he's been back east and the storm that hit them last night was nasty. Airports shut down and flights cancelled all over the place, just in time for Christmas. God knows when he will get out."

They walked in silence out onto a small pier and Jonathan turned to take her in his arms as they reached the end of it. After a long, crushing hug he pulled back a little and looked down at her face as he spoke.

"Well, I've had time to process what has been happening and I'm just going to put it all out there. Melanie, I can't believe I've found you. It feels like my entire life has led to this day. I know, I said we should take this a day at a time. So for today, I want to make it clear I want more of you in my life. I am really hoping you feel the same way."

Melanie smiled. "I do. It feels like I've been drifting alone somehow and now I've been washed ashore in an island paradise."

Jonathan smiled in relief and pulled her even closer.

"I'm glad. But you have a boyfriend, Melanie."

She shook her head. "Not any more. I sent him a message a few days ago telling him it was over. He didn't seem terribly surprised, but we are parting as friends."

"You sent it a few days ago? So it wasn't what happened yesterday that prompted it?"

A hint of guilt appeared on her face. "Yes, it was a few days ago. I know, I suppose I could have waited until after Christmas to do that, but I couldn't face spending time around the holidays with someone I really didn't want to be with. And besides, you are here and I guess I should have told you before now. We were already attracted to each other enough to spend the night together, remember?"

Jonathan laughed as they walked off the pier and resumed walking along the beach.

"And now we will have to talk about where we go from here."

After a half hour walk they both felt hungry and decided to head for the cafe. Two blocks from it they ran into James, who was heading for the same place. They asked where he had been the last couple of days, but James was deliberately noncommittal. Melanie sensed his desire to change the topic and moved on to filling him in on what had happened in the cafe. James showed interest on the surface, but Jonathan knew something was on his mind and couldn't resist asking him about it just before they reached the cafe. James appeared to wrestle for a moment with his answer, but he stopped outside the entrance and looked at them.

"Remember I told you the other day I looked in the mirror and wasn't happy with what I was seeing? Well, I—I've spent some time trying to deal with what happened the other day, because that just added to my misery, I'm afraid. I think Gwen and I both got messages and let's just say I've had to sort out what to do about it. Well, I'm going to talk to her about it now if she has time and do the best I can to help her understand. Wish me luck."

"Absolutely," said Jonathan. "Would you like us to make ourselves scarce?"

"No, no. I don't think your presence will make any difference, so let's get in out of the cold."

The warmth of the cafe was welcome. Gwen looked up from where she was sitting, nursing a cup of coffee, as the place was devoid of customers this early in the day. Jonathan couldn't help noticing Gwen locked eyes with James the moment he walked in the door, although he sensed she had made the expression on her face deliberately unreadable. But she composed herself and called out greetings, bringing coffee cups and menus over to the table Jonathan and Melanie chose to sit at.

As she finished dropping them off James pulled her aside and, after a quick conversation, Jonathan saw Gwen nod. James went and sat at the same table Gwen had been at and she followed him over with a coffee cup. After returning to fill all of their cups with coffee Gwen took Jonathan and Melanie's breakfast orders.

Once the order was placed Gwen joined James at his table. Gwen had more Christmas music playing in the background, so Jonathan was unable to hear what they were saying, but with their heads close together over the table it was obvious they were quickly in deep discussion.

"You think he's going to succeed this time?" said Melanie.

"I hope so," said Jonathan, telling her of the long conversation he had with James two days before. "I really think he's serious. I haven't known him as long as you, but he seems a good guy to me and I like him. God knows we all make mistakes and he obviously made some, but I've always felt if you are willing to atone for it you can find redemption."

As the conversation carried on both Jonathan and

Melanie couldn't resist surreptitiously making sidelong glances at the two of them, awaiting developments with anticipation. James pulled a piece of paper from an inner pocket of his jacket and pushed it across the table for Gwen to look at. As he did Willie rung the small bell he had in the kitchen to signify the breakfast orders were ready for Jonathan and Melanie. Gwen stared for a long moment at the piece of paper before looking up at James with the same unreadable look on her face she had shown before. Rising from her chair she went and got the breakfasts, bringing them over for Jonathan and Melanie. Jonathan couldn't help his stomach rumbling at the sight.

As they dug into their meals James and Gwen resumed their conversation, which from the looks on their faces appeared to be even more intense than before. James took one of her hands in his and they carried on that way for another two minutes before they both finally rose from their seats. They gave each other a long embrace before James turned away and made for the entrance.

As he passed by Jonathan's table he waved a hand and muttered he would see them later in the day. James wiped away the single tear that coursed down the side of his face, but not before both Jonathan and Melanie saw it. Gwen busied herself behind the counter, making a fresh pot of coffee and putting away their dishes. Jonathan wasn't certain, but he thought Gwen had discreetly wiped her own eyes with a tissue.

Minutes later she came bustling over with the fresh coffee and refilled their cups, but she appeared distracted. Melanie reached out her hand and put it on Gwen's arm.

"Gwen? Are you all right? James told us as we came in here he was going to make a pitch to you."

"Ah. Well, he did." She hesitated a moment and then sat down, putting the coffee pot on the table.

"So you know, the two of us were given some knowledge about ourselves the other day that took us a while to sort out," said Jonathan. "I am thinking the same happened to you two?"

Gwen nodded and was silent, before she gave a sigh.

"Yes. We've both—struggled with it. I guess coming to understand you've been a fool, which applies to both of us, is never easy. Anyway, the news from James is he has decided to apply for work here in town. You may have noticed that piece of paper he showed me? That is his resume, which he is taking over to give to Athena. She has already talked to the right people and has assured him the town fire services are ecstatic over the thought of having him on board. It brings him closer to his parents, but he's doing it for me, too, of course."

"My God, how do you feel about that, Gwen?" said Melanie.

Gwen was silent once again, this time for much longer as she stared with unfocused eyes away from the two of them.

"I—part of me is absolutely thrilled. Part of me has alarm bells ringing in my head. Stir it all together with what James told me, that he felt its time to grow up, and you get the mess I feel like I am right now. The spirit, or whatever that was, more or less told me to stop complaining about my lot in life and get on with it, you see. And the direction I'm being pointed to is James."

"We can relate. So what will you do?"

"The only thing I can do. I asked him for a little time to get my head on straight. You realize, of course, Dunstan has made it clear he wants me to run away with him. I guess I'm popular, but that is another wrinkle."

The door to the cafe opened and a group of six customers came in and took a seat. Gwen sighed and looked at them as she made to rise. Once again Melanie forestalled her by putting her hand on her arm.

"If you need to talk I can stick around a bit," said Melanie, but Gwen smiled and shook her head.

"I'm all right. I just need a little time." After picking up their dishes and the pot of coffee she went off to serve the new customers.

Melanie reached across the table and took Jonathan's hand for a moment.

"Let's hope they sort it out like we did."

After leaving money for breakfast on the table the two of them went their separate ways, both promising to be back for the meeting later in the day. Jonathan spent the afternoon staring at his work one last time and taking yet another nap. He knew having naps wasn't going to happen whenever he finally did get back to work, so he resolved to enjoy his naps to the fullest.

He woke with a start when the alarm went and for a brief, groggy moment he couldn't remember where he was, but it came back as he let his head fall back to his pillow. He lay there for a couple of minutes to shake away the cobwebs and as he did the thought came the time to move on was finally coming close. But he knew it wouldn't be today, so he gathered himself and stopped to get a coffee before heading out of the hotel on his now familiar path back to the cafe.

As he reached the entrance to the cafe he saw an old woman he didn't know was making her way to the same place, so he stopped and held the door open for her. She was peering at the building with interest and Jonathan wondered if she was the one they were going to meet. She was a petite, grey haired woman, wearing clothes of a fashion popular many decades before.

She stepped into the cafe and Jonathan had to crowd in and sidle around her to get fully inside, as she had stopped within a few feet of the entrance and looked about with even more intensity than she had done outside. Jonathan saw everyone else was already in the cafe and as they came in Athena immediately stood and came around to greet the old woman. Athena introduced herself and asked if she was Beatrice. Athena smiled on seeing her nod.

"Ah, thank you so much for coming today. We know it's a busy time of the year for people."

"It's my pleasure. I have some friends here in town I haven't seen for a long time, so this provided a good excuse to come by and see them. Besides, I haven't been inside the house here for decades and my curiosity got the better of me."

Gwen brought her a coffee and the rest of them made room for her at the table, doing introductions all around as they did. Even Willie appeared and joined them, as there were still no customers in the cafe. Athena had already given her a brief summary of what was happening in the cafe and what they were trying to do, but she took a few moments to fill in some of the details she hadn't provided. Beatrice stopped her a few times to ask for clarification, but let Athena carry on until she finished.

"So I hope you understand why we've approached you and I do hope this isn't stirring up any bad memories. We're just looking for a little information and we're trying to be helpful."

Beatrice laughed. "Ah, well, there were some rather bad memories, but they are also quite old now, like me. I gave up letting any of this bother me a long time ago. Time has a way of taking the sting out of these things and, as you get older, you start to wonder what the fuss was all about. What I find fascinating about all of this is it has taken this long for there to be a reckoning, if that is what it is."

Beatrice smiled and shrugged before she carried on.

"Well, I'll do my best to give you the facts, such as they are, and you can all decide whether or not any of it is of use. I'm not sure if you know, but Rose was my half sister. Her mother passed away when she was quite young and our father—well, lets just say he always had a roving eye. He finally settled on my mother as her replacement, but only after a parade of girlfriends. I don't know, my sister Agnes and I always thought Rose maybe became possessive of him because of the constant parade.

Anyway, the thing was he never married my mother. This was all a bit scandalous and unusual back then, but no one thinks anything of that kind of situation anymore, of course."

"So that must have made your relationship with Rose a bit awkward, did it?" said Tom.

"Exactly. Well, we got along, because we all lived together here and we had to, but it was never a positive relationship. It wouldn't be, of course, because being the oldest and the only legitimate daughter made her the boss, as far as she was concerned. Yes, there were more than a few cat fights as we grew older."

"Beatrice?" said Jonathan. "We came across a diary we think was hers. It looked like there was a big dispute over a young man?"

"A diary? Yes, I suppose that's possible. When I was finally able to sell the place I just wanted it gone and didn't care about the contents other than the few valuables we found. And yes, there was a young man. Our younger sister Agnes caught the eye of a fellow Rose had set her sights on. Oh, my, that was a battle! And things really went downhill from there."

"So you're mother never did marry your father, but you lived here all those years with him and Rose?" said Athena.

"Ah, Agnes and I lived here for a time, but not all of it. I don't know why Dad never married Mom, but he didn't. She got sick and passed away, you see, which left Dad stuck here with three daughters who were at odds with each other on a regular basis. He finally decided he'd had enough and prevailed on an aunt from my mother's side of the family to take Agnes and myself in. God, I still remember Rose standing at the door gloating the day Agnes and I left here for good. It must have been the happiest day of her life to that point. She was such a miserable bitch."

Jonathan cleared his throat to catch her attention.

"Uh, the diary I mentioned? To be honest, I had a sense the person writing it became—well, a little unhinged after a while. Does that make sense?"

"That doesn't surprise me in the least. But the question is, what does unhinged mean? After Dad passed away she was sane enough to grab everything she possibly could and do everything she might to try and ensure my sister and I got nothing. Dad was losing his faculties long before he died, you see, and she had power of attorney. God knows how much money she probably stole and squirreled away or squandered. But the fight was on once he died. My sister and I had my aunt to thank for anything we have as a result, because she made Dad give her a copy of his will, which gave the three of us equal shares of the estate, and Rose didn't know that. Anyway, if you read through the court case you know those details."

"I did a quick scan of it," said Athena. "For the benefit of everyone else, the gist is the most recent will was handwritten, giving Rose the right to live in the house the rest of her life, and giving the other two daughters little or nothing."

"Exactly, except the whole thing was quite suspicious. Dad was really in no shape to even legibly write his own name on the date he allegedly signed the new will. Suffice to say the lawyers did well out of it all and my sister and I finally got a little out of the estate, but Rose kept the house with the proviso it would come to us when she finally passed away. I expect that must have been somewhat galling to her, but that's what the judge decided. My sister Agnes passed away and wasn't able to enjoy any of the fruits of the sale, but I have."

Beatrice paused to laugh. "Going on a cruise ship around the world isn't cheap. I raised a glass of wine in toast to Dad in every port we stopped in. I'm certain Rose is turning in her grave over that. I suppose I shouldn't find this amusing, but I do. I guess that makes me an old sinner. I could never understand her naked greed. Anyway, that's the story and I hope it helps you. Unless you have any more questions, I should be on my way."

Miriam put up a hand to catch everyone's attention.

"You mentioned her grave. Is she buried nearby?"

"Why, yes, she's buried in the town graveyard just down the street."

"Could you show her grave to us?"

Beatrice looked puzzled for a moment, but shrugged.

"Certainly. It's on my way anyway. If you want to see it just follow me."

"Miriam?" said Dunstan, with an exasperated tone in his voice that was clear to everyone. "Look, I hope you've all noticed I've been playing nice here, listening to all of this, but why the hell do we want to go to a graveyard? The alleged ghost you're all chasing is here, not there."

"You know what, Dunstan? That's a good question."

Dunstan's eyes bulged wide before he responded.

"Christ, you mean I actually said something right around here? I should go buy a lottery ticket."

"I really don't know exactly why we should go there, but somehow it feels right," confessed Miriam, an uncertain look on her face. "As soon as Beatrice mentioned the word grave I felt— something, something in my heart, and I focused on that feeling. I think we are meant to go there."

"I agree," said Paula. "I felt that, too."

Athena and Tom both nodded and Jonathan saw Dunstan roll his eyes before he groaned softly.

"All right, all right, I give up. So we're all going to a graveyard, are we?"

"I think we are," said Melanie, as she rose from her seat and began pulling on her coat.

"Gwen?" said Willie. "We don't have any customers right now and, I don't know why, but I feel like I should be there. If you are coming too then what should we do about the cafe?"

Gwen looked around in thought for a moment.

"I'll leave the place unlocked and put a little sign on the table here that people should help themselves to a coffee. We won't be gone long. There's no point in making them stand outside in the cold."

Outside Jonathan found the gloomy, low clouds that had threatened to move in were now fully covering the skies from horizon to horizon. The only positive element was the temperature had climbed back to a few degrees above freezing, but the light steady breeze off the water made everyone huddle deeper into their coats as they stepped outside.

The little group halted at the entrance to the graveyard, as Beatrice took a moment to get her bearings. She finally pointed to a distant corner and they all began trudging through the now crusty snow that was slowly beginning to melt. After walking about for a bit in one area she finally called out.

"Ah, here it is! Sorry, everyone, the last time I was here was when Dad passed away. He's in that spot over here and Agnes is there. Rose has to be right here."

With effort she bent down and brushed away the remaining snow obscuring most of the gravestone embedded in the ground.

"These plots were all bought by my father for us, you see, so that's how I knew it would be here."

As everyone gathered around Jonathan helped Beatrice stand up again.

"Thank you, young man. Getting back up to your feet isn't easy at my age. Well, here we are. I confess I never thought I'd be out looking for her grave one day. I suppose it could only be at Christmas that I'd consider doing that. It actually makes me wonder if anyone even showed up here to watch her being buried. But I don't wish her ill anymore and if whatever you all do ends up helping her spirit, I guess I can live with that."

A long silence descended on the group and Jonathan knew it was likely they were all thinking thoughts similar to his own, which he struggled to voice.

"You know, every time I find myself in a graveyard the question that comes to mind is whether the only things that are eternal are the wind, the sun, the earth, and the water. We all have a destiny, but this is where it seems to lead."

"We all have a much greater destiny than this," said Miriam, with a firm tone in her voice.

"Well, I certainly hope so," said Beatrice. "At my age that destiny is a lot closer than it is for the rest of you. My, that wind off the water is biting."

As she made to turn away Melanie forestalled her.

"Beatrice? How did Rose die?"

"Good question. The postman is the one who got suspicious and called the police, as her mail wasn't being picked up. An empty pill bottle was found near her body, but the coroner said the cause of death was inconclusive. Personally, I don't think he spent a lot of time trying to figure it out. So I don't know if she killed herself or was thinking about it and God decided to help her along, who knows? She had spent many years living alone. I was told all her groceries were delivered to her and she rarely went out. Living that kind of life would likely make me want to do myself in too, I suspect. So, I'm getting a bit chilled. Any more questions?"

"Just one," said Miriam. "I almost forgot to ask you. Did Rose wear perfume?"

"Why, yes. All the women wore perfume back in those days."

"Do you remember what the scent was?"

"Of course. That's easy for her. She always wore

a rose scented perfume, naturally. It was in keeping with her name."

Miriam smiled. "Thank you, Beatrice. I think you've been most helpful. And unless someone else has another question, we should let you be on your way."

No one did, so Beatrice smiled too. She stopped for a brief moment beside her father and her sister's graves to pay respects as the others began moving back to the entrance of the graveyard. When they were all back on the street they thanked her once again and she went on her way. They turned as one to head back to the cafe and as they did Jonathan looked around in puzzlement.

"Hey, everyone? Where's Dunstan?"

The others gave a start and heads turned in all directions, until James called out and pointed back toward the cafe.

"There he is. He's just about to walk into the cafe."

"Huh," said Gwen. "I wonder why he didn't wait? Oh, well, let's go."

As they made their way back to the cafe James spoke up.

"So Miriam? We went to the graveyard, but I'm still not real clear as to why. Any more insight now that we've done it?"

"Maybe it's because contemplating our mortality and what it means for our lives is never a bad thing," said Paula.

"Yes," said Miriam. "I like what she said."

As they got closer to the cafe they saw Dunstan was standing in the doorway waiting for them.

When they were almost there he turned and went inside. Jonathan was walking beside Melanie and he gave her a questioning, sidelong glance she caught from the corner of her eye. She looked puzzled at his behavior too, and could only shrug in response. As they all made their way back into the warmth of the cafe Jonathan heard Gwen, who had been the first in the door, talking to Dunstan.

"You didn't have to wait outside, you know. I assume you were cold, so you left early. You could have come in and warmed up."

"I'm fine," said Dunstan, but he was staring at the table in front of him and wouldn't look up.

Gwen frowned, but went off to get a fresh pot of coffee brewing. No one else had come into the cafe while they were gone, so she was free to serve coffees all around and rejoin them. As she made her way about the table filling their cups with the last of the old pot Miriam spoke up.

"Well, I don't know about the rest of you, but I'm fully convinced this spirit we are dealing with was Rose Markleigh in life. Does anyone have any real doubt, now? Everything Beatrice gave us fits, and her confirmation Rose always wore rose scented perfume clinches it, at least to my mind. I think we should proceed with the meditation tomorrow. If we all meet here around ten o'clock, maybe?"

Dunstan grunted and mumbled something, before taking a sip of his coffee. Miriam gave him a puzzled look.

"What is it, Dunstan?"

Dunstan sighed. "Yeah, fine, I'll be here. Might as well see this through, although I'm not sure why.

But I think you're maybe jumping to conclusions about all this."

"What do you mean?"

"Look, we're only getting one side of the story. It's only natural this woman Beatrice would be painting her sister as a bitch, because this woman Rose ended up with the better of it all. Maybe this Beatrice was the bitch and was trying to screw Rose, and her Dad found out and didn't like it. Listen, money is at the heart of this story, and when it comes to money, in my experience, anything is possible. And if it comes down to it, I personally can't fault this woman Rose if she did what she had to do to keep her hands on her share of the loot. If the situation was fuzzy enough she managed to hang onto more than her share, so what? You got to look out for yourself. She sounds like my kind of woman, actually."

A long silence descended on the table as everyone contemplated what Dunstan had said, before Jonathan finally shook his head and sat forward to catch Dunstan's eye.

"Not buying what you're selling, Dunstan. Everything you just said simply doesn't feel right and the facts we do have don't support anything you said either. My God, have you listened to what you're saying? And you know what, I don't think you believe what you're saying either."

Dunstan glared at him. "And how the hell would you know that?"

"Because, strangely enough, I can feel it and don't ask me how that works, because I bloody don't know any more than you do. I think in your heart you are hoping someone can stick something tangible in front of you to prove all of this is real, because you desperately want and need it to be real."

"Wow, aren't you Mr. Sensitive. And tell me, why do I need it to be real?" scoffed Dunstan, but Jonathan could see the hint of a troubled look in his eyes.

"Probably because you're involved in so many shady things you haven't seen the sun shine in years and you know you're in too deep. Yes, I know, you told me you deal with bad debt collection and evictions for a living. You didn't mention the money laundering part of it, but that's no surprise, I guess."

Jonathan knew he was right when he finished speaking, as Dunstan's eyes widened and he gave a tiny flinch, so Jonathan pressed on.

"Yeah, lots of cash floating around from the proceeds of whatever crime generated it in Vegas. Drugs, loan sharking, prostitution, fraud, outright theft, the list is endless. And in order to enjoy the fruits of their efforts the bad guys have to find ways to make the money clean. Can't just walk into a bank with a million dollars in grubby twenty-dollar bills stuffed into a plastic garbage bag, right? Can't even buy a new Lamborghini to drive around in with it. And that would be where you come in."

"Dunstan, is what he's saying true?" said Tom.

For his answer Dunstan remained silent, letting his head drop to stare at the table. Jonathan nodded at Tom and continued.

"You see, the way this works is the bad guys provide the ready cash and Dunstan is the middleman who deals with the people who are going to do the dirty work, whether they like it or not. The bad guys find desperate people in need, like someone running a legitimate business that has a big cash flow problem and help them out. Middlemen really like businesses where a lot of cash is always involved, like restaurants or bars. Once they're hooked Dunstan gets to work."

Joanathan paused a moment to spread his hands wide in emphasis.

"Need some money to help keep you afloat? No problem. You monkey with your books with the help of our friend here and you get cash and lots of it. Dunstan gives you a fake invoice for, hmm, some consulting services. This is from an already established company and you give him a nice fat check back, which he can happily take to the bank. Yeah, the businessman taking the risk gets to keep a tiny piece of the cash flowing through his hands, just enough to help. He's now swallowed the hook and he'll never be able to spit it out, of course, so more little deals come his way. And if someday the taxman starts asking questions about the doctored books, well, that's your problem, isn't it? The shell company or companies Dunstan has providing him the funds will close their doors at a moment's notice and more new ones will be in business in no time flat. If the businessman on the hook is smart he will grab what he's got and run for it before problems start coming up."

"Seriously, Dunstan? Tell us he's wrong, please," said Gwen.

This time Dunstan openly flinched, but didn't

raise his head to look at anyone.

"Jonathan?" said Tom. "I would have thought the casinos would be the place to do this kind of thing."

"Yes, they have to be watched constantly, like everything else. The thing is, there's less going on there than you think because it is so obvious an avenue to use, although their hands certainly aren't clean. The casinos are also big businesses, you see. It isn't necessarily in their interest to be involved in messy little dealings like this. They don't need to, when there's people like our friend around. Anyway, folks, you get the picture. Money laundering comes in all shapes and sizes. Cars, real estate, horse racing, you name it and there can be a problem with it."

Jonathan paused to shake his head.

"All these money transfer businesses you see out there? Well, I suppose some of what they move around is legitimate, but more of it isn't. It's an endless game. And the scary part is the example I just gave of what Dunstan is doing is in some ways mere chicken feed. There are far bigger schemes out there involving high priced lawyers, big corporations, offshore banks, you name it."

"You seem to know a lot about this," said Melanie. "Tell me again what it is you do for a living?"

Jonathan gave them a guilty look and laughed.

"I don't think I got around to confessing all of the details. Yes, I suppose you could call me a cop, but I don't wear a uniform or carry a gun or anything like that. I believe I told you all I manage a small team of people that specialize in financial analysis for the government, right? Well, that is true. We look for clues that something suspicious is happening out there, and believe me, there is plenty happening. So it's just a matter of piecing it all together, which in turn allows law enforcement to do something about it. We use—large volumes of data collected from, ah, various sources to do our analysis on money laundering, both domestic and international. Money knows no borders, right?"

"Dunstan, are you as big an asshole as he is making you out to be?" said James.

"James, it's Christmas," said Miriam. "Let's remember what Christmas is about."

"Umm, Jonathan?" said Athena, glancing at Dunstan first to see if he was going to react before turning to look directly at Jonathan. "So why are you here and not at your job? Something happened, didn't it?"

Jonathan sighed. "Yes. Yes, it did. I was tested and I failed, you see. Umm, not a test a teacher would mark. More a situation that was—difficult, and I ran from it. My team and I came across something big, involving some very influential people. And I am not exaggerating when I say the word big. This would make international headlines in the media if it comes out and the story would stick for a while. Anyway, we were working on this file to get the goods on them all when I think somehow they got wind of it. People a lot higher above me in the organization were bought as a result and I'm certain of it. No, I didn't have hard evidence, but it was obvious from their behavior. So we were given a cease and desist order. I was told to stop wasting time with fantasies and find something else to look at, but this is no fantasy. There was even a very subtle hint that something bad might happen to me if I carried on. I think they gave the same veiled threat to members of my team, too. God, you have no idea how much that pisses me off. Bastards. Oh, sorry, Paula."

"It's all right," she replied. "I can understand why it would. So why did you leave your job, though?"

"I actually haven't left it, although I thought about quitting and just chucking it all. I guess the endless greed was all wearing on me and this just brought it to a head. So the part of me that wasn't reacting emotionally to the situation put in a request to take some personal leave. And here I am."

Jonathan paused and hung his own head for a moment.

"No, let me clarify that, because what I just said isn't entirely true. Yeah, the magnitude of the problem I was trying to expose was wearing on me, but another part of me I guess was just scared. Yes, the threats of violence are probably empty and I like to think if it were just myself it wouldn't be a problem. But the people I lead were a consideration along with the question of what I would do for a living, having to start over with a new job or whatever. Going through this bloody divorce at the same time wasn't helping, either. It just felt like my life was becoming a smoking ruin, so the truth is I just decided to run from it all. And I guess what really kills me is I failed as a leader. Leaders are supposed to deal with difficult situations. Stand up and be there when things get tough. I did neither."

A silence descended on the table as Jonathan sipped at his coffee and hung his own head, joining Dunstan in staring down at the table.

"Jonathan?" said Melanie. "I guess I understand all that, but where are you at now? I thought you mentioned you were doing some work in your hotel room? Are you still working on this file, as you call it?"

"Umm, yes, I have been. I don't know what made me do it, but when I left the office I took my laptop with a bunch of the raw data we hadn't sorted through yet. Not supposed to do things like that, since it's all highly confidential. I could get in serious trouble for it, but when I left I was—not myself. I just wanted to get the hell out of there. I couldn't take all the bullshit anymore. By the time I settled down and the reality of what I'd done sunk in I was halfway across the country."

"So have you found the remaining pieces of the puzzle?"

Jonathan was silent for a long moment, before looking up at her.

"Yes. I have, and now I have to decide what I'm going to do. You see, that day we did the meditation I was given a sense or thoughts about a few things. One of them was telling me what I had to do about this and you can probably imagine what it was. So I have a decision to make about it, but in reality I think there is a much larger decision for me."

"What's that?"

Jonathan looked up from the table and stared at Dunstan, who seemed to feel his gaze and looked up too.

"The question is, do I believe? You see, I guess at least on this point I'm not so different than Dunstan here. I don't think he believes in anything he can't see and I guess it's fair to say I've been no different. But I can't deny what has been happening around here and more importantly, what I've felt. So I think I'm at a point where I do believe and now I have to deal with what that means."

The two men remained staring at each other for several moments, before Dunstan once again dropped his head for a moment. After a few seconds he glanced at his watch and stood up, pulling a bill out of his pocket to pay for his coffee and putting it on the table.

"Interesting conversation, but I have to go. See you all tomorrow."

Everyone watched him in silence as he made his way to the door, pulling his coat on as he went. He was about to leave when Athena called out to him.

"Dunstan? Why in God's name are you still here?"

Dunstan stopped and stood still, staring at the door and not looking back at anyone. He finally sighed and hung his head, still not turning around.

"I'm still here because Dad is dying and he asked me to forgive him."

He paused for a moment as he finished speaking and then left. Silence descended on the room as the door closed behind him, before Cate finally spoke.

"I think the spirit has talked to him, too."

Miriam gave her a smile and agreed. "Yes, and I think this explains a lot of things."

As several people around the table nodded

agreement Miriam turned to Athena. "So, Athena, are we ready to do this tomorrow?"

"I think we are. I suppose we could have tried to do this today, but I have to go now and I don't think we want to rush it anyway."

"Excellent. And are you still okay with the thought of Dunstan being involved?"

"Certainly, and especially so after what has happened today. I'm not sure he would admit it, but my heart is telling me he will want to be here for it."

The door to the cafe opened and a group of customers came in, making their way over to a table. Gwen and Willie both got up from their chairs, but before she went over to the newcomers Gwen asked if anyone wanted anything else. Everyone looked about at each other and Jonathan's stomach rumbled as he thought about it, so he held out a hand for a menu.

"I don't know about the rest of you, but I haven't checked out everything on the menu yet. What's the special, Willie?"

As he finished ordering and several of the others joined in, Jonathan's thoughts turned to what could happen the next day. He felt an enormous relief to have finally opened up about his situation, but he knew he was now faced with truly dealing with it. What he hadn't told the others was he had already committed himself to acting, but the problem now was how to move forward. He had too many choices for his course of action and he had been over them many times in his mind, but he had found himself going in circles each time. He looked over at Melanie's pretty face and knew with certainty she too would have to be part of his future.

The hope now was that the ceremony tomorrow might bring forth yet more wisdom for him to use.

Chapter Ten

Jonathan left Melanie sleeping as he got up to fix
them breakfast and make coffee. The smell of the
rich, dark coffee she liked to drink filled the house
and woke her as expected. He could hear the taps
running in the bathroom and by the time she entered
the kitchen he was putting breakfast on the table.
After giving him a still sleepy hug and kiss they
both dug in. Jonathan suggested they shower and
take their second cup of coffee out with them for the
ritual they had settled into of a morning walk
together.

Another dusting of light snow had come in the
night, but Jonathan knew the weather had changed.
The radio told him yet another big wave of warm air
and heavy rain coming across the Pacific from
Hawaii was on its way. A misty marine fog was
already rolling in as the precursor, making the fresh
scent of nearby cedar trees seem even stronger than
usual. The forecast wasn't certain on exactly when it
would hit, but the children he saw playing in the
snow covered park were likely going to be
disappointed if they were hoping for a white
Christmas.

She took his arm as they headed for the beach and
sipped at her coffee before she spoke. Melanie
confessed to being curious about Jonathan's life on
the other side of the country now that she knew a
little more about him. Jonathan told her he had lived
and worked in a couple of the big cities back east,
so she peppered him with questions about them and
his work, to a point where he realized she was

asking for some kind of reason and not just casual interest. He did his best to answer all of them before finally quizzing her about it.

Melanie smiled. "You're pretty good at reading me, aren't you? Well, I think I've come to the realization my former husband and I drifted apart because we never had quite the same interests. And yes, that was one of the little thoughts that came to me. He loved to travel, you see, whereas I've always stuck pretty close to home here. But I'm asking myself why I haven't traveled much and am having a hard time coming up with an answer. So I've been doing some surfing on the net and, well, its like my eyes have finally opened. Don't get me wrong, because as far as I'm concerned I live in paradise here, but there are lots of other interesting places to visit in the world. I maybe wouldn't want to live in them, but I think its time I spread my wings."

Melanie laughed and Jonathan looked aside at her as she smiled back.

"You are probably standing there thinking I've been taken over by an alien at the moment, but you know what? I want to take a big trip with you to Greece. Maybe a cruise or something."

Jonathan laughed too. "Greece? Why Greece?"

Melanie shrugged. "Why not? Got to start somewhere and I was looking at some pictures of the Greek islands last night. Have you ever been to Santorini?"

"I confess I have not."

"Well, I'll show you what I was looking at later. Santorini looks like a stunning place to visit. It looks—romantic. They have all these whitewashed buildings perched on the rim of a huge volcanic crater, right? It all looks sunny and warm and bright, which is pretty much the opposite of what we have here right now."

They kept walking, going further out onto the beach itself because the tide was out, stopping to look at the tidal pools with myriad small fish and crabs trapped in them until the tide returned to free them. The tide was far enough out they were able to walk right out to some of the larger boulders covered with mussels and small sea urchins. The fresh tang of the ocean mingled with the rich smell of seaweed washed up by the constant storms. They walked along for another half hour in the steadily deepening, heavy mist, watching the sea birds pluck at mussels exposed by the retreat of the water from the rocks. Melanie linked her arm with his as she watched the birds fly into the air to break the shellfish open by dropping them from on high.

"Well, this may not be Santorini, but I do love it here. The birds are so clever at finding food, aren't they? This is so picturesque, even in this weather. But we should head for the cafe."

Jonathan agreed and they began retracing their steps. Melanie asked him if he had decided what he was going to do about his work and Jonathan shrugged.

"I think so, but we'll see. There are—options. To be honest, I'm also wondering if I might get more guidance today."

"Yes, I was wondering that, too. Actually, I'm wondering if Dunstan is going to show up at all. It must have cost him plenty to admit that to us yesterday."

"I expect it did, but my money says he'll be here."

As they reached the cafe they saw Gwen had put a closed sign out for customers to see, but the door was unlocked and they went in. Most of the group was already inside, with the notable exceptions of Dunstan and James. Everyone else was seated around two big tables that had been pulled to the side to make space for a circle of chairs Gwen set in place. Gwen brought them fresh coffees as they joined the others. A few minutes later James came in, gratefully accepting the coffee Gwen offered him. Jonathan noticed the look he shared with Gwen lingered a moment longer than necessary, but she kept her face unreadable.

"Well, everyone, we're all here except Dunstan," said Miriam. "I guess we should get going, as I don't know—"

"He's coming," said James, waving a hand to catch her attention. "I saw him about two blocks away coming this direction. He should be here in a moment."

A minute later Dunstan walked in the door and came over to join them. Jonathan saw the haggard look on his face and immediately wondered if Dunstan had gotten any sleep at all the night before. Others saw it too.

"Dunstan, are you all right?" said Melanie. "Forgive me for saying this, but you look like crap."

"I feel like crap. Didn't sleep well, but I'm here. Let's get on with this."

Athena stared at Dunstan for several seconds and Jonathan began to wonder if she was going to object, but she nodded and looked for Miriam, who turned to the rest of them to speak.

"All right, everyone. Athena and I discussed this and we are going to work together. We are first going to begin a meditation and then do a simple prayer, like we did a few nights ago. For those of you that weren't here, listen up and I'll fill you in."

After briefing them and answering a few questions, she continued. "So the purpose of the meditation is to focus everyone's consciousness and make a group connection, if you will. Probably five or ten minutes in, when she feels it is time, Athena will begin."

Miriam turned to Athena who nodded. "I will be opening the door to the verandah and some of the vent windows to the outside for this. You may wish to keep your coats on, as it could get cold as a result. Please understand we must all approach this with good intentions and the utmost respect. Once I begin you may open your eyes. I will be saying a brief and simple prayer, asking for the Creator to help the spirit. I ask each of you to join me silently with that prayer. You may continue to pray silently on your own and, if you wish, you need not wait for me to begin. Even just saying your own prayer of gratitude during your meditation or praying that the spirit receive the guidance and help it needs will be beneficial."

Athena looked around the room, waiting a moment for any questions before continuing.

"Once I finish the prayer I will go to the corners of the room. In each corner I will say a brief prayer asking for help to purify and cleanse the room and, in reality, the entire house. We expect the spirit will be making its presence felt by this point, if not sooner. Are there any questions?"

"Yes," said James. "So how does this end? What will happen to the spirit?"

"That a spirit has attached itself to this house and not moved onward is in reality a negative event," said Miriam. "We all know this isn't how it is supposed to work. I must caution you should not think the spirit is evil or something like that. It simply hasn't moved on. We don't need to know or understand why. We just need to help it with a little kindness. It needs cleansing of this negative energy, you see?"

James frowned. "Sorry, just one more question. I can't wrap my mind around something and I confess this has been nagging at me for a while. You once spoke of this as perhaps being our task to help this spirit, right? So if this spirit is the one in such dire need of help, how is it that it's managing to give us all these, uh, helpful thoughts? Like, who needs the help around here, us, or this spirit?"

"Excellent question. I've spent a lot of time contemplating this the last couple of days and I think I finally have a better understanding. I'd like to see if we succeed with the ceremony before answering that. May I suggest we come back to that question afterwards?"

James shrugged. "Sure. Let's do it."

"Athena?" said Paula. "Is Joker okay to be here with us?"

"I don't see why not. I suggest lets see what happens."

Everyone did as she asked and began taking spots in the circle of chairs Gwen had set up. Joker settled down between Paula and Cate and closed his eyes. Shadow made an appearance, winding his way between the chairs before jumping onto a chair in a corner, in a spot where he could settle down and watch everyone with ease. When everyone was in place Miriam began with the same brief, simple prayer she had spoken the first time they did a meditation. Athena opened the door and the windows before sitting down and as the minutes passed the room began to cool steadily.

Jonathan was feeling the same sense of peacefulness as before when Athena broke the silence in the room. After offering a brief, simple prayer to the Creator to help the spirit, she rose from her seat and went to stand in the center of the circle. This time she said a simple prayer requesting everyone and everything in the old cafe be cleansed and purified. She returned to her seat when she finished.

The marine fog and mist outside was even heavier than before and it carried the faint, but fresh smell of the cedar trees outside into the room, filling Jonathan's senses. Jonathan felt the scent somehow sharpen his mind and he knew somehow the meditation was doing exactly what it was intended to do. And even as that thought came to him Joker gave a low whine and everyone knew the spirit had come into the room. Jonathan opened his eyes to see Shadow was alert and crouched with muscles tensed, but the cat remained where he was, staring intently at the scene while whisking his tail back and forth hard.

"Ah, I see it," said Miriam, staring at the hallway near the kitchen. "And it is now about to join us in the circle. Everyone please stay where you are."

Miriam stood up and stepped to the side, remaining standing and staring intently at the space in the center of the circle before them. Jonathan could see nothing, but the now familiar scent of roses mingled with the faint smell of the cedar trees. The first time he had encountered the spirit he had felt a chill, but this time it was impossible to tell if that was happening again because the doors and windows were open.

The one major difference this time was the strange sense of a tangible presence in the circle. The sensation was like nothing he had ever felt before, but as he came to realize he could sense the presence a feeling of awe at what was happening came over him. And with a flash of insight he understood he was sensing more than just the spirit's presence.

A strange, indefinable feeling stole over him of being surrounded by an energy as ephemeral as mist permeating every fiber of his being and everything around him. The energy filled and flowed through him, giving him a sense of being connected to everyone and everything in the room. And once again, Jonathan found a little voice inside his mind whispering to him. But the presence in the center of the circle stood out, emanating a different kind of feeling. Although he felt no fear and he had no sense of threat from it, Jonathan immediately sensed its presence was not in harmony with everything else.

Miriam stood and spoke her simple prayer a second time, before telling the spirit it was forgiven and that the time had come for it to leave and move onward. As she finished speaking Athena came over to join her and did the same. The two women came forward and stood on either side of the center of the circle, motioning to the open door with hands open wide.

"It's leaving," said Miriam, turning and stepping toward the door in time with Athena, as if they were escorting the spirit between them. Both women stopped short of the doorway and after a few moments Athena was the first to speak. Jonathan could sense the wonder she felt from the tone of her voice and the look of delight on her face.

"It has gone. I felt it pass me and go outside."

"Yes," said Miriam. "I saw it leave. The spirit has cut its bonds and returned to the Creator as it should. The cafe has been cleansed, Gwen."

"One last thing, everyone," said Athena. Please join me in silent prayer to give thanks for the help we have received today."

A long minute of silence descended on the room before Athena finally spoke again.

"Thank you, everyone. I will give thanks to my friend for the advice I was given."

The silence continued for a brief moment before everyone slowly began to shift about, as if reaching the surface of the water after a deep dive. Cate turned to her mother, a look of wonder on her face.

"I felt it, Mom. Did you feel it, too?"

"I did, honey. I feel a sense of—blessing for

everyone. We did what we were supposed to do."

"I got that as well," said Willie, nodding his agreement, with the tone of his voice revealing the marvel he felt at the experience.

The others nodded their agreement, but Tom had a puzzled expression on his face. Athena came and sat beside him.

"Are you all right?" she asked.

"Hmm? Ah, yes, I am. It's just—I think I was given one of these thoughts along the way, maybe like the rest of you."

He turned to stare at Athena and the two of them held each other's gaze.

"You got one, too," said Tom. "I know you did."

Athena took his hand and nodded. "Let's talk later."

"Dunstan?" said Gwen.

As everyone turned to look they were shocked to see Dunstan staring blankly into the center of the circle with tears streaming down his face, making no effort to stem the flow. Gwen went over the cafe counter and returned quickly with a box of tissues for him, but he made no effort to take one. Gwen bent down and gave him a hug.

"My God, Dunstan, what's wrong?"

After a long moment he finally sighed and pulled several tissues from the box to wipe his face. While still staring blankly at nothing he finally spoke in a voice that trembled a little.

"I got some—messages, too. That, and Dad died just after I got home last night."

Everyone converged on Dunstan to offer condolences. The women took turns giving him hugs, but all Dunstan seemed capable of doing was to sit wordlessly staring into space for a long few minutes. Eventually, though, he sat up straight and made a visible effort to pull himself together. Gwen went to brew fresh coffee for them all and offered Dunstan a shot of brandy, but he shook his head. When everyone had settled back down James spoke up.

"Miriam? You were going to talk to us about these little thoughts we all seem to have gotten? What is going on here?"

"Ah, yes. So as I said I spent a fair bit of time meditating on this and, of course, this is one of those times when the answer is so obvious you begin to wonder why you've been walking around in a fog of misunderstanding for so long. I don't believe the little voice intruding on your consciousness or the feelings you've experienced came from the spirit we were trying to help. Rather, it was the Spirit, with a capital S."

"So you're saying that Cate was correct? It's God talking to us?" said Gwen, a strange look on her face.

"More or less," said Miriam, smiling at him. "Some people might see this as their higher selves in action, others might call it guardian angels, but I prefer to keep it simple and just focus on it being from the Spirit."

"Uh, can you fill in some of the gaps here, Miriam?" said Jonathan. "How does this link to what we were doing and why would we be getting these messages while we were focusing on helping the spirit?"

"Well, as I told you before, I really believe we were given this as a collective task, to help the spirit, right? But suppose it wasn't just the spirit that was in need of help? Suppose we collectively needed a little help, too? By making a conscious, collective effort to be open to helping the spirit, we have ourselves become open to receiving aid ourselves. I mean, please correct me if I'm wrong here. Something has come to all of us here, right? And whatever you got has come in the form of help. Can I get a show of hands, please? Is there anyone who hasn't felt or experienced anything like that as a part of this?"

Jonathan looked around the circle and saw no one had put up their hand, but a few people were staring openly at Dunstan. His tears had finally stopped, but he looked even worse than he did when we entered the cafe. Athena came over and put her hand on his shoulder.

"How about you, Dunstan? Are you all right? You got something helpful, too. I can feel it."

Dunstan slowly nodded, his lips pressed together hard. "Yes, and not just today, they came on more than one occasion. I wasn't particularly—receptive at first, but I've come to realize I have to pay attention. Whether I like it or not."

Dunstan stood up and looked around the room, pulling on his coat.

"I should go. I have some things to take care of at home."

"Are you sure you are all right, Dunstan?" said Gwen, a look of concern on her face. "You don't need to be alone on Christmas Eve, you know.

Willie and I were planning to make a bunch of appetizers for us and maybe watch some Christmas movies together. I have a cable connection in here and we can bring a television in. You are more than welcome to join us. Actually, any of you that want to come over are welcome to do so."

"And I'm cooking a turkey tomorrow for lunch," said Willie. "You'd all better show up to help us eat it, because I bought one big enough to feed everybody here."

"Yes," said Gwen. "We know some of you will be having dinner with family, but we thought it would be nice after all this to have a lunch together here. So everyone please come if you can. Dunstan?"

Dunstan hung his head in thought for a moment, but finally nodded.

"I doubt I'll be here tonight. I feel rather—drained right now. But yes, I'll come for lunch tomorrow."

As Dunstan turned and left the cafe the others began putting on their coats to leave as well. Melanie looked up at Jonathan, raising an eyebrow in question with a small smile on her face. Jonathan laughed.

"Sure, why not? I'll come by tonight if you're going to. Might as well spend Christmas Eve with friends and have a good time."

Melanie grinned and put on her coat so the two of them could leave together. And outside the rain that had been holding off for so long finally began, making a steady, relentless patter on the windowpanes. Melanie was surprised when Jonathan announced he had to go do some shopping, but would meet her back at the cafe. She had put her hands on her hips and tried to wriggle an answer out of him as to what he was up to, but he simply smiled and refused to give in.

They set no alarm for Christmas morning and both slept late as a result. With none of the normal traffic sounds outside there was nothing to intrude and wake them early. The continuous rhythm of the now heavy rain tapping on the windows of their room was the only sound to penetrate their consciousness. Leaving Melanie in bed, Jonathan went to the window and looked out. As he expected, the rain was heavy and warm enough that most of the snow was already gone.

Jonathan rubbed his face and went to splash water on it, hoping it would wash away the effects of one too many drinks the night before. Both of them had gone to the cafe as promised, where a few of the others had appeared. The musicians who had played at the cafe a few days before came in unexpectedly along with a few other people who were at the earlier party and what was supposed to have been a quiet night turned into the exact opposite.

Gwen and Willie seemed prepared, almost as if they were expecting something like this would happen. Willie soon had a steady stream of all manner of appetizers flowing out of the kitchen in between making appearances to dance with all of the women present. The night had felt like one great, joyous release of celebration, as if somehow everyone and everything had been knocked asunder, but was now back in balance and in place the way it should be.

After Melanie dragged herself out of bed to shower with him, Jonathan made himself presentable and went downstairs to make breakfast. As he stared into the depths of the second cup of coffee and went through the motions of making breakfast, he realized he knew he would do what the little voice had told him to do. Jonathan smiled to himself, as understanding came that the choice he had made was in reality not a choice, for it was the only way forward. He knew with certainty he had a task to perform and all that was left was to go out and do it.

As they finished breakfast Jonathan gave Melanie a kiss and told Melanie he would meet her at the cafe for lunch. Seeing her puzzled look he winked and gave her a smile, saying he had to pick up something from his hotel room. Back in his room Jonathan finished wrapping the presents he had bought for everyone and stuffed them all in the carry bags he had purchased. He knew they were likely all going to be mad at him for doing it.

When the lunch hour finally came and it was time to leave he was glad the bags were plastic and he could tie them up, as the rain was still coming in a steady downpour. But even with his raincoat he still felt like he had been soaked to the bone by the time he made his way through the entrance to the cafe.

Most everyone was already there and they greeted him with smiles. The only one missing was Dunstan. The air was filled with the wonderful smell of roast turkey, making his mouth water at the thought of the lunch to come. Gwen and Willie had pulled enough tables together to seat everyone around them and covered it all with a white tablecloth. The places had all been set with fine linen napkins and real silverware to use. Jonathan set his bags off to the side and shrugged out of his wet coat, accepting hugs of greeting from the women when he was done. Jonathan was surprised to find everyone already had drinks in hand, but Gwen appeared with a beer for him and smiled, seeing his puzzled look.

"We're celebrating, Jonathan. Athena and Tom are going to get married!"

"Really?" said Jonathan, turning to see the two of them standing with their arms around each other. "That's wonderful. Congratulations!"

"Thank you," said Tom. "I know this may be a bit of a surprise. It's actually a surprise to us, too, believe it or not. We'd kind of talked about this before, but we'd always shied away from it. Both of us are kind of—independent, I guess. But we both got a little thought yesterday and guess what? It was the same for both of us and after everything that has happened here, well, I think we both knew we'd better pay attention. So I asked Athena to marry me last night and she accepted."

Tom laughed, reaching for her left hand and holding it up for Jonathan to see she wore no ring.

"It was too late to go buy a ring last night, but we'll fix that soon enough."

"That's great news, you two. Have you thought about a date?"

"There's no rush," said Athena. "The truth is we've been seeing each other for years. We're also both pretty set in our ways about having our own space, but I figure if we find a big enough place for both of us to live in we'll make it work. So maybe some time this summer, once we sort out the details."

She glanced at the windows of the cafe and grimaced.

"No point getting married in the rain, is there?"

Jonathan laughed and reached for the bags he had brought, shuffling through the presents to find the ones for Athena and Tom.

"Well, these are intended as Christmas presents, but you can maybe put these to use to start your celebration with."

Jonathan distributed the presents to everyone and called Willie out from the kitchen to collect his. Several of them chided him for spending the money, but they all eagerly opened their packages. The women found boxes of chocolates while the bottles of scotch the men received brought smiles to everyone's face. When he came to Melanie he gave her an envelope along with the package containing chocolates.

"I went shopping, remember?" said Jonathan as he watched her face crinkle with a puzzled look while she peered at the envelope with her name on it. Jonathan just grinned at the rest of them, waving away everyone's protests at his generosity as the door to the cafe opened and Dunstan came in. He too was carrying a large bag.

"Merry Christmas, Dunstan," said Jonathan, handing him his present. "I was just about to tell everyone how much I appreciate having found so many new friends so easily and to show my appreciation I bought everyone a present."

Dunstan looked around and saw everyone holding their chocolates and bottles of scotch, before turning back to look at the package Jonathan was holding out to him. He looked up at Jonathan with a strange expression on his face.

"It's a bottle of scotch, Dunstan, just like the others have."

Dunstan burst out laughing. Jonathan stared at him, unable to understand what had set him off.

"What? What's so funny?"

For answer Dunstan reached into the bag he had brought, rummaged around, and pulled out a present covered with Christmas wrapping paper.

"I'm sure you'll enjoy this bottle of scotch I got you for Christmas. The women will like their chocolates too, I'm certain."

Everyone joined Dunstan in laughing as he handed around his presents. Jonathan put out his hand and Dunstan gripped it in a friendly handshake. Jonathan was pleased to see Dunstan appeared much fresher than he had the day before.

"You look a lot better today. You got a good night's sleep?"

"Yeah," said Dunstan. "I confess I was exhausted. Crashed and burned at eight o'clock last night and didn't get up till eight this morning. But I feel a whole lot better. I feel—I feel like today is a new day and it will be all right. I know I can make everything all right."

Gwen handed Dunstan a drink and explained why they were celebrating. As Dunstan went over to offer his congratulations to them Melanie gave a delighted cry behind him, coming over to Jonathan with her eyes alight and a wide smile on her face as he turned to her.

"Yes! I would love to go to Greece and the Mediterranean!"

Jonathan laughed. "I thought you might. That's a tentative booking, you understand. We'll have to make sure this fits our schedules. If it doesn't work on those dates we can find others that do."

"What are you two talking about?" asked Tom.

"Jonathan has booked a Mediterranean cruise for the two of us that starts in Italy and goes to Greece. He's also booked a week to stay in Santorini. My God, I've been dreaming about how wonderful it would be to see that part of the world. And now I will. Thank you so much!"

As she finished speaking she wrapped her arms around Jonathan and gave him a kiss.

"I think she's more excited about it than I am," said Jonathan with a laugh as they stepped apart and he looked at the others. "We've got a bit of time to wait though. The cruise ship season doesn't really start until spring. We're going in early June."

Tom came over and stood in front of Jonathan with hands on hips looking chagrined.

"I am very glad for you, but you do realize I'm going to have to find a way to top that for Athena, don't you?"

Athena laughed as she came over to pull him away. "We'll think of something, Tom."

Melanie turned to look at Jonathan once again, her face serious this time.

"Jonathan. It's like—like my eyes have been

opened and I can't understand why I had them closed. It feels I've been waiting for someone to open them and only now can I truly see."

Jonathan smiled. "Maybe we both just needed to bring a little romance into our lives."

The others resumed finishing unwrapping the remaining presents as Dunstan turned to face Cate, wearing a long face. Both Melanie and Jonathan saw it and they turned to see what was happening. Dunstan put his hands in his pockets and let a look of frustration show.

"I'm sorry, Cate. I don't have a present for you to unwrap."

Cate gave him a curious, hesitant look, before letting a tiny smile appear.

"That's okay. Mom will share a few of her chocolates with me, I'm sure."

"Ah, but just because I don't have something for you to unwrap, it doesn't mean you'll get no present."

Dunstan laughed as Cate's face wrinkled in confusion.

"You know that expensive treatment your Mom can't afford for you? Well, I have plenty of resources and I can afford it. You're going to get your treatment and you'll be just fine. I know you will."

Cate stared at him openmouthed for a long moment before turning to Paula, who appeared equally stunned by what Dunstan had said. Dunstan nodded and grinned at Cate to reassure her he was serious and in a rush Cate came over, wrapping herself around him in a ferocious hug. A second later Paula joined her daughter in crushing Dunstan between the two of them. Paula was too overcome to speak, but Cate looked up at him.

"I don't know how to thank you or how I will ever be able to repay you."

"No need to repay me. Making you better is reward enough."

Miriam came over and looked at Dunstan as Paula finally pulled away and sat down again, wiping away the tears that had streamed down her face.

"Dunstan, that is so very generous. I can't help but ask, did you receive a thought suggesting you should do this?"

"Actually, no, I didn't, or at least I don't think so. But the thought has been percolating in my mind for a while now and I have no idea how it got there. I did as you suggested, though. Every time it came up I looked into my heart and tried to see how it felt. Thinking about doing it made me feel—happy. And I know I probably don't deserve to be happy, but there you have it. I like this feeling and I'd like to keep it."

Miriam gave him a hug as Willie appeared from the kitchen.

"Lunch in fifteen minutes, everyone."

Gwen came over from where she was standing with James and gave Dunstan a hug, too.

"Thank you, Dunstan. I agree with Miriam."

Dunstan smiled. "Thanks. I wish you and James all the best, by the way. Planning to get married?"

Gwen gave a start and a quick glance at James, who slowly smiled and came over as Dunstan offered them a wry grin.

"Well, if you aren't going to marry her you're a fool, you know. So yes, I know you've made your decision, although don't ask me how I know that. I'm very glad for both of you."

"Yes, Dunstan, I have. James has been hired by the town and will be moving here early next year. This is home for me and I think I can manage the cafe better with someone who can help me when I'm in a pinch. I'm so glad you understand."

"I do. I wish it was otherwise, but I'm okay. But you didn't answer my question. Hey, you two could come hang out at my place in Vegas and get married by Elvis!"

James laughed. "Well, this isn't exactly how I'd been thinking this was going to work, but what the hell."

James took Gwen's hand and got down on one knee, pulling a small box out of his pocket.

"Oh, my God," said Gwen, putting her other hand over her mouth in shock.

"Marry me, Gwen," said James.

"I will. Yes, I will. My God," she said, unable to hold back the tears any longer.

James opened the little box and pulled out a ring, sliding it onto her finger as he stood up and gave her a crushing hug. The pandemonium of everyone clapping hands in appreciation and all talking at once drew Willie out of the kitchen, looking puzzled. When he learned what had happened he pulled the two of them together into an enormous hug of his own.

"Well," said Tom. "The wedding planners are

going to have a banner year around here."

Willie finally let the two of them out of his embrace, before cautioning Gwen that while he didn't want to spoil the occasion he would be serving lunch soon and would need her. Gwen nodded and wiped away her tears as best she could. As everyone was focused on congratulating them Melanie came over and put her arm around Jonathan for a brief moment to catch his attention.

"So you're going to leave me soon, aren't you?"

Jonathan turned to look at her, as did some of the others who had overheard her question.

"Yeah. I guess that was obvious, huh? I've told the hotel I'm checking out tomorrow or maybe the day after."

"We'll have to talk about what is next for the two of us, won't we?"

"Oh yes. I'm going back to have at them, Melanie. However, I was thinking of heading south for a week or two to find some sunshine and warm weather first. As much as I've enjoyed being here with you and everyone else, I'm sure you've noticed it does rain around here. In fact, I've had all I want to see of it. So what does your schedule look like for work? Feel like taking a little trip with me to the sunshine in the next day or two? Maybe you could come back east with me afterwards?"

Melanie laughed, before turning serious. "I can rearrange my schedule. Besides, I work remote and online anyway. But you are going to confront them at work?"

"Absolutely. The little message I got about this made it clear this is my task, as if it's what I've been waiting to do my whole life. But the question was how best to do it, you see. I could have anonymously leaked a few things to the media or maybe found some sneaky ways to bring some key facts to the attention of other law enforcement that might pick up on it all, but none of that feels right. So I'm just going to barge in and stir up some shit. I'm quite certain the team will be totally behind me. You may be seeing my name in media reports in the not too distant future if they don't take me seriously or they try to sweep it all under the rug. Actually, I think you'll be seeing my name one way or another, because however it gets out the fan will spread the crap around far and wide."

James reached out with his hand and Jonathan took it. As they shook hands James smiled.

"Welcome back. Sometimes even tough guy firefighters have to take time and step back from it all. But they're all good guys and they always jump right back in if at all possible. I'm not surprised you're back in the fight. You'll get it done."

"I'm sure you will, too," said Dunstan. "Still planning to check me out when you get back to spook headquarters?"

Jonathan smiled. "Don't know. Should I?"

"I don't think you need bother. I've decided I'm packing that shit in and moving on to running a legitimate business for a change. Not sure what yet, but that will come to me. It'll take me a while to disentangle from everything anyway and in the meantime I can maybe help out a few charities. I have a few things to take care of around here with Dad's estate, too."

"Sounds like a good idea to me. Going to stay in Vegas?"

"Actually, yes. There are enough people in that town in need of a little help I'll never run out of things to do. And by the way, I've been thinking I could point you in the right direction of a few people you may be interested in having a look at. Discreetly, of course."

"Of course. I'll give you my contact information. Always looking for new things to do. And Dunstan? Never thought I'd be saying this to you, but welcome to the fight."

Jonathan reached out and shook Dunstan's hand as the two men smiled, while Miriam came over and put her arms around both men.

"I'm always happy when I see how life has a way of balancing. The pendulum swings one direction and then the other. But listen, you two are both coming back for the weddings, whenever they are, right?"

"Wouldn't miss them," said Jonathan.

"Just give me enough warning of the date and I'll be here," said Dunstan.

"Lunch, everyone," said Gwen. "We're setting up a little buffet on the cafe counter here so you can all take what you want."

As everyone lined up Gwen and Willie began bringing out trays of steaming food and everyone was soon seated at the table with a full plate before them. Willie was the last to join them, only removing his kitchen apron once the food was all out. As Willie sat down with his meal Gwen pulled out a box of Christmas crackers and gave one to each person before reaching for her drink.

"Merry Christmas, everyone!"

As Gwen raised her glass everyone echoed the toast and did the same. The sharp snaps of crackers being opened came around the table and everyone put on their bright colored paper hats. Gwen smiled as she looked around the table at the people examining the little prizes stuffed into the crackers.

"I don't know if Christmas crackers are a tradition for any of you, but they are for me. Willie and I want to thank all of you for coming. This would have been a lonelier place with just the two of us and no one should be alone or lonely at Christmas."

"I agree," said Willie, wearing a big smile on his face. "I think that's another one of the reasons I like working in a cafe, there's always people around and I've never felt lonely here. Even if I don't talk to anyone, I still have others around and, if I wanted to, I could talk to them and make new friends."

"There are lots of lonely people outside these walls, but we aren't in that category, and for that we should be grateful," said Tom.

"Maybe if everyone understood the whole world is a cafe and that every day is Christmas it would be different," said Cate.

Everyone around the table smiled at the image. Jonathan laughed before responding.

"So the world is just a cafe and we are all just the customers, is it then?"

Cate smiled back at him. "God bless us all."

"Look people, I can't stand all this happiness and probably don't deserve it anyway," said Dunstan. "Can we eat?"

Everyone laughed once again they picked up their forks and dug into their meals. Jonathan looked over at the cafe windows, as outside the rain lashed particularly hard once more against the house. He knew it was washing away any last remnants of the snow and with the earth saturated, there was only one place for it go.

And outside on the beach the waves came crashing to the shore once again, reaching out to welcome the rivulets of snowmelt and rain returning to the endless, dark blue sea.

The End

Author Notes

Every time I finish writing a book I take a bit of time to look back and contemplate the way I did it, making notes for the next one with an eye for what I could have done better to improve the process. Having done this with a number of books now I've noticed I still find myself feeling a sense of wonder at how it all starts from a tiny seed of an idea. The way I see this, the primary task of an author is to deal with the magic when an idea grabs you and simply won't go away.

Anyone familiar with the brilliant author Charles Dickens and his work A Christmas Carol or with the equally brilliant 1951 British movie adaptation of it entitled Scrooge will recognize that my novel shares a few common elements with these works. I'm certain more than a few readers of The Christmas Cafe have already assumed the inspiration for my project somehow came from the countless times I've viewed the movie or the occasions I've read A Christmas Carol.

But that isn't how this came about.

I was enjoying lunch with an old friend a couple of years back and we were discussing spirits and the spiritual world, as we had done once close to forty years ago now. During our more recent conversation she made reference to that time and linked it to her more recent life. The connection she made on the subject of spirits stuck in my mind long afterwards. That linkage was the seed for this story and, I can assure you, there was no hint of Christmas being involved whatsoever at this point.

Stories are everywhere. People are stories. We have a beginning, middle, and end. We are the hero of our own story, filled with drama, comedy, action, adventure, and sometimes tragedy. The thing is, not every story has elements that will interest other people enough they want to read or hear or see the story. So recognizing when an idea has the potential to become a story other people could be interested in is the essential art of being an author, at least to my mind. You can display amazing technical skills as a writer, but it's all for naught if your story doesn't have the magic to hook even yourself. If it doesn't hook you, the lack of inspiration will shine through and no one will be buying your book.

I confess this one had me scratching my head for a while. The idea of a spirit who wouldn't or couldn't let go, and of living people who perhaps needed a little help themselves giving it aid to deal with its situation felt like a possible story that could work. This idea also had the telltale sign of continuing to creep back into my consciousness every time my mind wandered in the days that followed. For me, this is the sign that I'm onto something and I have to start paying attention.

I don't know if this is how it works for other authors, but it is what happens to me. In my case, paying attention generally means a lot of sitting around and staring off at the sky or at nothing in particular while processing the idea. Ideas percolate in my mind even when I'm out doing everyday tasks and, in reality, I think my subconscious is what is actually paying attention. Eventually, more ideas crop up that link to the central seed to carry the concept further. When that starts happening I know the process has begun for certain.

In this case I started thinking my ghost story needed a place. Since your basic haunted house is a far too well used staple of the horror genre, I knew I needed something different. Along came the notion of a seaside cafe that was somehow haunted and I thought I could work with that. I also knew there was no way I would be setting this around Halloween, since I was well aware it was not a horror novel I was writing. So the idea of a seaside resort town populated with storm watchers around Christmas time popped into the picture and, once again, I felt it could work.

By this point I was now well on my way, beginning to map out scenes and chapters and building pictures of the characters in my mind. Imagine, then, what happened in my head when it dawned on me that some other guy named Dickens had already written a wonderful story about ghosts around Christmas time. Progress on the story ground to a halt while I struggled to wrap my mind around this. The thought of going back to the drawing board and shifting the timeframe came, but in the end I was certain The Christmas Cafe was its own story.

The more I thought about it I also felt comfortable this would serve as a personal homage to Dickens and to the amazing work that was done with the movie Scrooge. Writing styles have evolved since the time of Dickens, but his brilliance is on display in the many wonderful characters he created and the compelling stories he wrote them into.

As for the 1951 movie Scrooge it is certainly dated by the technological limitations of movies of this era and it has its imperfections, but in my humble opinion the acting is stellar, as is the work that was done on the screenplay and the production. Every year at Christmas time when I watch the movie I find myself quoting aloud the lines before they are spoken because they are so memorable and wonderful. Not everyone may agree with my assessment and that's fair. These are qualitative judgments and what works for me doesn't necessarily work for someone else.

Readers of this work will have noticed the obvious theme of greed and its impact on people that permeates the entire story of The Christmas Cafe. The story of A Christmas Carol shares this theme and, on more than one occasion while writing this book, I confess I found it appalling to know Dickens would likely not be surprised by the scale of greed at play in our world of today, were he somehow able to experience it. Sadly, I suspect he would not see much difference from the world he knew in his own time. But the truth is people with massive, staggering degrees of wealth have been present in every century of human existence to varying degrees.

At this point you may be thinking I am perhaps cynical about human behavior and don't see much of a future for mankind. The consequences of unfettered greed in our world are on display everywhere on a daily basis and it can be disheartening. But not everyone with vast wealth behaves badly and there are lots of decent, ordinary people out there making a positive impact on our world. Those people serve as a counterbalance to the negative energy of greed and give plenty of cause to be optimistic. And keeping a positive balance in our lives is a good thing.

I sincerely hope you have enjoyed reading The Christmas Cafe.

www.ingramcontent.com/pod-product-compliance
Lightning Source LLC
Chambersburg PA
CBHW071111250626
47159CB00002B/689